$\sqrt{\text{summer}}$

THE SQUARE ROOT OF

√summer

HARRIET REUTER HAPGOOD

ROARING BROOK PRESS
New York

Text copyright © 2016 by Harriet Reuter Hapgood
Published by Roaring Brook Press
Roaring Brook Press is a division of Holtzbrinck Publishing Holdings Limited Partnership
175 Fifth Avenue, New York, New York 10010
fiercereads.com

Library of Congress Cataloging-in-Publication Data

Names: Reuter Hapgood, Harriet.
Title: The square root of summer / by Harriet Reuter Hapgood.
Description: New York : Roaring Brook Press, [2016] | Summary: Gottie Oppenheimer,
    a seventeen-year-old physics prodigy, navigates grief, love, and disruptions in the
    space-time continuum in one very eventful summer.
Identifiers: LCCN 2015022270| ISBN 9781626723733 (hardback) |
    ISBN 9781626723740 (e-book)
Subjects: | CYAC: Love—Fiction. | Grief—Fiction. | Space and time—Fiction. |
    BISAC: JUVENILE FICTION / Love & Romance. | JUVENILE FICTION /
    Social Issues / Death & Dying. | JUVENILE FICTION / Science Fiction. | JUVENILE
    FICTION / Fantasy & Magic.
Classification: LCC PZ7.1.R47 Sq 2016 | DDC [Fic]—dc23
LC record available at http://lccn.loc.gov/2015022270

Our books may be purchased in bulk for promotional, educational, or business use.
Please contact your local bookseller or the Macmillan Corporate and
Premium Sales Department at (800) 221-7945 ext. 5442 or by
e-mail at MacmillanSpecialMarkets@macmillan.com.

First edition 2016
Book design by Elizabeth H. Clark
Illustrations by Kristie Radwilowicz
Printed in the United States of America

1   3   5   7   9   10   8   6   4   2

For my parents, for everything

{1}
PARTICLES

---

*The Uncertainty Principle states that you can know
where a particle is, or you can know where it's going, but
you can't know both at the same time.
The same, it turns out, is true of people.*

*And when you try, when you look too closely, you get
the Observer Effect. By trying to work out what's going
on, you're interfering with destiny.*

*A particle can be in two places at once. A particle
can interfere with its own past. It can have multiple
futures, and multiple pasts.*

The universe is complicated.

Saturday 3 July

[Minus three hundred and five]

My underwear is in the apple tree.

I'm lying in the grass, staring up through the branches. It's late afternoon and the rest of the garden is lemonade sunshine, but under here it's cool and dark and insecty. When I tilt my head back, the whole garden is upside down—and my laundry with it, festooned like the world's saddest bunting.

Déjà vu flattens me, and I have the stupidest thought: *Hey, Grey's home.*

When our clothesline broke a few years ago, my grandfather Grey was underneath it. "Balls and buggery to the flames of hell!" he roared, flinging the wet clothes into the trees to dry. He loved the effect so much, he insisted we repeat it every time the sun came out.

But Grey died last September, and we don't do things like that anymore.

I shut my eyes and recite pi to one hundred decimal places. When I open them, the apple tree still blossoms with underwear. It's a throwback to how things used to be—which means I know exactly who's responsible.

Then I hear his voice saying my name, floating towards me over the bushes.

"Gottie? Yeah, still a total Mensa patient."

Rolling onto my front, I peer through the trees. Across the garden, my brother Ned is coming out the back door. Six foot of stubble and snakeskin leggings, and a clothespin clipped to his T-shirt. Since coming home from art school a couple of weeks ago, he's been making a pastiche of Grey's summers: dragging our grandfather's things out of the shed, rearranging furniture, playing his records. He settles himself on the grass, swigging a beer and air-guitaring with his other hand. Perpetual motion.

Then I see who's following him and instinctively duck into the grass. Jason. His best friend and bass player in their band. He slouches slowly to the ground, where I stare a hole in the back of his leather jacket.

"It's past seven," Ned is saying. "Grots'll be home soon, if you wanna say hi."

I wrinkle my nose at the nickname. *Kla Grot—little toad.* I'm seventeen!

"It's that late?" Jason's voice is a low rumble. "We should call the others, have band practice here."

No, don't do that, I think. *Shoo.* It's been one thing, having Ned home these past couple of weeks, bringing the house alive with music and noise and mess. I don't want Fingerband here too, squawking their guitars all night and talking, talking, talking. Not when I've been an elective mute since September.

Then there's Jason. Blond, bequiffed, blue-eyed. Beautiful. And, if you want to get technical about it, my ex-boyfriend.

Secret ex-boyfriend.

Ugh.

Aside from the funeral, this is the first time I've seen him since the end of last summer. This is the first time I've seen him since we were having sex in the sunshine.

I didn't even know he was back. I don't know how I missed it—our village, Holksea, is the size of a postage stamp. Barely enough houses for a Monopoly set.

I want to throw up. When Jason left for college, this was not how I pictured us seeing each other again—with me lurking in the shrubbery like Grey's vast stone Buddha. I'm frozen, compelled to stay where I am, staring at the back of Jason's head. It's too much for my heart to take, and not enough.

Then Umlaut appears from nowhere.

A ginger blur through the garden, landing with a *meow* next to Ned's cowboy boots.

"Yo, midget," says Jason, surprised. "You're new."

"That's Gottie's," Ned non-explains. Getting a kitten wasn't my idea. He appeared one day in April, courtesy of Papa.

Ned stands up, scanning the garden. I try to blend, a five-foot-nine-inch leaf, but he's already strutting towards me.

"Grotbag." He raises one cool eyebrow. "Playing hide-and-seek?"

"Hello," I reply, rolling onto my back and staring up at him. My brother's face is a reflection of mine—olive skin, dark eyes, beaky nose.

But while he lets his brown hair fall unbrushed around his shoulders, mine hasn't been cut in five years, and is twisted up in a permanent topknot. And only one of us is wearing eyeliner. (Clue: it isn't me.)

"Found ya." Ned winks. Then, quick as a flash, he whips his phone from his pocket and snaps me.

"Uuuhhhnnn," I complain, hiding my face. One thing I haven't missed while he's been AWOL all year: Ned's paparazzo habit.

"You should come and join us," he calls over his shoulder. "I'm making *Frikadeller.*"

The prospect of meatballs is enough to coax me out, despite myself. I stand up and trail him through the shrubbery. Out on the grass, Jason's still lounging among the daisies. He's obviously found a new hobby at college—there's a cigarette half-smoked in his hand, which he lifts in a half wave, half smiling.

"Grots," he says, not quite meeting my eye.

That's Ned's nickname for me, I think. *You used to call me Margot.*

I want to say hello, I want to say so much more than that, but the words vanish before they reach my mouth. The way we left things, there's still so much unsaid between us. My feet grow roots while I wait for him to stand up. To talk to me. To mend me.

In my pocket, my phone weighs heavy, untexted. He never told me he was back.

Jason looks away, and sucks on his cigarette.

After a pause, Ned claps his hands together. "Well," he says brightly. "Let's get you two chatterboxes inside. There's meatballs to fry."

He struts off to the house, Jason and me walking silently behind. When I reach the back door, I'm about to follow them into the kitchen, but something stops me. Like when you think you hear your name, and your soul snags on a nail. I linger on the doorstep, looking back at the garden. At the apple tree, with its laundry blossoms.

Behind us, the evening light is condensing, the air thick with mosquitoes and honeysuckle. I shiver. We're on the cusp of summer, but I have the sense of an ending, not a beginning.

But perhaps it's that Grey is dead. It still feels like the moon fell out of the sky.

Sunday 4 July

[Minus three hundred and six]

I'm in the kitchen early the next morning, scooping *birchermuesli* into a bowl, when I notice it. Ned's reinstated the photographs on the fridge, a decorating habit of Grey's I always hated. Because you can see the gap where Mum should be.

She was nineteen when Ned was born and she moved home to Norfolk, bringing Papa with her. Twenty-one when she had me, and she died. The first photo I show up in after that, I'm four and we're at a wedding. In it, Papa, Ned, and I are clustered together. Behind us towers Grey, all hair, beard, and pipe—a supersize Gandalf in jeans and a Rolling Stones T-shirt. I smile toothlessly: prison-cropped hair, shirt and tie, buckled shoes, trousers tucked into grubby socks. (Ned is in a pink rabbit costume.)

A couple of years ago, I asked Grey why I'd been dressed as a boy, and he'd chuckled, saying, "Gots, man—no one ever dressed you any which way. That was all you. Right down to that weird jam with the socks. Your parents want to let you and Ned do your own thing." Then he'd wandered off to stir the dubious stew he was concocting.

Despite my alleged childhood insistence on dressing like Mr. Darcy, I'm not a tomboy. They might be in a tree, but my bras are pink. Awake all last night, I painted my toenails cherry red. Hidden in my wardrobe— albeit underneath a hundred doppelgänger sneakers—lurks a pair of black high heels. And I believe in love on a Big Bang scale.

That's what Jason and I had.

Before leaving the kitchen, I flip the photo over, sticking it down with a magnet.

Outside, it's an English cottage–garden idyll. Tall delphiniums pierce the cloudless sky. I scowl at the sunshine and start heading to my room—a brick box annex beyond the apple tree. Almost immediately, my foot hits something solid in the long grass, and I go flying.

When I pick myself up and turn around, Ned is sitting up, rubbing his face.

"Nice dandelion impression," I say.

"Nice wake-up call," he mumbles.

From the house, through the open back door, I hear the phone ring. Ned cat-stretches in the sun, unruffled. Unlike his velvet shirt.

"Did you just get home?"

"Something like that," he smirks. "Jason and I headed out after dinner—Fingerband rehearsal. There was tequila. Is Papa around?"

As if cued by a hidden director, Papa floats from the kitchen, a mug in each hand. In this house of big stompy giant people, he's a *Heinzelmännchen*—a pixie-pale elf straight out of a German fairy tale. He'd be invisible if it weren't for his red sneakers.

He's also about as down-to-earth as a balloon, not batting an eye at how we're scattered on the grass as he perches himself between my upside-down cereal bowl and me. He hands Ned a mug. "Juice. Here, I have to talk both of you to a proposition."

Ned groans but gulps the juice, emerging from the mug slightly less green.

"What's the proposition?" I ask. It's always disconcerting when Papa tunes in to reality enough to run ideas past us. He seriously lacks *Vorsprung durch Technik*—German precision and efficiency. Not just a blanket short of a picnic—he'd forget the picnic too.

"Ah, well," Papa says. "You both remember next door, the Althorpes?"

Automatically, Ned and I turn to look across the garden, at the house beyond the hedge. Almost five years ago, our neighbors moved to Canada. They never sold the house, so there was always the promise of a return along with the For Rent sign and its constant parade of tourists, vacationers, families. It's been empty for the past few months.

Even after all this time, I can still picture a grubby little boy in coke-bottle glasses squeezing through the hole in the hedge, waving a fistful of worms.

Thomas Althorpe.

Best friend doesn't even begin to cover it.

Born in the same week, we'd grown up side by side. Thomas-and-Gottie—we were inseparable, trouble times two, an el weirdo club of only us.

Until he left.

I stare at the scar on my left palm. All I remember is a plan to swear a blood brothers pact, a promise to talk to each other. Three thousand miles wasn't going to change anything. I woke up in the E.R. with a bandage on my hand and a black hole in my memory. By the time I came home, Thomas and his parents were gone.

I waited and waited, but he never wrote me a letter, or emailed, or Morse code–messaged, or anything we'd said we'd do.

My hand healed; my hair grew long. Little by little, I grew up. Little by little, I forgot about the boy who forgot me first.

"The Althorpes?" Papa interrupts my thoughts. "You remember? They're getting divorced."

"Fascinating," croaks Ned. And even though Thomas abandoned me, my heart skips a little on his behalf.

"Indeed. Thomas's mum, I was on the phone with—she's moving home to England in September. Thomas is coming with her."

There's a strange sense of inevitability to this announcement. Like I've been waiting for Thomas to come back this whole time. But how dare he not even tell me! To have his mum call Papa! *Chicken*.

"Anyway, she'd like that Thomas is settled back before starting school, which I agree," he says, adding a *harrumph*, a classic Papa telltale sign that there's more to the story than he's letting on. "It's a bit last-minute, her plan, but I offer that he stay with us this summer. That's . . . that's my proposition."

Unbelievable. It's not enough that he's coming home, but he'll be on my side of the hedge. Unease blooms like algae.

"Thomas Althorpe," I repeat. Grey always told me saying words out loud made them true. "He's moving in with us."

"When?" asks Ned.

"Ah." Papa sips from his mug. "Tuesday."

"Tuesday—as in *two days' time*?" I shriek like a tea kettle, all calm evaporating.

"Whoa," says Ned. His face has reverted to hangover green. "Am I meant to share a bunk bed with him?"

Papa harrumphs again, and launches the Götterdämmerung. "Actually, I offered for him to stay in Grey's room."

Four horsemen. A shower of frogs. Burning lakes of fire. I may not know my Revelations, but disturbing the shrine of Grey's bedroom? It's the apocalypse.

Next to me, Ned quietly throws up on the grass.

Monday 5 July

[Minus three hundred and seven]

"Spacetime!" Ms. Adewunmi scrawls on the whiteboard with a marker-pen swoosh. "The four-dimensional mathematical space we use to formulate—what?"

Physics is my favorite subject, but my teacher is way too energetic for 9 a.m. For a Monday. For any day after I've been awake all night, which since October is basically always. *Spacetime*, I write down. Then, for some inexplicable reason—and I instantly scribble it out—*Thomas Althorpe*.

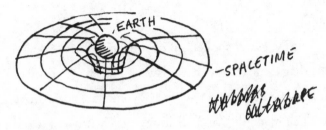

OBJECTS CAUSE SPACETIME TO CURVE

"E equals McSquared," mumbles Nick Choi from the other side of the classroom.

"Thank you, Einstein," says Ms. Adewunmi, to laughter. "That's the theory of special relativity. Spacetime—space is three-dimensional, time is linear, but if we combine them, that gives us a playground for all sorts of physics fun. And it was calculated by . . . ?"

Hermann Minkowski, I think, but instead of raising my hand, I use it to stifle a yawn.

"That guy, Mike Wazowski!" someone yells.

"What, from *Monsters, Inc.*?" asks Nick.

"They travel between worlds, don't they? *McSquared*," I hear from behind me.

"Minkowski," Ms. Adewunmi attempts over whoops and catcalls. "Let's try to focus on reality . . ."

Good luck with that. It's the last week of term, and the atmosphere is as fizzy as carbon dioxide—probably why Ms. Adewunmi's given up on the curriculum and is making her own fun.

"Anyone else for interstellar dimensions? How would you describe a one-way metric?" *A wormhole*, I think. A one-way metric is a blast from the past. That's how I'd answer. Ned bringing back Grey by repatriating his Buddhas, leaving crystals in the bathroom sink, cooking with way too much chili. Jason, smiling at me in the garden after almost a year.

Thomas Althorpe.

But I've never spoken up during any of Ms. Adewunmi's lessons. It's not that I don't know the answers. And back at my old school, I never minded saying so and having everyone stare at the math-genius-prodigy-freak-show-nerd. We'd all known each other since forever. But like a lot of the villages along the coast, Holksea's too small to support a real high school. At sixteen, everyone transfers to the giant school in town. Here, classes are twice the size and full of strangers. But mostly, it's that ever since the day Grey died, talking exposes me. As though I'm the opposite of invisible, but everyone can see right through me.

When Ms. Adewunmi's gaze lands on me, her eyebrows go shooting off into her Afro. She knows I know the answer, but I keep my mouth clammed shut till she turns back to the whiteboard.

"All right, then," she says. "I know you guys have fractals next period, so let's keep moving."

Fractals, I write down. *The infinite, self-replicating patterns in nature. The big picture, the whole story, is just thousands of tiny stories, like a kaleidoscope.*

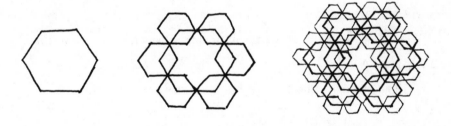

Thomas was a kaleidoscope. He turned the world to colors. I could tell you a hundred stories about Thomas, and it still wouldn't be the big picture: He bit a teacher on the leg. He got a lifetime ban from the Holksea summer fair. He put a jellyfish in Megumi Yamazaki's lunch box when she said I had a dead mum, and he could thread licorice shoelaces through his nose.

But it was more than that. According to Grey, we were *wolf cubs raised in the same patch of dirt*. Thomas didn't belong on his side of the hedge, where the lawn was neatly clipped and his scary dad's rules were practically laminated. And I didn't quite belong on mine, where we were allowed to roam free. It wasn't about like or love—we were just always together. We shared a brain. And now he's coming back . . .

I feel the same way as when you flip a rock over in the garden, and see all the bugs squirming underneath.

The bell rings, too early. I think it's a fire drill, till I see everyone around me holding worksheets in the air. The whiteboard is covered in notations, none of them about fractals. The clock suddenly says midday. And, one by one, Ms. Adewunmi is plucking paper from hands, adding them to her growing pile.

Panicked, I look in front of me. There's a worksheet there, but I haven't written on it. I don't even remember being given it.

Next to me, Jake Halpern hands in his worksheet and slouches away, his bag knocking against me as he slides off the stool. Ms. Adewunmi snaps her fingers.

"I . . ." I stare at her, then back at my blank paper. "I ran out of time," I say, lamely.

"All right, then," she says, with a small frown. "Detention."

I've never had detention before. When I check in after my final lesson, a teacher I don't recognize stamps my slip, then waves a bored hand. "Find a seat and read. Do some homework," he says, turning back to his grading.

I make my way through the hot, half-empty room to a seat by the window. Inside my binder is the college application packet I got in homeroom this morning. I shove it to the bottom of my book bag, to be dealt with *never*, and pull out Ms. Adewunmi's worksheet instead. For lack of anything better to do, I start writing.

THE GREAT SPACETIME QUIZ!

Name three features of special relativity.

(1) The speed of light NEVER changes. (2) Nothing can travel faster than light. Which means (3) depending on the observer, time runs at different speeds. Clocks are a way of measuring time as it exists on Earth. If the world turned faster, we'd need a new type of minute.

What is general relativity?

It explains gravity in the context of time and space. An object—Newton's apple tree, perhaps—forces spacetime to curve around it because of gravity. It's why we get black holes.

Describe the Gödel metric.

It's a solution to the $E = MC^2$ equation that "proves" the past still exists. Because if spacetime is curved, you could cross it to get there.

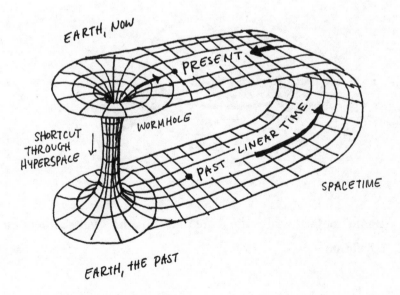

EARTH, NOW

PRESENT

WORMHOLE

SHORTCUT THROUGH HYPERSPACE

LINEAR TIME

PAST

SPACETIME

EARTH, the PAST

What is a key characteristic of a Möbius strip?

*It's infinite. To make one, you half twist a length of paper and Scotch
tape the ends together. An ant could walk along the entire surface,
without ever crossing the edge.*

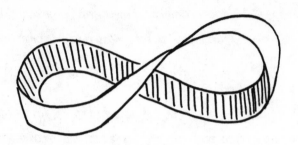

What is an event horizon?

*A spacetime boundary—the point of no return. If you observe a
black hole, you can't see inside. Beyond the event horizon, you can
see the universe's secrets—but you can't get out of the hole.*

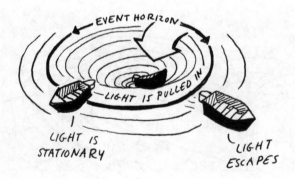

**Bonus point: write the equation for the Weltschmerzian
Exception.**

?!

Even after I stare at the final question for several centuries before giving up, it's still only 4:16 p.m. Forty-four minutes till I can escape.

Resisting the urge to nap, I start doodling. The Milky Way, constellations of question marks. Geometry jokes, spaceships, Jason's name written then scribbled out, over and over and over. Then Thomas's, same thing.

When I look down at the worksheet again, it's a total mess.

4:21 p.m. I yawn and open my notebook, planning to copy my answers onto a clean page.

$E = MC^2$, I begin.

And the second I write the ^{2}, the whole equation starts to shimmer.

Um . . . I yawn and blink, but there it is: my handwriting is definitely *shimmering*. All it needs is a pair of platforms and a disco ball.

I flip the notebook shut. It's a standard college-ruled pad. Heart fluttering, I fumble a couple of times opening it back to the right page. Those ruled lines are now rippling like sound waves across the paper.

Once, I read that lack of sleep can make you hallucinate if you stay awake long enough. But I thought it meant migraine aura-type black spots in front of your eyes, not cartoon-animated notebooks. As if to prove me wrong, the equation begins to spin. Distantly, I'm aware I should probably be panicking. But it's like trying to wake up from a dream—you give yourself the instruction, and nothing happens.

Instead, I yawn and look away, out the window, and begin counting backwards from a thousand in prime numbers: 997, 991 . . . My curiosity gets the better of me around ninety-seven, and I glance back at the notebook. It's not moving. There's my pen scrawl on lined paper, nothing more.

All right, then, as Ms. Adewunmi would say. It's the summer flu, or the temperature in here, or the being-awake-since-yesterday. I shake my shoulders back, pick up my pen.

I'm writing Jason's name again when the notebook disappears.

Seriously.

My pen is hovering in the air where the page should be and suddenly now isn't. It's so ludicrous, I can't help it: I laugh.

"It's not giggle time, Miss Oppenheimer," warns the teacher.

Ms., I correct in my head. And then, *"Giggle time"? What, are we, seven? I've had sex! I've made irreversible decisions, awful ones, huge ones. I'm old enough to DRIVE.*

He frowns at me—I'm grinning like a loon, so I pretend to write on an invisible notebook until, satisfied, he turns away.

I look back at the absence-of-notebook and swallow another cackle. Because I'm wrong: it's not invisible. If it were, I'd be able to see the desk underneath. But instead, there's a rectangle of nothing. An absence. It looks sort of like the black-and-white fuzz of an old TV that won't tune in, or how I imagine the indescribable gloop beyond the boundaries of the universe, the stuff the Big Bang is expanding into.

Am I going bananas?

I bend down, peering underneath the desk. Lumps of gum, a Fingerband sticker, and graffiti on solid wood.

But when I sit upright again, there's still that rectangle of television fuzz.

It's not growing, or changing, or moving. I slump in my seat and stare at it, hypnotized. Drifting back to five years ago. When there was a boy.

An attic.

And a first kiss that wasn't.

"Bawk, bawk, bawk," Thomas says from the other side of the attic. "Chicken. Bet there's not even arteries in your hands."

"Mmmm." I don't look up from the anatomy encyclopedia. Like everything else in Grey's bookshop, it's secondhand, and there's graffiti on the pictures. "Let me check."

He's wrong, you do have arteries in your hands, but I'm planning to do the blood pact anyway. I just want to look at this book first. The pages with boy parts especially. I turn it on its side, tilt my head. How does that even . . . ?

"G, what are you doing?" Thomas peers over my shoulder.

I slam the book shut.

"Nothing! You're right. No arteries," I lie, my face bright red. "Let's do it."

"Gimme your hand," he says, waving the knife. "Oops."

The knife flies through the air. When Thomas turns to get it, he topples over a stack of books.

"What are you kids doing up there?" Grey bellows from the floor below.

I yell down the stairs, "Nothing. Thomas is just reshelving. We thought we'd use this wacky new system called the al-pha-bet."

There's a muffled curse and a giant rumble of laughter. I turn back to Thomas, who's retrieved the knife and is carving our initials into a bookcase. He won't be here tomorrow. We'll never see each other again. On what stupid planet is that even possible?

And it means there's about four hours left to do something I've been thinking about for weeks.

"Thomas. No one is ever going to kiss you," I announce. He looks up, blinking owlishly behind his glasses. "And, no one's ever going to kiss me either."

"OK," he says, and takes a huge inhaler puff. "We should probably do that, then."

We stand up, which is a problem. I grew ninety-three feet this summer.
The eaves are low and I hunch, but I'm still six inches taller than him.
Thomas clambers onto a stack of books, then we're the right mouth height.
He leans forward, and I suck peanut butter off my braces. Here we go . . .

"Ow!"

His head hits my chin. The books slide out from underneath him. Our
hands flail in the air, grabbing at each other, and we smash into the book-
shelves. We're still untangling ourselves when Grey comes bellowing in, chasing
us downstairs to the front door, hands flapping like big hairy butterflies.

"It's raining," I pretend to whine. It's the seaside; I don't mind getting
wet, but I want to hear what he'll say—

"You're a twelve-year-old girl, not the Wicked Witch of the West," Grey
booms, slamming the door behind us as I giggle.

Outside, Thomas and I teeter on the porch, the air soggy. He looks at me,
his glasses smeared, his hair curly with humidity. His hand forms a fist.
Little finger pointed straight out at me.

A salute, a signal, a promise.

"Your house?" he asks. I don't know whether he means for a kiss or the
blood pact. Or both.

"I don't know how to be, without you," I say.

"Me either," he says.

I lift up my hand, and curl my finger into his. Then we jump off the step.
Into the rain.

———————

A paint-stained finger taps on the fuzz in front of me, and instantly, it's
a notebook again. I blink, looking around me, dazed.

"What are you doing?" Sof is standing in front of the desk.

Silhouetted against the windows, she's just an outline—pointy hair, triangle dress, stalk legs, light blazing all around her. An avenging angel, come to rescue me from detention!

I'm confused, sleepy. Sof and I have barely been on corridor nodding terms all year, yet here she is, throwing her portfolio on the ground and her body into the chair next to mine.

After blinking the sun out of my eyes, I blink again when I see her curly hair done up like fro-yo, red lipstick, rhinestone glasses. Sometime between now and whenever I stopped noticing, my erstwhile best friend has remade herself into a fifties musical.

"Uh, hi," I whisper, unsure whether we're allowed to talk. Not because it's detention, but because we don't hang out the way we did at our old school.

She leans over to peer at my notebook.

"Huh," she says, tapping my doodles, where I've scribbled out both Jason's and Thomas's names so they're illegible. I suppose this explains my dream. "Is this your artistic comeback?"

It's a pointed remark. Back in ninth grade, Sof opted for art, geography, German. I went with her choices to save making my own, which sums up our entire friendship. I never told her I had different plans, once we switched schools right before junior year—it was easier to wait for her to notice I wasn't at the next easel.

"Physics quiz," I explain.

"Whatcha do to get thrown in the gulag?" she croaks. For a white-witch-tiger-balm-super-hippie, she sounds like she gargles cigarettes for breakfast.

"Daydreaming." I fiddle with my pen. "What about you?"

"Nothing," she says. "It's time to spring you."

When I look up at the clock, she's right. The teacher's gone. The room's empty. Detention ended an hour ago. Huh. It doesn't feel like I've slept for that long.

"They lock the bike sheds at five." She stands up, fiddling with the strap on her portfolio. "Do you want to catch the bus with me?"

"Okay . . ." I say, only half paying attention. I stare at the notebook: it's only paper, but I shove it right to the bottom of my book bag like it's to blame for what just happened.

Was I really asleep? Is that where the last hour went? I think back to Saturday, a whole afternoon lost before I found myself under the apple tree.

Perhaps I am insane. I take that thought, and shove it as far down as it will go too.

Sof's waiting for me at the door. The silence that rides between us all the way home is so heavy, it deserves its own bus ticket.

Monday 5 July (Evening)

[Minus three hundred and seven]

Schere. Stein. Papier.

It's after dinner, and we've been standing outside Grey's bedroom door playing rock-paper-scissors for twenty minutes. Food was eaten in silent disbelief after Papa suggested Ned and I might want to clear out Grey's room.

"Dare you," says Ned. *Stein* beats *Schere*.

"You first," I say. *Papier* beats *Stein*.

"Best out of, uh, fifty?"

I've only been in there once all year. It was right after the funeral. Ned was leaving for art school in London and Papa was falling apart and pretending he wasn't by hiding at the bookshop, so I did it. Not looking left or right, I took a garbage bag and I swept in everything I needed to—deodorant sticks, beer bottles, dirty plates, half-read newspapers. (Grey's cleaning philosophy: "Here be dragons!")

Then I went through the house, picking out the things I couldn't bear to look at—the enormous orange casserole dish and the Japanese lucky cat; his favorite tartan blanket and a lumpy clay ashtray I made; dozens of tiny Buddha statues tucked into shelves and corners—and I put it all in the shed. I did the same with his car. Papa didn't notice, or didn't say anything, not even when I rearranged the furniture to hide the spectrum of crayon marks on the wall, marking our heights as we grew up—Mum, Ned, me. Even Thomas, occasionally.

Then I shut Grey's bedroom door, and it hasn't been opened until now.

Paper beats rock, again. I win.

"Whatever." Ned shrugs, no big deal. But I notice his hand rests on the doorknob for a full minute before he turns it. His nails are pink. When he finally pushes the door open, it creaks. I hold my breath, but no swarm of locusts emerges. There are no earthquakes. It's exactly as I left it.

Which is bad, because there are books everywhere. Double-shelved from wonky floor to sloping ceiling. Piled up against the walls. Stacked under the bed. Word stalagmites.

Ned clambers past me and yanks open the curtains. I watch from the doorway as the evening sunlight pours in, illuminating approximately eleventy million more books and sending up dust tornadoes.

"Whoa," says Ned, turning around, taking it all in. "Papa told me you cleaned it."

"I did!" God. I lurk in the doorway, afraid to go in any farther. "Do you see any moldy coffee mugs?"

"Yeah, but . . ." He turns away and starts fiddling with cupboard doors and pulling things open. There are more books inside a chest of drawers. After Ned opens the wardrobe, he lets out a long, low whistle.

He doesn't say anything, just stands there staring as if he's seen something . . . odd. As in disappearing-notebook-hole-in-the-universe odd.

"Have you found Narnia in there or something?"

"Grots."

"What is it?" I take a step into the room, keeping my eyes on Ned and not the rest of it—the photographs of our mum everywhere. The huge painting on the wall above the bed.

"Grots," Ned says again, not looking up, talking to the wardrobe. "Fuck. Gottie. His shoes are still in here."

Oh. There's that swarm of locusts.

"I know."

"Couldn't face it, huh?" Ned gives me a sympathetic look, then turns to sit on the piano stool. When Grey was steamed on homemade wine, he'd leave his door open and tunelessly pound out music hall hits. "It's not the melody that counts, it's the volume," he'd boom, not listening to our many declarations otherwise.

Ned runs his hands up and down the keys. The notes emerge in a series of muffled plinks, but I recognize the song.

Papa's left a stack of flattened cardboard boxes on the bed. I walk round to the other side so I don't have to see the painting, and start assembling them. I'm careful not to touch the bed itself, even though it's covered in a dust sheet. This is where Grey slept. In twenty-four hours, Thomas is going to erase his dreams.

"Man, this is going to take forever!" Ned exclaims, even though he hasn't done anything yet. After a final ten-finger kerplink on the piano, he spins round idly on the stool. "You shouldn't have to be in here, doing this. It's Papa's grand plan."

"Do you want to tell him that, or shall I?"

"Ha." He bounds past me to a book stack and starts shuffling through it—not so much organizing as rearranging. Fiddling. Flicking through and reading bits of things. He glances up at me. "Grotbag. What do you think Thomas did?"

"What do you mean?" I frown at the box in front of me. I'm trying to line up the books perfectly perpendicular, but one of them has warped pages from being dropped in the sea, and it's wonkifying everything.

"You know," says Ned. "To get sent back here. Banished to Holksea."

"Banished?"

"C'mon, there's no way this settle-in-for-the-summer story holds up," Ned continues, juggling a book. "It's so last-minute—the flight must have cost a fortune. Nah, it's punishment for something—or getting him away from whatever he's done. I bet he's pulled a Mr. Tuttle."

Mr. Tuttle was Thomas's hamster. A furball who escaped at bedtime seventeen nights in a row, until his dad worked out what was going on and bought a padlock. "Oh dear," Thomas would sorrowfully declare, having opened the cage not five minutes before. "Mr. Tuttle has got out *again*. I'll sleep over at G's in case he's there." His bag would already be packed.

"C'mon," insists Ned. "*You* know what Thomas was like."

Huh. It hasn't occurred to me to wonder *why* he's been sent home so quickly.

A hammering on the bedroom door breaks my thoughts wide open.

"Yo, Oppenheimer! Answer your phone much? I've been looking all over, have you seen the time—" Jason stops when he sees me. There's a pause as he literally shifts and readjusts: stepping back and leaning against a bookshelf by the door, arranging himself just so, before he smiles lazily and amends, "Oppenheimer*s*."

My throat plays rock-paper-scissors and settles on *rock*.

"Gottie." He meets my gaze this time, blue eyes searching mine before he weighs out his words, one by one. "Again. All. Right?"

I have a book in one hand, the other opening and closing on empty air, trying to hold on as we look at each other.

Oblivious, Ned drops the book he's holding onto a stalagmite, which promptly topples. He leaps across the falling books, offering his fist for Jason to bump.

"Shiiit, mate," Ned says, as they perform a complicated handshake. It seems to involve a lot of thumbs. "Is Niall going ballistic?"

"The usual." Jason reverts to slow motion as the handshake ends. He sighs. "You ready?"

"Grots." Ned's practically out the door already as he turns to me. "Swaps?"

I concentrate on assembling another box, fumbling over the corners. "What's the swap?"

"I forgot, we've got a Fingerband meeting. Look, do the books? Get them in the car, and I promise I'll take care of the rest of it." When I look at him, he adds softly, "His clothes."

"Seriously?" I can't decide if Ned's trying to get out of packing the books or shield me from everything else. Grey's shoes. The photographs. *The Wurst.*

I steel myself to look up at the painting on the wall. My final art exam from last year. It's hard, being the straight one in a house with Dumbledore and Peter Pan and Axl Rose, being friends with bangle-wearing glittered artists. So I'd tried, and I'd painted the canal. At the school exhibition, Papa had taken one look at it—a giant blue sausage—and christened it *The Wurst*. Ned had laughed himself silly. I'd pretended I didn't mind, and laughed too.

"Gots, dude." Grey had clamped my shoulder in one giant hand, holding me steady. "You tried something different. You think your brother would attempt anything he wasn't already good at?" We contemplated the sausage for a minute, then he said, "Your mum liked blue."

I tear my eyes away from *The Wurst* and see Ned is hovering in the doorway, waiting for me to make up my mind.

"Deal," I say.

"Cheers, Grots!" he yells, disappearing across the sitting room. "Jase, I'll grab my gear, see you outside in five."

Then I'm alone with Jason for the first time since the day Grey died.

Soft as a sunset, he smiles. And says, "Margot."

The way it ended between us, a text message from a hundred miles away, I never had the chance to let him go. Instead, I stuffed all my heartbreak in a box like the one I'm packing now, and waited. When he says my name, it floods the room.

I could melt into him. But instead I grin, teeth and terror, try to speak, and—

. . .

. . .

. . .

. . .

Jason finally breaks the awkward to murmur, "How's. It. Going?"

"Okay!" I answer too loud and too fast. Then, squeakily: "How is . . ."

Shit. My brain blanks on where he's been. We talked every day last summer, I Internet-stalked him for weeks in the autumn, but I can't remember where he went to college.

"Nottingham Trent," he fills in with a slouchy shrug, his eyes not leaving mine. "It's all right."

There's no air in the room, no air in my lungs, as Jason peels himself off the doorway and approaches me. For a second, I let myself hope he'll slide his arms around my waist, help me forget about this whole horrible year by giving me someone to belong to. Then he flops backwards next to the half-empty box, onto Grey's bed. I wince.

It's too much: the combination of Grey's room and Jason, so close to me. Last October, alone in this empty house and after weeks of trying to work out what we were to each other, I'd asked him. And he'd texted, *I think I can only manage friends for now.* For now. I bet my heart on that caveat, and now here he is.

I grip the side of the box, trying to breathe. Concentrate on stacking Grey's diaries inside the box. Don't look at *The Wurst.* Don't remember how Jason had laughed at it too, a bit.

"Hey, daydreamer." He reaches out and touches my arm. "What about you? Had a good year?"

And as he says it, everything inside the box blinks out. It's no longer a box of books, but a box of nothingness. TV fuzz. Like in detention this afternoon.

Not like detention.

This time, the fuzz is tuning in, forming a picture, swirling, more like, more like—smoke. I can even smell a bonfire. And there's a flicker of light. My fingers tremble. This can't be happening, not with Jason here. I lean closer, to check if he dropped a cigarette or something, and I swear I can see the tartan check of our picnic blanket. Our dandelion-strewn lawn. Hear music. I reach my hand out, I can almost touch it—

"Margot? Gottie?" Jason says. "You seem . . ."

His voice is far away, and I feel a sudden tug as though I'm being

      y   e d   i   e   b

    a   k   n   d   t   e   o

         n   s   i   h   x

I close my eyes as the universe contracts and expands.

———————

"Hey, daydreamer. Brewski?" Jason asks, handing me a can of beer.

I take it, even though I don't want another drink. Sof has been sneaking vodka all night, but one sip left me woozy—floaty. And parties aren't my thing. When Grey wants to celebrate the existence of trees, or the migration of birds, or his annual Last Day of Summer hootenanny, I hover at the edges. Tonight, it's Midsummer's Eve, and I've hidden myself under the apple tree, where I can see everyone, and everyone can't entirely see me. Except, apparently, Jason.

He's already opened it—the "brewski." Fingerband has started doing this stupid dude-backwards-baseball-cap in-joke. Everything's brewski and broseph and fist bumps. It's idiotic.

"This way, we don't have to keep getting up and down," Jason adds, plonking a six-pack in front of us, then flopping onto the blanket. Next to me. Um. Okay?

"Cool thinking, bro," I say in a deep voice, then take a sip of the beer— it's warm.

He laughs. "You know we're being ironic?" He twists to look at me, and I look back. In the dark, his eyes are practically navy. "You can't be called Fingerband and go full metal."

"Full metal?" I take another sip, wishing the beer were cold. It's a hot night, but Grey has insisted on a huge bonfire. Earlier he was leaping across it, yelling about Vikings. I smile in the dark.

"KISS makeup, safety pins in our noses, shouting about Satan." Jason attempts devil horns, but it's tricky when you're resting on your elbows.

"Isn't that punk?" I ask.

Jason laughs, a low rumble as though we're in on a joke together, but I'm not trying to be funny. I don't have a clue. Ned's the musical encyclopedia. I listen to whatever's on the radio—which Grey tunes to static. I'm not sure why Jason's even over here, talking to me about music. The most he's ever said to me in ten years of knowing Ned is, "How's it hanging, oddball?"

"The point is, it's cooler if we play metal but act dorky." He cracks open another can. The clunk-sploosh is as loud as a firework in the dark garden, but no one looks over at us as he edges closer and murmurs, "Margot. How come you never come to see us rehearse?"

Because you've never asked. Because I'd rather watch paint dry. Because Sof worships Ned and if I tell her you've invited me, she'll make us go— and Fingerband sounds like a goat in a lawnmower.

Across the garden, Sof's on a blanket with this week's girlfriend, both of them laughing at Ned's air guitar. I mentally add Jason's invitation to the tally of secrets I'm keeping from her.

"You should come along," he says again. "School's over, huh?"

"Yeah. I finished my last exam on Friday." My elbows are getting fuzzy; pins and needles. Is that why he's talking to me? School's out, and I'm rolling with the cool kids now?

Across the garden, Ned hollers something and jogs off inside, into the house. When he's out of sight, Jason leans over my shoulder, nudging me with his chin. "Give me a taste."

I turn to him, to say he can have the beer, it's gross, and he all of a sudden plants his mouth on mine. I squeak with surprise, into his tongue, but he doesn't laugh. His lips are firm against mine, a question. I kiss him back, but I don't know what to do. I've never kissed anyone before. It's warm and beery, and it's Jason! Why is he kissing me? And then it's . . . I'm . . . We're . . . I float away, closing my eyes.

When I open them, I'm still standing in Grey's bedroom. Only now it's dark, and Jason's gone—and we just had our first kiss.

That's what it seems like, anyway. A memory so vivid, there were sights and sounds and smells and touches. I could sense the scratch of the blanket we were lying on, smell the wood smoke in the air. The taste of beer on his tongue, the roughness of his face against mine. The first of a summer of secret kisses, something that belonged to just me.

And the loss of him is suddenly so real and so raw, I want to cry.

I take a big, juddering gulp of air, trying to fill my lungs, which are pinched and small. I'm so overwhelmed by how much it hurts—missing Jason, *seeing* Jason—it takes me a moment or two before I catch up with what just happened and think: WTF?

I unpack the thought I pushed down after detention today. How a daydream shouldn't last more than an hour. How it shouldn't leave me standing alone in the dark. Why can't I remember Jason leaving, saying goodbye? And what *was* that, inside the box? It felt like I was looking the wrong way through a telescope, to another time. A time when Grey was alive.

A vortex. A one-way metric. But that would mean—

I stumble towards the door, switch on the light, turn around.

Everything's packed. All the books are gone, the boxes too. There are little dust outlines on the shelves. Book ghosts. And the room seems smaller, now that it's empty. The ceiling is lower and the walls are closing in.

Perhaps that's my panic. I don't remember doing this. I sit on the floor because my legs have forgotten how to do "upright," and I try to think.

I touched the television fuzz, and I was with Jason, last summer. An optical illusion? A daydream? *C'mon, Gottie—are you seriously saying it was a wormhole?*

The boxes are packed. The room is empty. I must have done that. My pocket beeps and when I fumble for my phone, there's a text from Jason: Nice to see you again . . . Nothing about me getting sucked into a box, but maybe that's not the kind of thing you put in a text. A text that trails off into three dots, like there's more to come.

Is there such a thing as a split-screen vortex? Last summer on one side, this room on another. And you can only tune in to one viewpoint at a time.

It makes total sense. Except for the part where I'm completely crazy!

There's one box still on the bed, and I clamber to my feet to dig through it, fingers fumbling, hoping to find something to explain what I thought I saw. To tell me I'm not going nuts.

There's nothing but odds and ends. A framed photo of my mum where she's a few months older than I am now, and we look so alike it hurts. And a stack of Grey's diaries. He used to note everything down: a new recipe for spaghetti with apricots (really), a bird's nest on the lawn, when the village shop briefly stopped selling Marmite. He's the only one of us who ate it.

When my scrabbling fingertips hit cardboard, I admit defeat and tell myself I imagined the whole thing. I've lost a few hours, that's all. Slept on my feet, like a horse in a stable, and dreamed about Jason. Hitting the light switch with my chin, I carry the box outside, to Grey's crappy old VW Beetle.

The car is parked on a hump of grass, skewed at an angle into the hedge, sitting so low that Papa will barely be able to get it over the speed bumps to the Book Barn tomorrow. I have to stand sideways on the small slope to reach the latch, balancing the box on my knee, and as the trunk springs up, the box slides off, bursting open on the grass in a scatter of coins and pages.

"*Scheisse!*" I kneel in the half-dark to pick everything up, chucking the half-open diaries clumsily back in the box.

ROAST CHICKEN AND POTATO SALAD IN THE GARDEN.

Grey's scrawling handwriting catches my eye in the light spilling from the kitchen. *Beech leaves on the fire. I dream of being a Viking.*

Potato salad. He meant *Kartoffelsalat*, the German sort served warm with mustard and vinegar, not mayonnaise (i.e., not totally disgusting). The entry is from Midsummer's Eve last year: the night of my first kiss with Jason. My first real kiss, ever.

It's a thump to the heart. But it's also an explanation: I spent the afternoon studying spacetime, and I was reading the diaries while I packed. That's why I remembered it so vividly. Ned's home, I hung out with Sof, Jason's back and smiling at me . . . This is why my mind's on last summer. I didn't lie on a blanket in the grass or smell the bonfire. I'm imagining things.

Because otherwise I'd have to admit that there is such a thing as a wormhole, and that I've seen two today. But Thomas is arriving tomorrow, and that's about as much as I can deal with.

I reach forward and slam the diary shut.

Tuesday 6 July

[Minus three hundred and eight]

After I text Jason back—a breezy *You too! :)* that takes two hours to compose—me and Umlaut stay up all night, reading Grey's diaries and breaking our hearts. I couldn't quite bring myself to put them in the car. And a small part of me is hoping that the wormholes are real, and I'll be blasted back to when he was alive.

The entries are all semi-cryptic, but this one makes me laugh, because I remember the day he means:

GOTTIE ON A FRUIT AND VEGETABLE BOYCOTT AFTER LEARNING BIRDS AND BEES.
SOMETHING ABOUT A CONDOM ON A BANANA.
(BUY VITAMIN PILLS?)
CONSIDER DUNGEON. SHE LOOKS SO MUCH LIKE CARO.

Caro—my mum. Grey was pretty accepting that his only daughter got pregnant at nineteen by a tiny blond German exchange student—but he was also clear history wasn't going to repeat itself. That day, I'd hurtled home from sex education at school, convinced Grey would say "Make love in the sea, Gottie! Tangle among the waves! Let Neptune protect your vital eggs!"

But instead he thundered, "I don't know if I believe in all the things I'm doing, dude, or if I half believe them and it's cosmic insurance. But you can get pregnant upside down, the first time, in the sea, on the grass, under a full moon—most especially under a full moon; all that romance and you forget your own name, let alone the rubber in your wallet. So take the pill, for God's sake. Take all the pills. Use a condom, get a diaphragm."

It's dawn by the time I stop reading, the sun coming up as bright as a magnesium flame. No freak rainstorms have shut down the airports. Which means Thomas is arriving in T-minus eight hours.

Let the *Sturm und Drang* begin.

First, though, I have to make it through this end-of-year assembly. We've barely finished our year, and already they're hustling us out the door—every week there's a talk about college applications, personal statements, student loans, next year's exams . . .

"This Is Your Last-Chance Summer," Mr. Carlton, the college advisor, is stage-whispering. "Entrance Exams Start In September, People—Do Not Waste Your Summer Vacation."

In the row ahead of me, Jake rests his head on Nick's shoulder, unconcerned with the doom-mongering. The girl next to me is on her phone, tweeting about the *unfairness* of having summer homework. Across the room I can see Sof, head-to-toe in pink and frantically writing a million notes as Mr. Carlton starts whispering about the Process For Art School. I should text her and say not to bother—Ned went through all that a year ago.

But I'm too busy freaking out.

And not just about what happened last night: the memory-wormhole-whatever. Losing a huge chunk of time. *Jason*. But also: Thomas being halfway over the Atlantic by now. Ned retuning the kitchen radio to static, which was how Grey used to listen to it. ("Cosmic noise, man, you can't beat it! It's the sound of the universe expanding.") And Papa, ballooning around the bookshop—he drifts in and out of the house, replenishing cereal supplies and springing surprise kittens and summer visitors, but he's not *there*.

All of that, and then there's Mr. Carlton striding around, telling me I need to decide what to do with the rest of my life, and for the next four years, and where to do it. Right Now!

You can practically hear the exclamation marks as he talks. That I'm expected to be excited about it. Everybody else is. Happy to escape our sleepy seaside villages, embroidered along the coast, where we've been our whole lives and nothing ever happens.

But I like sleepy. I *like* nothing-ever-happens. I buy the same chocolate bar from the same shop every day, next to our village pond with its minimalist duck population of three, and then I check the Holksea village newsletter with no news in it. It's comforting. I can wrap my whole life up in a blanket.

I don't want to "Think About The Future," as Mr. Carlton keeps proselytizing. It's hard enough living in this present.

While he keeps finding new and terrifying ways to hiss about The Rest Of Our Lives, I tune out and start making notes on my notebook. I might not be able to stop the inexorable forward motion of applying for college, Ned's *What Would Grey Do?* summer agenda, or Thomas's plane, but there is one thing I can control.

I can work out what really happened last night.

By the end of the assembly, I've got a notebook full of equations to justify my split-screen-meets-telescope hypothesis. As everyone scrapes their chairs back, Sof half waves at me across the room to join her in the escape-gaggle at the doors. I shake my head, pointing to my physics teacher, and she gives me a closed-lip smile.

Ms. Adewunmi's lingering in her seat, frowning at a timetable, but I'm hoping she'll welcome such out-of-the-blue questions as—

"How does spacetime work?" I blurt.

She looks up sternly. "I *knew* you weren't paying attention yesterday."

"No, I mean—I was. I did the quiz, in detention. In class, sorry . . ."

My apologies trail off, and she laughs: "Kidding! What is it you want to know, exactly?"

"I wanted to ask—vortexes. Wormholes. What do they actually look like?"

"Is this a curriculum question, or do I need to worry about Norfolk getting sucked into the fourth dimension?" Ms. Adewunmi asks.

"It's hypothetical. I mean, theoretical! I'm interested in the math behind it," I assure her. "I know you can't create a wormhole without dark matter, or travel through one. But could you see through it? Like a long-distance TV?"

My teacher considers me, then darts a glance from left to right. There are still stragglers at the doors, and she watches them leave before leaning forward to whisper urgently, "What's the thousandth prime number?"

"Um?" I don't understand, compute it anyway. "7,919."

She jerks her head to the doors. "Follow me."

Ms. Adewunmi doesn't say anything the whole way along the corridors. Every time I try to ask a question, she gives a tiny head shake. I start to wonder if I'm in trouble. When we get to her office, she sits behind the desk, then pushes the other chair out with her foot, wordlessly asking me to sit. It's completely badass.

I scramble into the chair. Is she going to give me detention again? Normally she's all smiles, even when covering boring stuff like topology, but she's watching at me seriously. Then she finally speaks.

"Welcome," she says, fixing me with a stare, "to the Parallel Universe Club."

I stare back, heart thumping.

"God! *Kidding*, again!" She cackles loudly. "You kids are so gullible." She wipes her eyes, still laughing. Hilarious.

"Gottie, every year one of my students acts like wormholes are real. And c'mon, this is the first peep I've heard from you all year. You've got to let me have my fun. All right, then. Theoretically—who knows what you'd see? Maybe the vortex would be so curved the event horizon would prevent you from seeing round the corner. And if we imagine you *could* see through a wormhole, the gravity inside might be so strong it would distort the light waves—like a fish-eye lens."

In English: you'd see nothing, or fun house mirrors. But Jason's kiss last night was a live-action, Smell-O-Vision, Technicolor, 3D, IMAX replay. With popcorn.

"Okay, but," I push, "mathematically. In theory. Say with the Gödel metric, the past still exists, because spacetime is curved. If you *could* see the past, like through a—" I mumble the next bit, aware of my supreme ridiculousness. "TV-wormhole-telescope, and it wasn't distorted. Would watching the past make time work, um, differently? From the viewpoint. Affect it, somehow?"

"You mean, the way a clock on a speeding train runs slower than one in the station?"

"Yes!" I beam. The clock thing is both true and *amazing*. "I was thinking . . . if you watched twenty minutes' worth of the past through the wormhole, you'd lose a couple of hours of real time."

"Could do." Ms. A contemplates me for a moment. Then she reaches for a pen and starts to write. "If you're interested in pursuing quantum mechanical theory at college, you'll want to read these. You should also"—she points her pen at my notebook, which is open to a doodle of Jason's name—"concentrate on your applications."

I nod, putting my hand out for the list. She doesn't give it to me.

"Have you thought about a branch—pure mathematics or theoretical physics?" she asks, holding the paper just beyond my reach. "We don't want to lose you to the biologists. Ha-ha!"

"I'm not sure yet . . ." The thought of committing to a subject for life gives me the dry heaves. I can barely commit to an emotion for five minutes.

"Don't take too long to decide—I'll need time for your recommendation. In fact . . ." She waves the paper. "I'll let you have this if you write it up for me. Your take on wormholes."

"Homework?" I grimace, though I suppose a summer in the library is one way to avoid Thomas.

"Think of it as your personal statement. I want the math behind it too. You give me a kickass essay on this telescope-time theory, I'll write you the kind of recommendation that will take you a million light-years from Holksea—scholarships, grants, the works."

She dangles the paper at me. I don't want to be a million light-years from here. I don't know where I want to be. But I do want to know what's going on. So I take it.

———

Unsurprisingly, hardly any of Ms. A's list is in the school library. I check after my last lesson, but among nine thousand poetry anthologies there's not so much as a battered *Brief History of Time*. The couple of books that should be there are checked out—I reserve them at the desk, then head to the bike sheds.

I know where I can find what I need. The Book Barn. Grey came at the universe from a different angle than me, but he had a whole floor stacked full of science—from fiction to physics. The only problem is, I haven't been there all year. Whenever Papa's floated down to earth and asked, I've made excuses—homework. Biking. Swimming, even when the sea froze in November, or lying on my bed and staring at the ceiling for hours.

If you turn people away enough times, eventually they stop trying to find you.

When I get to the gate, I stop and dig through my book bag for my helmet. See Grey's diary instead. I brought it with me this morning, a sort of talisman. Now I flip it open to find out—what was I doing, this day last year?

G SHOULD MOVE BACK INTO NED'S ROOM WHEN HE LEAVES FOR ST. MARTINS. REJOIN THE WORLD.

Underneath, there's a little doodle of a cat, and I know exactly what day this is. Exams were long over, but I was tucked inside the bookshop attic, reading. Until Grey sat down next to me, plucking the book from my hand.

"Schrödinger, huh?"

I watched him scan the text a little, the famous cat theory. It was pre-Umlaut.

"Let me get this straight," said Grey. "You put a cat, uranium, a Geiger counter, a hammer, and a jar full of poison in a box. What the hell kind of Christmas present is that?"

I laughed, and explained the uranium has a 50 percent probability of decaying. If it does, the Geiger counter triggers the hammer to break the jar full of poison, and the cat dies. But if the uranium doesn't decay, the cat lives. Before you open the box and find out for certain, both things are therefore simultaneously true. The cat is both dead and alive.

"You want to know a fun fact about Schrödinger?" Grey asked, handing me the book back and standing up.

"All right."

"He was a champion shagger," Grey boomed. "Screwed his way round Austria!"

I could hear his laughter as he made his way down the stairs, even as I went back to trying to work out how two opposites could both be true. Jason was my Schrödinger. Inside the box was us: a secret, something special; no one else could take it over or spoil it. But we'd been together a few weeks, and now there was another thought inside the box: I wanted him to claim me out loud.

Before I left the bookshop, I went into the biographies section and looked it up—about Schrödinger, and the shagging. Grey was right.

I don't know how Papa manages to work there every day.

But once I pedal away from town, on the coastal road back to Holksea, I begin to relax. The air is honey on my skin, and after a while, the world is nothing but sun and sky and sea. Occasional pubs and churchyards flutter in my peripheral vision. I speed up till they blur, salt air filling my lungs. I breathe it deep, and then I'm a kid again and for a moment nothing matters—not Thomas, not Grey, not Jason.

After a few minutes, a cluster of old buildings approaches in the distance—the outskirts of Holksea. The bookshop is on the sea side of the village, and you can see the sign from space: the Book Barn. It's huge, flashing neon-pink capitals, dim in the sunlight but still as bright as Grey himself, and the letters imprint themselves on the back of my retinas.

I'm fifty feet away and still going fast when they disappear. Just—*blink*—and gone.

No.

My heart speeds up, my feet slow down, but not much. I'm compelled to keep going. Thirty feet now. Where the letters should be, there's nothing but space. And this time I don't mean emptiness, nothing, a negative integer, the square root of minus-fucking-seventeen. I mean, literally: outer space. There's a hole in the sky where the sky should be.

Twenty feet now. I'm half a mile from the sea, 52.96 degrees north, and a billion light-years away from Earth. This isn't a telescope. It's the *ficken* Hubble.

And at the edges of the hole, where the sky turns back to blue, the same untuned-television fuzz that I've seen before, twice now. What did Ms. Adewunmi say, about vortexes? That the image would be distorted? This is crystal.

I'm sick with terror, but I can't make my feet stop pedaling. Because, oh shit, oh shit, oh shit. Grey's bedroom. Grey's diaries. Grey's bookshop. Whatever this is—and there's definitely a *this*, yesterday I saw last summer, and today there's a hole filled with the Milky Way!—it has to do with Grey. And Grey's dead. Which means it has to do with me . . .

At ten feet away, instinct jerks my handlebars, aiming for the footpath to the sea. I lean my body into the turn, one I've taken a million times before, and faster. But this time, for whatever reason, I'm in trouble.

I hit the turn too hard, it's more of a swerve, and adrenaline floods me. This is going to be bad. There's a shot of fear as I try to correct my balance, jerking to the right. But then my front tire veers from a rock to a pothole, and I'm down—and it hurts—but I don't stop moving, even when I hit the path. My elbow meets the ground first, and a throb shoots up my arm. There's fire in my thigh as I slide along for a few feet, leaving my skin behind. I crumple to a halt when I land in the hedge—but the bike keeps sliding, my foot trapped in the pedal. It drags my leg round, twisting my ankle, before discarding me and spinning away with a crash. Leaving me alone.

Tuesday 6 July (Later)

[Minus three hundred and eight]

I lie in the hedge for an eternity, looking up. All I can see is the sky—the real sky, the one that's supposed to be there. It's huge and cloudless, bright and blue, and very, very far away.

A century or so later, I check my watch—smashed, the LCD digits scattered—and my phone—dead, however hard I mash the buttons. But even so, I know I haven't lost any time at all. I felt every second. Because

Jesus

Fuck

Ow

it hurts.

My heart hurts. I want Jason. I want the mami I've never had. I want Grey. I *want*.

"Hello?" I say eventually, experimentally, my voice wavering. "Hello?"

And I wait and wait, but nobody comes to find me. I've been making myself smaller and smaller for a year, and now I'm barely here at all.

Finally, eventually, I stand up, testing my ankle. It's not broken, I don't think—I'd have heard it snap, like when Thomas dared me to jump off the pier and I spent three months in a cast that he drew swears all over. But *shit*, it kills. I stumble on it a few times till I'm able to lean against the hedge and look around.

On the other side of the road, the bookshop sign flashes pink neon. Normal as pie. My bike is at an angle in the ditch, taking a bubble bath in the white wildflowers. I hobble over and see it's mostly unharmed: the front wheel is twisted and the chain has come off, but it's all stuff I can bash back in place. I haul it out of the ditch and lean on it while I hop, wincing, to the bookshop.

After avoiding it forever, it's the only place I want to be.

———————————

The door is locked, Papa at the airport picking up Thomas. It takes a couple of tries of fumbling with the key. Inside it's dark and quiet, the smell hitting me in a whoosh—paper, old wood, pipe smoke, and dusty carpets. Home.

I leave the door open and the lights off as I inch my way through the narrow shelves, emerging into a small, book-lined cavern. A maze of more bookshelf corridors leads off it in all directions. The boxes I packed last night are piled in a corner, next to the desk. Behind it looms Grey's giant armchair.

I crawl into it, throbbing, and try to shut out the too-loud, off-kilter tick of the grandfather clock that Grey refused to have fixed. I examine the desk, squinting through the gloom for the first aid kit. The top drawer is overflowing with scraps of paper—it reminds me of the wildflowers in the ditch. Fishing through the receipts and order forms, I find chocolate bars, essential oil, a tin of tobacco, a brown glass bottle. I rattle it. One of Grey's hippie remedies. He swore by ginkgo biloba, Saint John's wort, evening primrose. I swallow two pills dry, forcing them down around the lump in my throat.

Everything hurts. My leg is gravel-scraped and gross. I'll have scabs for days. When I was a kid and fell over, my grandfather would be there to give me a Band-Aid and kiss it better.

I rest my head against the velvet chair, breathing in its Grey scent, falling apart over and over. Papa's kept the bookshop exactly as it was—dusty and disorganized, a shrine to Grey's admin policy. ("I'm a keeper of books, not a bookkeeper!") His ginormous chair, I'm tiny inside it, the desk where he sometimes wrote his diaries, and that stupid broken clock, its tick-tick . . . tickticktick . . . -tock. Tears blob my eyes so I can't see, and the mottled velvet blurs until it looks like the untuned TV, the monochrome fuzz I saw outside, right before I crashed. Tick . . .

Tock.

Tick-tick.

"Make it look good, okay?" I say. We're in the apple tree, which is all full of slimy wet leaves, and my bum is cold, but Grey says you have to feel the earth underneath you. "They can't know it was us."

It's Ned's tenth birthday party and he uninvited me and Thomas. Grey says we are invited and that Ned is on thin ice, but I think we should steal his cake anyway. Thomas came up with the plan to do face paint like bandits.

"Obviously," says Thomas, rolling his eyes. "Okay, I'm going to give you a mustache as well."

"Yes," I agree. It's always yes when it comes to us, and I close my eyes. The paint tickles as he starts drawing. "Remember the signal: when Grey shouts 'Trouble times two . . .'"

"That's when we run," Thomas finishes. "G, open your eyes."

When I do, Thomas is laughing and holding up a permanent marker—

"—what happened? Gottie? Gottie, open your eyes."

Papa's voice breaks through the darkness. My eyelids are thick and heavy, rusted over. I must have fallen asleep. I've been dreaming of Thomas and me in the tree, but not the right day, not the day he left . . .

When I open my eyes, the images fade away. I blink. Papa is in front of me.

"Fell asleep. Oh. And off m'bike," I tell him, mumbling into the chair's velvet wing, twisting a bit to the side to show him.

He makes a sucking-in-air sound, out of proportion to a scraped leg. Papa hates the sight of blood, winces when me or Ned gets a paper cut. How did he deal, when Mum died, if there was blood? Did he disappear down wormholes looking for her?

I can't keep hold of the thought, of any of my thoughts; they scatter like autumn leaves.

"*Ist* your bike outside?" Papa's asking. My bike is pink with a basket and cereal box clackers on the spokes, so I don't know whose else's he thinks it might be.

I force myself to sit up, wincing in anticipation of cotton balls and hydrogen peroxide sting. The sense memory of childhood cuts and scrapes wakes me up enough to smile at Papa, convince him I'm all right.

"Good." Papa smiles. "The car's parked down at the beach. I go and fetch, so wait here?"

"Okay."

"Keep her company," I hear as Papa turns away, and I sneakily close my eyes again, snuggling back into the velvet. It's the Milky Way. *Who her?* I think. *I'm me.*

Footsteps, and the bookshop door banging in the distance as Papa goes outside. But maybe not, because he's still here, holding my hand. Being annoying, too, he keeps on tapping on it.

"Gerroff." I try to shake the hand away, but warm fingers slide into mine, squeezing me awake. "Papa, ztoppit."

"G?" someone says. A boy's voice, coming out of the stars. "Your dad's outside. It's me."

Me has a funny accent; it's English but not English at the same time, and I open my eyes to look at it. There's a boy my age leaning over me, holding my hand, his face glasses and freckles and concern.

And he's surrounded by stars, all the time, everywhere. There's an entire galaxy inside the bookshop, hanging in the air.

"You're covered in stars," I say.

His mouth crinkles. That's how Thomas Althorpe always smiled—like his face couldn't contain how hilarious he found the world, and it overflowed into dimples. This version has added cheekbones, and canine teeth that push into his bottom lip. Oh. Glasses. Freckles. It's him.

"Hello, G." Thomas smiles as a comet whizzes by his head. "Remember me?"

"I remember you. You came back. You promised you would. But I don't remember you being this gorgeous."

Those are the last words I say before I pass out.

Wednesday 7 July

[Minus three hundred and nine]

I wake up sweating under a patchwork quilt and six blankets I didn't put there, see my clock and realize that I'm late for class, decide not to care, then turn and vomit over the side of my bed. There's a plastic washing-up bowl on the floor, waiting for this to happen. This sequence takes place smoothly in about thirty seconds before I flop back against the pillows.

I'm not going to school today.

The sun through the ivy has turned the air Aurora Borealis green. I feel heavy—my bedroom has its own gravitational force, pushing me into the mattress. There's a throb in my leg from falling off my bike, a pounding in my head, and the ubiquitous Jason-and-Grey-shaped hurt in my heart.

Grey. I stare across the room at his diaries. There's something else, something pushing at the edges of my consciousness, something I need to remember . . .

Grey's bedroom. And Thomas Althorpe, across the garden, sleeping in it.

Oh.

I don't remember you being this gorgeous.

Cringe. Maybe I manifested these blankets into being with the thermodynamics of mortification, so I'd have something to hide under.

That reminds me of yesterday's theory, right before I fell off my bike: that the strange occurrences are a manifestation of Grey, and guilt. And me.

I shouldn't have taken his diaries. I shouldn't be reading them. But it's more than that. It's this whole year, it's how I was on the day he died—

Stop. I force my brain back to Thomas—by contrast, an easier mental topic. I make a clucking sound with my tongue until Umlaut jumps onto my bad leg. Why is he here? Thomas, I mean, not the kitten. Ned says banishment. But Thomas never did anything leave-the-country bad. Letting the pigs out at the summer fair—an annual cluster of raffles and homemade jam on the village green. Eating all the stripy Jell-O Grey made for my birthday party, then throwing up rainbows. But he's not *criminal*.

My head hurts thinking about it. My head hurts, period.

"I'm going to go to the kitchen to get a glass of water," I say out loud to a skeptical-looking Umlaut. "I'm extremely dehydrated."

Not because I'm curious about Thomas. Not because I want to find out why he's back, or why he never wrote to me. Not because the picture I have of him from yesterday—freckles against dark hair—is blurred by shooting stars. I want some water, that's all.

It takes me ten minutes to limp through the garden, Umlaut trotting beside me, barely visible in the shaggy grass. When I get to the kitchen, Ned's bedroom door is shut. There's a message on the blackboard in Papa's handwriting for Thomas to call his mum, and a wonky loaf of bread in the middle of the table. We've been mostly cereal people this year, eaten in handfuls out of the box. No me and Papa gathering for breakfast, two people at our huge table. The empty space where Grey always sat highlighting that Ned wasn't here, that Mum should always have been.

It's like Grey's death left a hole bigger than even he was.

"Curiouser and curiouser," I say to Umlaut as I sit down opposite the bread.

"What's curious, Alice?"

I jump at Thomas's voice behind me, my heart in my ears. Half of me freezes. Half of me swivels in my seat. Consequently, I almost fall off the chair as he walks into the room. Dark hair shower-wet, bare feet, a cardigan buttoned over a T-shirt. He looks *clean*. I run my tongue surreptitiously round my dry, post-vomit mouth.

Thomas gives this shy little wave and disappears behind the fridge door, which is now a Ned-orchestrated blur of photos and magnets, leaving me to compute the updates on the boy who left. He'd been half my height, round, and topped with thick-lensed glasses that boggled his eyes. This version is a hundred feet taller and has *arms*. Obviously he had arms before, but not like this. Not like you had to think about them in italics.

I'm leaning to one side and duck back in my seat as Thomas emerges from the fridge, his arms laden. He doesn't say anything, giving me the tiniest smile as he piles butter and jars of jam and Marmite and peanut butter in front of me.

"Tea?" He smiles again, his hand hovering over the mugs that hang from the cabinet. One night and he's completely at home. *Duh*, I remind myself: he practically used to live here. With Grey's roars and Ned's Nedness and Papa's DIY approach to parenting—"Chocolate? Hmmm, take the whole bag"—Thomas and I spent most of our time on this side of the hedge. It was more interesting (not to mention his dad was a yeller).

As Thomas fills the kettle, silence builds in the air. There has to be The Conversation—you don't come back after leaving and say "Tea?" Actually, Jason did. Ned did. That's what boys do. They leave, and when they come back, act like it's no big deal.

Thomas hacks the wonky bread into slices while he waits for the kettle to boil. I peek at him when he's not looking, adding details to my mental file: Thomas has hairy toes! Thomas wears hipster glasses! Thomas is *cool*. From his vintage haircut—too short at the sides and tousling into curls on top as it dries—to his obscure-organic-coffee-brand T-shirt. And his cardigan. It's a betrayal. How dare he grow up *cool*. How dare he grow up at all.

Finally he plonks a stack of toast and a mug in front of me and sits down opposite, nodding as if to say "Well, here we are." As if to say five years is nothing.

He's made my tea the perfect shade of brown. My toast is burnt the way I like it. It's infuriating, that he's got this right. I push the Marmite out of sight and scrape on hard curls of butter, then take a bite and let out an involuntary "Mmm."

When I look up, Thomas is staring at me, puzzled.

"What?" I wipe my chin for crumbs, conscious of my sweaty hair, my grungy pajamas, my bralessness underneath them. The second I think this, my brain goes: *breasts, breasts, breasts.* My skin flushes.

"Nothing." He shakes his head, then again. "Yesterday. At the Book Barn." His voice is deeper than when he left, and not quite Canadian. Apparently my brain is on a roll with embarrassing thoughts, because it goes: his mouth must taste of maple syrup. *Wie bitte?*

"Your dad says that's the first time you'd been there for a while? The bookshop?" Thomas is still talking, and I try to focus.

This must seem weird to him—the Book Barn was always our rainy-day refuge. An escape when his parents were fighting—especially then, when his dad would redirect ire to Thomas—or when Ned was refusing to play with us. We'd cycle out of the village towards the sea, and Grey would take us in until we got too noisy. I don't know how to answer, so I cram a piece of toast into my mouth.

"Right. Sorry. How—" Thomas immediately holds up a wait-a-minute finger. After digging in his pocket, he emerges with an inhaler and takes two puffs before saying, "How are you feeling this morning?"

"Huh?" I'm distracted—I'd forgotten about his asthma. I add a mental wedge of Scotch tape to his glasses, and my memories start to shift and rearrange themselves. Past Thomas and this one, beginning to coalesce.

"Falling off your bike, remember?" prods Thomas. "Hang out with me—Ned said to tell you to pull a sick day; he'd fake a note for you."

Ned said that?

"I'm fine," I lie automatically, a year's practice. It's practically my catchphrase.

"Actually, you ralphed. You'd taken a couple of pills, morphine; you said there were shooting stars coming out of my head." Thomas waves his hands around when he talks, grabbing invisible bats. He used to do that when he was excited, or freaked out, or nervous. I don't know which one this is. I'm trying to get my brain to speed up: *morphine*?

"We got you in the car, your dad muttering in German the whole time, and WHOOSH. You hurled all over my pants. With the bloody leg, it was like the day I left. Remember? That day with the time capsule."

Thomas pauses his insane monologue—he's used more words in a minute than I have in ten months. And I can't keep up, what time capsule?—and he looks at me. His eyes are muddy, with a flaw in the right iris like an inkblot. How had I forgotten that?

"You had short hair that day," he says, like he's planting a flag on the moon and declaring his knowledge of me.

But if an old haircut and a scar on my hand is everything he has—I was wrong. He doesn't know me at all.

"G." Thomas tilts his head at me. "Do you think that email—"

Screenwipe.

I don't know how else to describe what happens. One minute, Thomas is tilting his head, holding his mug, mentioning an email. Then there's this ripple across the air, for a few seconds. Cling wrap peels off across the room. Revealing what's underneath: everything looks exactly the same, except the clock has jumped forward a minute, and Thomas is holding his toast and laughing, shoulders and curly hair shaking, as he says:

"—Okay, so what's the plan this summer?"

It's as though time skipped. Not for long, but like a jumpy DVD stuttering through a scene. I think I'm alone in noticing this glitch, which reinforces what I thought about yesterday's space trip: that it's to do with me. Me and Grey. Something I did has made time go all *Eternal Sunshine.*

Thomas is waiting for me to answer, acting as though nothing has happened. I don't know—maybe it hasn't. Maybe this and the worm-holes are all in my head. Maybe it's this alleged "morphine." Is that Canadian slang? Grey spurned traditional medicine—he was once caught trying to fish for leeches in the village pond, and I never saw him take so much as an aspirin—so I'm more inclined to believe it was a legal high or something potently herbal.

"G," he repeats, poking my good leg under the table. "This summer—what's our plan?"

"Our plan?" I repeat, incredulity and annoyance helping me find my voice. "Are you kidding? You can't drop off the face of the planet then come back wanting there to be a *plan*."

"Canada," he says mildly, sipping his tea.

"What about it?"

"It's in the northern hemisphere. About three thousand miles west of here?"

"So?"

"It's on this planet."

If you didn't know Thomas, you'd say he sounded calm. But there's nothing I find more infuriating than someone refusing to have a fight when I'm picking one, and he knows that. And I hate that he knows that.

"Whatever. I'm going to have a bath." I can't quite storm off, but I swallow the pain as I limp out of the kitchen as fast as I can. When I get to the bathroom, I lock the door and crank the taps till they thunder. I sit on the edge of the bath and stare at the sink. Four toothbrushes in the mug, where all year it's been two. Baking soda toothpaste. An explosion of Ned's hair products and boy deodorant and joss sticks jostling for space. Above them, the mirror fogging up with steam, revealing a finger outline of Ned's band logo.

As I watch, the steam pixelates. And even though it doesn't tune in to anything yet, I know, when it does, where it will take me. It's time to admit it.

Whatever I told Ms. Adewunmi—theoretical this, hypothetical that—the mirror, Jason's kiss, yesterday's galaxy in the sky, even Thomas and me in the Book Barn. They're all wormholes. They're all real tunnels to the past.

{2}
WORMHOLES

From a billion light-years away, a Schwarzschild black hole looks exactly like a wormhole. They're the same thing.

Our universe could itself be inside a black hole, which exists inside another universe, inside another, like a set of nesting dolls.

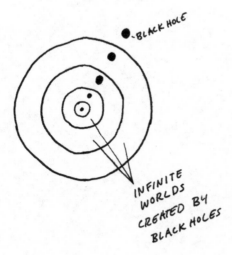

Infinite worlds, infinite universes. Infinite possibilities.

Thursday 8 July

[Minus three hundred and ten]

When I emerge from my bath, Thomas is curled up in the sitting room, asleep. Umlaut too, tucked inside his cardigan. His glasses are folded on the sofa arm—without them, it's even harder to connect this cheekboned troublemaker with the round-faced boy who left.

There's a laptop on the table; I don't suppose Papa warned him we're the last house on Planet Earth not to have Wi-Fi. "Keep your swipe cards and hoverboards, dude," Grey would tell me when I asked for a decent Internet connection. "Talk to me about the cosmos. What's new in astrology?" "Astronomy," I'd correct, and we'd be off, arguing over Pluto's planetary status or Gaia versus Galileo.

A little part of me wants to wake Thomas up and ask him why he disappeared. Instead I limp-lurch past him to the kitchen, grab a box of cereal, and spend the rest of the day in my room.

But if I want to figure out the wormholes—and the screenwipe!—I can't keep hermiting. The next morning, after covering my bruises in jeans and a long-sleeved flannel shirt, I ambush Papa early and ask him to drive me to school. On the way, I spring a plan on him: vacation shifts at the Book Barn.

"Good idea," Papa says. "You'll do the same days to Thomas?"

I nearly swallow my tongue. Thomas is going to help out at the bookshop? "Um, maybe we should work different shifts. That way, you get more help," I suggest, then add, as an oh-so-casual-afterthought: "I'm sure Ned would want a shift too."

Swaps. You put the photos of Mum all over the house; I make you work on Fridays.

To my delight, Papa agrees, and I generously offer to work out the schedule for everyone.

"Phone me when you need the lift home," he says when he drops me off. It's only as he's driving away that I remember: my cell phone is broken.

After my math lesson, I collect the two books I reserved and spend lunch in the library, printing diagrams from the Internet and googling theorems to research. When my computer slot is up, I tuck the pages and myself away in a corner. Then I take Grey's diary out of my book bag, and look up the entry for Midsummer's Eve again.

I'm going to read about last summer. I'm going to blow my heart away. My sandwich leaves crumbs on the page—I wish I were eating *Kartoffelsalat*, not Cheddar on stale white sliced—and I brush them off, flipping ahead a day, a week, a fortnight later, to:

*R.

DRUNK ON PEONIES. CLOUDS OF THEM EXPLODING ALL OVER THE GARDEN.

GOTTIE IS IN LOVE.

I choke on my sandwich. Grey knew?

This time, I feel the wormhole before I see it, a tingling in the air. The sound of the universe expanding. Hauling myself up, I hold on to the shelves as I limp along the aisle, searching the spines. Latimer, Lee, L'Engle. When I pull *A Wrinkle in Time* from the shelf, I catch a glimpse of television fuzz and smell salt before I—

Jason is waiting when I come out of the sea.

It's sunny, and his eyes are the same blue as the sky. This bit of the beach is empty. Only locals come this far down the sands, and anyway, it's Monday.

"Yo, Margot," he says when I sit down next to him. "You're welcome, by the way."

"Huh?" I put my head on one side and try to shake the water from my ears.

"I watched your stuff for you," he clarifies with a sweeping gesture. "I mean, you might not worry about thieves, but . . ."

My "stuff" is a biography of Margaret Hamilton (the scientist, not the witch). A towel. A pile of clothes. The key to my bike lock. It's sweet, though.

"It's Holksea," I point out. "I'm the most dangerous person here."

He laughs and says, "You are dangerous. That bikini is criminal."

I don't know how to reply to that. It's the same one I've always worn, but the boobs in it are brand-new, arriving by overnight express a couple of months ago. Sof's been trying to educate me about the difference between a B cup and a balconette ever since.

The easiest response is to kiss him . . . The sun hot on my skin and the sea a distant sparkle as I close my eyes and we lean into each other. My lips are salty, my face wet and cold, our mouths warm. It makes me want to crawl all over him. But after a second, Jason pulls away.

"Listen," he whispers, smoothing my wet hair back up into its topknot. "Maybe we shouldn't do this here . . . Someone might see."

"Like who? Holksea's notorious criminal underworld?"

Jason smiles, then sighs, then stretches flat out on the sand. I'm never sure if I've done something wrong; his moods come and go like the tide.

"Hey." I lean over him, put my face close to his, try to kiss him again.

"Ned would get all chaperoney," he murmurs. "You're younger than me. He'd keep an eye on us at every party, make sure we're never alone."

I'm pretty sure Sof would disapprove if I told her about me and Jason: he's two years older. He's in a band. I've never had a boyfriend, and Jason isn't exactly training wheels. She'd definitely disapprove if I told her about this conversation. Which is why I'm not going to.

Even though school's finished and our choices are narrowing—we've already had letters about college—strangely, oppositely, I can feel myself expanding. Changing. I want to stretch out like a tree towards the sun, the world at my fingertips. And Sof's friendship is beginning to feel like a cage. She wants me to stay exactly the same.

Jason curls his fingers under my bikini strap, his hand brushing against my skin just where my tan fades to pale. He's right about Ned. My brother's seventies fashion sense also translates to his gender politics, when it comes to me. And I like this bubble we're in. This club.

"Let's keep us a secret," I say, and it sounds like my idea. "For a bit."

I float home on the promise of us.

———————

—then I'm not sitting on the library floor anymore or floating home from Jason and the beach. I'm walking across the school car park, directly towards Sof. Aargh.

My hand is raised in a wave as I stagger in surprise, then try to incorporate it into my limp. Time has passed in real life, exactly like detention and the wormhole in Grey's bedroom. The opposite of how things worked in Narnia.

Sof's sitting on the wall in a sundress, sipping something green and frothy. Hubble, bubble, toil and wheatgrass. Her hair is a cloud of curls that wobble as I approach. I'm unsure if it's a nod of welcome.

I shake my own head, trying to focus on the present, and perch next to her, sweating in my jeans. My mind is still wrapped up in Jason, remembering how I'd felt in those early days, like my heart was expanding at a million miles a minute with a hundred new senses, till I was ready to explode. It takes me a moment to think of something to say, and eventually I have to settle for, "Do you mind if I get the bus with you?"

"'Course not," she says. She sounds both wary and pleased. After a few seconds, she glances at me and adds, "You're not biking?"

"I crashed my bike."

"Oh, shit. You okay?" Sof turns towards me and I show her my ankle. "Eurgh. Put arnica cream on it."

That's Sof. Offering advice where none was asked for. But it's meant kindly, and it's the sort of hippie remedy Grey would suggest, so when she asks what happened, I say, "Went round the Burnham corner too fast. It's not so bad."

"You were at the Book Barn?" she asks lightly, no-big-deal, tearing a sheet of paper from her sketch pad and folding origami, fingers deft. She doesn't know I've not been there since September.

"Yeah."

We lapse into silence, something that never used to happen with us. We used to talk all the time, nonstop, about everything: boys, girls, homework, the infinite possibilities of the universe, which flavor milk shake was best to dip your chips into, whether I should let Sof cut my hair into a bob.

I'm digging in my book bag for one of the books I checked out— H. G. Wells's *The Time Machine*—and noticing a cinnamon muffin has materialized in there since the wormhole, when Sof nudges me. She's flicking her origami open and shut—a fortune-teller.

"Why does your bag smell like Christmas?" she asks. "Never mind: pick a color."

"Yellow."

"Gotcha." Sof counts it out and unfolds the square, then pulls an exaggerated would-you-believe-it? face. "Gottie will come to the beach on Sunday."

Summer vacation starts this weekend, and we always spend Sundays at the beach. Rain or shine, whether Ned and his gang go or not. It's one of our friendship traditions, like making up stupid bands and songs to go with them, writing each other's names on the soles of our shoes, or watching the same film while texting incessantly. Not that we've done any of those things since last year. Sof's taking this bus ride as an olive branch.

"Okay," I agree. Then I open my book bag again for the Mystery Muffin. It's slightly squashed, but I hold it out as a further peace offering. "Here. I think Ned made it."

Sof hero-worships my brother, because he sings in front of people and she wants to, but is too shy. Half the bands she makes up are for his attention—when she coined "Fingerband," Ned high-fived her and she didn't wash her hand for a week.

"You're eating white flour?"

I look up. Standing in front of us, wrinkling her perfect nose at the muffin, is Megumi Yamazaki. Of Thomas-put-a-jellyfish-in-her-lunchbox fame. Her family moved along the coast to Brancaster, so we went to different secondary schools, but I've seen her around this year. If Sof's from the fifties, Megumi's the sixties, one of those weird, arty French films: striped T-shirt, short hair—and shorter shorts.

"Meg, you remember Gottie? Actually, weren't you at kindergarten together? And now"—Sof indicates the switch with her hands, ignoring the muffin—"we're in art and drama. I do the sets, Meg does the stardom."

They beam at each other. Sof's new crush? It seems to be reciprocated. And I don't have the right to be hurt by her not telling me. Then Meg says, "I keep trying to get her to perform, but would you believe she has stage fright?"

Um, yes? She's only ever done bedroom karaoke in front of me.

The bus arrives. It trundles slowly to a stop, but Sof still leaps up anxiously to flag it down anyway. Grey used to tease her: "Are you definitely a hippie, Sofía? You need to relax."

I limp on after Meg and Sof, who are already curled up next to each other, feet tucked up on the seats, by the time I flop down opposite. Meg fishes out her iPod and I hope she's going to plug in and ignore us, but instead she pops one headphone in her ear and another in Sof's.

"Sorry," Sof says to me. "Bus tradition."

I nod and try to give them privacy while they whisper to each other. I break off a piece of muffin: it tastes like autumn, even though the sun is high in the sky.

"Sof, are we on for Fingerband tomorrow?" Meg murmurs.

"Ned's Gottie's brother," Sof reminds her, with a glance at me. I hadn't known the band was playing.

"Oh, yeah." Meg leans over Sof, running her eyes over my outfit, presumably confused how I'm related to Ned. He thinks leopard print is a neutral. "Are you going to be at rehearsal? This end-of-summer party sounds like a kick, doesn't it? Did Ned's grandpa honestly sacrifice a goat one year?"

Her words pop-pop-pop in my ears. Grey threw a bacchanalia in the garden every August. Last year, he wore his hair in bunches, asking Ned to push the piano outside so he could sit in the rhododendron pounding out "Chopsticks." How can Ned think having this party is okay?

"You know Jason, then?" Meg speaks in questions, and doesn't wait for answers. I want to ask how *she* knows Jason, when they spoke, why isn't she sure I know him, has he not talked about me, are we still a secret? "Is it true some boy is moving into Ned's house?"

Shit. Thomas's mysterious return isn't the same for Sof—she moved here the year he left—but she's aware of who he is. I spent the first six months of our friendship complaining about his bizarre disappearance. It's unclear yet if she and I are friends again or what, but as she owl-neck-twists to stare at me, it's pretty obvious: she thinks I should have told her this already.

Too late and blushing furiously, I tell her: "Uh, Thomas Althorpe moved back. Yesterday."

Meg wrinkles her nose, oblivious, as she texts and talks and drops bombs, all at the same time: "Thomas from kindergarten? Is he really living in Ned's grandpa's room?"

I *definitely* should have mentioned the part where he's in Grey's bedroom.

Sof doesn't speak for a minute, then turns pointedly to Meg and says, "Dramatical Grammatical."

Meg doesn't look up. She's texting rapidly, her rings flashing in the sunlight.

"All-female hip-hop collective," Sof tries again, nudging her. "We'll rap about romantic dramas and punctuation."

The way it used to go, I'd come up with lyrics, or a supporting act. But that's obviously not what Sof wants. Playing our game with Meg and not me—she's making a point.

Meg frowns, somehow graceful as she slides her phone into her ridiculously tight short-shorts pocket. "What are you talking about?"

Sof's still not looking at me, but I can *feel* her bristling. The bus is practically vibrating. When I can't bear the tension anymore, I address the seat in front of me.

"Cheating on me is impermissible. Gonna leave her dangling like a participle."

Silence. Then: "Never mind," Sof rasps to Meg, who flicks her eyes back and forth between us, confused. *Sof was my friend first*, I want to yell, like I'm five years old. *Only I'm allowed to know she has stage fright! She tells everyone else she has adenoids!*

Grey would say I'm a dog in the manger.

I go back to staring out the window as the countryside blurs by, green and gold. A few minutes later, the colors reassemble into trees and fields as we pull up at the Brancaster stop.

"This is me," says Meg, standing up. "Nice to see you again, Gottie. We're going to the beach on Sunday. You're welcome to come."

It's an invitation—to something I'm already part of—but it makes me feel left out.

Meg saunters off down the aisle. Sof stands up too, gesturing after her. "I . . . we . . . art project," she mumbles, dropping something in my lap. "For you."

She darts off. Through the window, I see her catch up to Meg, polka dots flying. As the bus trundles on, I look at what she gave me: the paper fortune-teller. Under every single fold, she's written: *remember when we used to be friends?*

When I get home, Thomas and Ned are playing a very Grey version of Scrabble in the garden—minus the board, half the words are lost in the daisies. I think I can see D-E-S-T-I-N-Y, but it could equally be D-E-N-S-I-T-Y.

Thomas smiles up at me.

"G," he says, "want to—"

"Nope." I stomp past them, leg throbbing. I'm suddenly, irrationally, furious. I want to turn back the clock. I want a do-over on this whole year. Because I'm pretty sure I fucked it up.

That's twice now I've found Jason at the end of a wormhole—and with him, the girl I used to be.

That's the world trying to tell me something.

I grab a pen and write on the wall above my bed, in big, black, marker-pen letters:

$$\langle e_\mu, e_\nu \rangle = \eta_{\mu\nu}$$

The Minkowski spacetime equation. It's an "I dare you" to the universe. I wait for a screenwipe, like in the kitchen yesterday, or a wormhole. Anything to take me away from this crappy reality.

Nothing happens.

Friday 9 July

[Minus three hundred and eleven]

On Friday night, we eat fish and chips in the garden, straight from the paper, drinking *ein prost!* to Thomas's arrival with mugs of tea.

I pick at scraps of batter, barely speaking except to say, "Please pass the ketchup," until Papa drops the bookshop bomb on Thomas that he'll be working Tuesdays and Thursdays. "Until your mother arrives. Oh, Ned," he adds, "Gottie's suggestion is you do Wednesdays and Fridays."

Ned glares at me, and I say innocently, "I volunteered for Saturdays."

I'm half hoping Ned will laugh and threaten some childish revenge, but our sibling simpatico is out of sync.

"Hmmm," he says, before peppering Thomas with questions about the music scene in Toronto, naming nine thousand Canadian metal bands, and asking if Thomas has seen them play. The theme of the responses is *no*, and I get the sense Thomas isn't half the scenester his T-shirts paint him as. Ned doesn't mention the party.

Finally he runs off to Fingerband's rehearsal in a cloud of hair spray. Papa floats off inside with a vague "Don't stay up too late" and a reminder for Thomas to phone his mum.

Then it's just me and him. It's the first time we've been alone together since the squabble in the kitchen, two days ago. I refuse to apologize.

Twilight's just gloaming and the bats are here, swooping in and out of the trees. Searching for bugs that haven't yet arrived.

I scooch my knees up to my chin, wrap my arms round my legs, feeling gangly. After all of Ned's chatter, the silence is palpable. When Thomas and I were little, we could not-talk over entire afternoons, side by side and fingers linked in a tree house or a pillow fort or a den, days that stretched on forever. Sort of the opposite of how me and Sof were. And we never had to check what the other was thinking, because we were telepathic.

I peek at Thomas, who's holding scraps of fish in the air to make Umlaut play jumpy-jumpy. This is a terrible silence. He's bored and wishes he were back in Toronto and hanging out with a girl who actually speaks. Someone *cool*. His insanely beautiful Canadian girlfriend, who he wants to call and tell all about his bizarro childhood pal.

The mosquitoes are beginning to bite when Thomas sneezes. And again. And again. "G," he sniffles eventually, after an inhaler puff. "Evening pollen. Can we hang out inside?"

"Um, okay." I stand up, attack of the fifty-foot woman while Thomas is still on the grass. Today's cardigan is fuzzy and moss green. Then he unfolds himself too, a flash of flat stomach above his jeans. He turns towards the trees, not the house. Oh. He means hang out *in my room*.

"I've been wondering about this," he says as we walk through the garden. "I wanted to ask all week—since when do you live in the annex?"

"Five years ago?" I say, as if it's a question, holding back a bramble, thinking how the years he's missed are the ones that matter. I got my first period and my first bra. I left school and had sex. I've been in love. I've made bad choices.

I've been to a funeral.

"About six months after you disappeared," I explain, pointedly, "Ned was going through a farting stage. So Sof—my friend Sofía Petrakis, she moved to Holksea right after you left—made me march on the kitchen, waving a picket sign and demanding my rights. A-room-of-one's-own, type thing."

At the apple tree—which is now, thankfully, underwear-free—Thomas pauses, trying to twist early, unripe fruit from its gnarly branch. I lean against the trunk opposite him, the air between us fuzzy with gnats.

"Oh wow," he says, peering up into the branches. "It's there—"

Thomas yelps in surprise as the nascent apple finally comes away in his hand. The branch springs back, ricocheting us with flecks of ancient, lichen-sticky bark, and sending him staggering towards me. "Oops."

He stuffs the apple in his cardigan pocket, then looks up at me and laughs. His face is spattered with gross tree grot. Mine must be too.

"Sorry," he says, not sounding it. "I've given you bark freckles."

Thomas's real freckles, beneath the bark ones, are faint and translucent, like stars on a foggy night. He yanks his cardigan sleeve over his hand and lifts it to my cheek. I hold my breath. What happened under this tree five years ago, to make him go silent on me?

All the stars in the sky flicker out.

Literally. The only light in the garden is from the kitchen. There's no moon, no stars, no reality.

Thomas doesn't notice. It's as if we're in two separate universes: for him, everything is normal. For me, the sky has gone blank. It's a super-sized screenwipe.

When he drops his hand, stepping away, all the stars ripple back. The whole thing only lasted for a moment—a fluorescent light on the fritz, spluttering in and out.

"There you go." Thomas stares at me, confused. Maybe he *did* notice how the world just got a Ctrl+Alt+Del reboot. But all he says is, "You know, I was expecting you to have short hair."

Whatever just happened, it definitely only happened to me. Or it happened to us both, but I'm the only one who saw it—we're at opposite sides of the event horizon. The point of no return. I don't want to think about which side I'm on.

"Whoa," says Thomas, once we're inside my room. "This is, as Grey would say, a trip."

I scuttle to the bed. I'd forgotten about the emptiness. Thomas peers at what's on my chest of drawers—hairbrush, deodorant, telescope. That's it.

"Minimalist," he says, prowling around.

It wasn't always a monastery. When I moved in, Grey painted the floorboards, assembled a bed, and gave me a flashlight and the advice to never wear shoes when I cross the garden—"Feel the earth between your toes, Gottie, let it guide you." (I always wore sneakers.) Papa gave me a twenty, which Sof commandeered to play interior decorator. I couldn't stop her from buying cushions and Christmas lights, or putting stickers on my wardrobe.

When I cleared out the house last autumn, I got rid of almost everything in my room too. Made it negative space. It had felt cathartic. Now, seeing it through Thomas's eyes and nothing on my corkboard but a handwritten school schedule, it just seems sad. There's nothing to show that I'm here, that I exist. That this is where I live, breathe, don't sleep.

"Where are the stars?" Thomas is turning in circles, looking at my ceiling, while I'm looking at him, and the way all the parts of him fit together. *Arms* and shoulders and chest.

"What?" I say, once I work out a response is required.

"On the ceiling." He twists to look at me. "You always had stick-on stars. They glowed in the dark. Like magic."

"Like zinc sulphide," I correct.

"That was what I meant by the stars. You got all the references, right? In my email?"

The

    room

        screenwipes

           again

              and

                I'm

                   confused.

This is the second mention of an email—and the second occasion it's made time go flooey. I don't get it. And even if he had my address, *I* don't. I deleted everything, after Jason. And why would Thomas send me an email now, after five years? A warning of his surprise arrival? That means I should forgive him. But I'm committed to resentment.

I can't screenwipe my brain into a new emotion.

Now Thomas is sitting on the bed, still gazing around as he shucks off his shoes. I'm a little weirded out by how at ease he is in my room. He picks up my clock from the windowsill and starts fiddling with it.

"What's that?" he asks suddenly, pointing the clock at the equation on the wall.

"It's math," I explain. Then, duh, because it's obviously math, I add, winningly, "An equation."

"Huh." Thomas drops the clock on the duvet and brushes past me as he shuffles on his knees to get a closer look. There's a hole in his sock and I can see his skin. I was naked with Jason a dozen times, we even skinny-dipped, and this is just a *toe*, but it's surprisingly intimate. "And this is on your wall, why?"

I reset my clock and nudge it back into place on the windowsill as Thomas flops around on the pillow end of the bed, getting settled.

"It's homework." That's all I have to say—I don't feel like explaining Ms. Adewunmi's offer, I'm not even sure I want to take her up on it—but Thomas just impassively waits for more. "I'm supposed to come up with my own mathematical theory. I'm working on this idea that the time it takes to travel back and forth through a wormhole is less than the time an observer would spend waiting for you. You'd emerge late."

"Reverse Narnia." Thomas nods—the same conclusion I'd come to. Telepathy. "Okay. You were always Ms. Astronaut Science Girl Genius." He nods at the telescope across the room, then looks around at the nothing else. "But what happened to your stuff?"

"I have stuff." I'm instantly on the defensive. I point to Grey's diaries, still stacked on my desk, and—ha!—"Look, see, there's a cereal bowl on my chair."

"Ooh, a *bowl*." He waves his hands. "You need THINGS. My room's like a monkey cage—plates, mugs. A Maple Leafs poster, cookbooks,

Connect Four . . . I have postcards—all the places I haven't been. Felt-tips, comics. You could walk in and immediately know, okay, this guy draws, he wants to travel, he likes Marvel more than DC, which tells you a lot."

I gaze around my room, thinking, *No, it doesn't. It doesn't tell me if you've ever been in love, or if you still don't like tomatoes, or when you switched from sweatshirts to cardigans. It doesn't tell me what happened when you left, or why you're back.* Then again, all I have are Grey's diaries. Sof's stickers. Other people's things. Martians would be baffled.

"My room is a time capsule of me—" Thomas widens his eyes dramatically, stressing the words, as though I'm supposed to think, *Oh, of course, a time capsule.* Like the one he mentioned in the kitchen earlier this week.

"—of who I am right now," he continues. "Thomas Matthew Althorpe, age seventeen. Archaeologists will conclude: he was messy."

There's silence again as I imagine him in Grey's room now. Without all his *things*. Then Thomas pokes me with his holey sock and non sequiturs. "I poured whiskey on Grey's carpet."

"Wait—what? Why?"

"It was a ritual. A commemoration. That was his room, you know?"

"Yeah . . ."

"I didn't think it through, where I'd sleep when I got here. Your dad gave me Grey's room for the summer, and I didn't want to act like it wasn't a big deal," he continues, "move in and take it over. It needed a ritual."

"It needed whiskey?"

"Exactly." He rolls up his cardigan sleeves and mimes pouring it out. I try to absorb this. That Thomas not only understands his being in Grey's room is A Big Deal, he was thoughtful enough to do a supremely

[81]

Grey-like thing about it, pouring whiskey on the carpet—equal parts superstition and ritual and mess.

"This is different—you coming back—than what I expected," I admit to him.

"You thought I'd jabber aboot moose and maple syrup, eh." Thomas dismisses the comment, rummaging for the apple and a handful of coins, piling them on the windowsill. "There," he beams. "Grey's room needed whiskey. Your room needs things. All the way from Canada. And, er, your garden. A time capsule of you: Margot Hella Oppenheimer, in her eighteenth summer."

I feel a flicker of irritation. Those are his things, not mine—that's not a time capsule of me. Mine would contain silence, lies, and regret, and I'd need a box the size of Jupiter.

"What is it with you and time capsules?"

"I like the idea of a permanent record," he explains. "Something to say, This Is Who I Am, even when I'm not that person anymore. I left one back in Toronto."

"What was in it?"

"Sharpies. Comics. My old glasses. A key ring for my car, which I had for all of two months before selling it to come here. I guess I don't need it to escape my dad anymore, though. That's Toronto. It's like this—" He holds out his left hand, showing me the two-inch pink scar nestled there. "I'm not twelve anymore. We may not have talked for years"—he glances at me—"but I always had this, so I could remember that day."

Whoa. His scar matches mine. I didn't know he had one.

But it doesn't mean he knows me.

"I don't want to open our time capsule," I say, not caring whether we really made one or not as my irritation gathers steam. "I don't want to remember being twelve. Big deal, you have a scar too. That's not a good enough reason never to write to me!"

Mum, Grey, Jason—none of them can answer me. It's exhilarating, finally having someone to yell at.

Thomas hops off the bed and grabs his shoes. My words have slapped the dimples right off his face. His voice is flat as the landscape when he says, "Have you even considered it from the other way around? That you never wrote to me?"

After he stalks out the door, across the garden, the kitchen light stays on for hours.

I stay up with it. First I count the coins into neat stacks on the windowsill—they come to $4.99 exactly. Then I pick up my marker pen and draw a circle around the Minkowski equation, and write underneath:

WORMHOLES—TWO TIMES AT ONCE.
SCREENWIPES—TWO REALITIES AT ONCE.

And at the top of the wall, I write: *The Gottie H. Oppenheimer Principle. v 1.0*

Sunday 13 July

[Minus three hundred and fifteen]

"Synthmoan de Beauvoir."

"What?" I'm highlighting excerpts from *A Brief History of Time* and only half-listening to Sof. When she snatches the book out of my hands, the pen leaves a fluorescent-yellow squiggle across the page, an electrical storm.

"Hey!"

"Synthmoan de Beauvoir deserves your full attention."

"Who?" My mind is on wormholes, not here at the beach with Sof. I had my first shift at the Book Barn yesterday, working with Papa and avoiding Thomas, and I've finally got hold of all the titles on Ms. A's reading list.

When Sof rang the bookshop to make peace, I thought showing up here today would be enough. But she keeps pushing to re-create our former dynamic, not noticing we can't slip back into our old groove, like happiness is a dress you wear. Neither of us mentions her fortune-teller, or her note.

It's a grey, grizzly day, the cold air fuzzy with impending rain. Sof and I used to hit the beach on Sundays, weather be damned—but Ned and Fingerband only showed when the sun was cranked up. I remember whispering to Jason, confused, "But I thought you were goths?" He chuckled and explained how goth and punk and metal were totally different. I don't know; they all wear a lot of black.

There's a glimmer of weak sunshine. He might show.

"It's my stage name," Sof rasps, waving my book in front of me. "Lead singer of a feminist disco-punk band. Grrrls, guitars, glitter, and Gloria Steinem lyrics."

Is disco-punk a genre? I stop trying to grab the book back and start rubbing arnica cream—the homeopathic stuff Sof recommended—into my bruises. I found some, new, in the bathroom cabinet. Along with coconut oil and a big lump of rose quartz. Ned. He and Sof are working from the same script, putting on a play of *Last Summer*. Only I've forgotten my lines.

"What's the band name?" I ask, finally.

"Get this." Sof peers over her heart-shaped sunglasses. They match her heart-print bikini. If she could, she'd probably make her goose pimples heart-shaped. "The Blood Wagon."

"*Gross*," I say, trying to make an effort. "Are all your songs about tampons?"

Sof chuckles and flips my book over to read the back. "Ugh, do you have anything a normal person can read?" She rummages through my bag. "Oh my God." I worry she's found Grey's diary, but she emerges with a battered copy of *Forever*: "*Definitely* extracurricular."

Actually, it was one of two books on Ms. Adewunmi's list that the library had. I even checked on the last day of term that she meant the Judy Blume. She just laughed, wagging a gold-nailed finger, and told me to have a good summer—and write her that essay.

"I haven't read this in—ha, forever. Why do you have this?" Sof thumbs rapidly through the pages, murmuring to herself, "Oh my God, *Ralph*. I'd forgotten that. Straight people are so weird."

"I've never read it."

"Why are you—oh my GOD," Sof says for the third time. She looks from the book, to me, shocked. "Are you having sex with someone?"

"What? No! Give me that." I snatch *Forever* back from her. What the hell is this book about?

"Whoa. Gottie, I'm joking. I *know* you're not having sex. You'd ask me first," she says, superior and certain of herself as she stands up, pulling her dress on. "Okay, I'm going to get a drink."

"Could you get me a Creamsicle?" I ask when she doesn't offer. It's not ice-cream weather, but I skipped breakfast.

She holds out her hand for my money, and I can hear her singing loudly "T-A-M-P-O" as she goes marching up off the beach. There's no one else in sight.

I immediately crack open *A Brief History of Time* again, and try to wrap my head around the two parts of string theory. 1. Particles are one-dimensional loops, not dots. 2. There are threads of energy that run through spacetime.

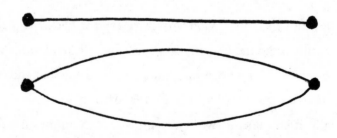

Grey claimed the term was "cosmic strings" and insisted it referred to a giant harp in the sky. If he's right, the universe is out of tune.

I look up when a shadow falls across the page.

"That was quick, you—" I break off as I see Meg standing above me.

"Hi." She waves.

"Sof's at the snack bar."

"Yeah, I just saw her," she says lightly, and helps herself to a large fraction of blanket. I can't figure out if she and Sof are together or friends. "She said you'd be over here."

I peer over my book as she takes a small green bottle out of her bag and starts polishing her toenails. It's not that Meg's horrible. But since Grey died, I barely know how to talk to my own friends, let alone someone else's. All my words were cremated along with him.

Thankfully, I hear Sof's voice seconds later—except she's not alone. The full Fingerband entourage is here. And trailing them is Thomas. I haven't seen him since he walked out of my room on Friday night. One benefit of Papa being head-in-the-clouds—no enforced family dinners. That's how I'll score my Nobel: one girl's experiment to live off cereal in her room for an entire summer.

Ned and Sof lead the pack. He's got his arm slung round her neck, and she's laughing. Possibly at his outfit. Where do you even get an orange playsuit in Holksea? Behind them are Niall, Fingerband's drummer, and Jason, the only one of us dressed weather-appropriate in spray-on black jeans and ever-present leather jacket. Full bad-boy regalia, except I know his mum knitted his jumper. Seeing him here isn't a surprise—this is north Norfolk, there's nothing to do besides cow tipping and the beach—but my body reacts anyway. I turn cold, and hot, and cold, and my throat constricts.

He smiles lazily at me, and I think of that moment in Grey's room, when he touched my hand and called me Margot.

I shiver, no longer wanting the ice cream Sof's flapping at me.

"Take it, it's freezing my fingers," she says, as everyone clusters round. "They only had ice-cream bars. You're twenty pence short."

"Thanks."

Thomas is lurking at the back of the group, his hands shoved in his pockets, shoulders hunched up. He nods at me, and I focus on unwrapping my ice-cream bar so I don't accidentally stare at Jason in front of him for nine hours. I'm so busy fake-concentrating, it takes me a minute to notice everyone's still standing up, waiting for me to move.

"Blanket reshuffle," Sof explains. She glances at Ned. "Actually, that's a good name for a band."

"All right, shoegazer," he teases, gesturing for everyone to huddle together for a photo. "I bet I'll have you rocking out to Savage Messiah by the end of the summer."

"You can pay up at the party"—Sof bats her eyes—"when I get you dancing to Blanket Reshuffle."

I stand up, somehow ending up sandwiched between Thomas and Jason while Ned fiddles with the settings. It takes forever, because today he's brought one of his eight thousand film cameras instead of his phone. Thomas and Jason both sling an arm round my shoulders for the photo, and they clash just as Ned bellows, "Okay, everybody say 'Ziggy Stardust.'"

There's a clunk-click and a mad chorus as everyone shouts something different—I think I hear Thomas yell, "Trouble times two," but his face is innocence when I look at him.

When he finally lets us sit down, there's a scramble for the center of the blanket. Niall's all hair and piercings, and he stumbles around, heavy-footed in DMs, so I'm pushed into the corner. Everyone ends up paired off: Sof with Ned in the middle, Thomas with Niall, and Meg next to Jason, who glances my way. I'm squished behind Thomas and Niall, on the edge of the group. *Guten tag*, my entire life. Except . . . last summer, I had Jason, and before that I had Sof, and before *that*, I was Thomas-and-Gottie. How did I end up here?

The weather has gone from grey to almost-drizzling.

Ned and Sof are loudly debating playlists for the party, which he still hasn't actually told me about directly. Papa hasn't mentioned it—he might not even know. He's not the kind of parent to deny permission for much, except when Ned wanted to get a neck tattoo, but, then, mostly we don't ask for anything. We muddle along.

I bite a lump of ice cream that I can't swallow, then point at my mouth so I don't have to talk to Niall. He's got so many studs you could peel his ear off like a stamp, and I never know what to say to him: "Nice holes"? He puts his headphones on and ignores me.

Thomas turns around, awkwardly, twisting the blanket underneath his feet to a chorus of complaints. His glasses are sea-speckled, and his hair is as curly as Sof's. "Hey."

"Hey," I mumble back, regretting my ice-cream lump.

Apologizing was never part of the Thomas-and-Gottie vocabulary. It was part of our unspoken agreement. I settle for asking, "Have you been introduced to everyone?"

"G, I already know you, Ned, and everyone," he points out. "It's only Sof who's new, and she rather boldly introduced herself."

"Oh." I seem to still be having trouble connecting *this* Thomas with *that* Thomas.

"Does putting a jellyfish in my lunch box count as knowing me?" Meg calls out, and Thomas turns around again to answer her, retwisting the blanket, so I end up bumped out onto the cold sand. With his back to me, I can't hear what he says. I stare at the freckles on his neck while he and Meg and Sof laugh. I catch the occasional word—it seems to be a comic-book discussion.

Using Thomas as cover, I switch my stare to Jason. His collar is popped, his blond hair swept back. He twists in my direction to give Ned's camera the best moody seascape profile. The last time I saw him was in Grey's room, when—*when what, Gottie? Do you honestly believe you went back to last summer? But that you also stayed here? That your consciousness split in two?*

I need to ask Jason what happened, from his perspective. I need to get Jason alone, again. Explain that I'm not ignoring him; my phone's broken.

He catches me staring, and smiles. Then steals a chip from Ned, makes a joke to Meg about her nail polish, flips the bird at Sof. This could be a scene from last summer—but I'm only near him, not with him, and it makes my rib cage feel two sizes too small for my lungs.

I stare at my book, penciling formulas in the margins and trying not to mind that I don't have a secret bubble anymore, or that Ned's shouting about a party I don't want to happen. Tiny raindrops fleck the page and smudge my numbers. A big fat tear joins them.

I'm surprised when Niall shoves a tissue into my hand. It's gross—dirty and shredded, probably snotty—and he doesn't say anything or look at me, 'cause I'm clearly too pathetic. I need to stop sniffling and do something. Otherwise the time capsule of Margot H. Oppenheimer, in her eighteenth summer, will be a soggy mess.

I shove the snot rag into my bag, on top of Grey's diary. It's one from five years ago, bookmarked to the day Thomas left. Hearts and flowers are doodled all over the page. He used to do that on our school reports and permission slips. (Asking Papa to sign anything is like trying to catch a helium balloon in a tornado.) I nearly didn't get my measles shot because there were smiley faces in all the *O*s on the form.

When I look up, I notice two things. 1. There's a wormhole, twenty yards from shore. And 2. Thomas is looking between me and Jason with a frown.

"I'm going to swim," I announce, standing up. Better a watery vortex than here.

Everyone stares up at me.

"You just ate," says Sof. Her feet are in Ned's lap. "And the water'll be like icicles."

"All right, Mum. I'll paddle," I say, standing on the backs of my sneakers to take them off.

"Okay, well, I'll go with you," she says reluctantly. Her teeth chatter as she peels off her sundress. Meg claims she has a volleyball injury and can't swim. And I think, meanly: *we didn't invite you.*

Then we start walking down to the tidal line, lurching as our bare feet hit the strip of sharp pebbles and seaweed. It takes a few minutes—the flats at low tide stretch on for miles—and we don't say much. It's even colder when we get to the water's edge, wind whipping in off the sea. Aside from the wormhole, it's empty. Sof jumps up and down, making exaggerated "Brrr" noises.

"If you're cold now, wait till we're in the water," I tell her.

She puts one toe in and hops back. "Shit. Yeah, there's no way I'm going in."

"Duh." I copy her, dipping my toe in—then brave my whole foot. I hold it there. It's not *so* cold . . . I take another step forward, putting both feet in. Take another step, and another.

"Gottie," Sof hisses when I'm calf-deep. "Come back, I'm freezing."

"In a sec," I say, without turning round. The sea and the sky and the wormhole are grey. Grey. I want to swim. All the way to the Arctic and away from my life. Then I turn round and splosh back to Sof.

"Ugh, thank God. If you'd gone in and I hadn't, your brother would think I was chicke—wait, what are you doing?"

I'm peeling off my jumper and I hand it over to her, along with my shorts, then step back into the water in my T-shirt and underwear. The salt water stings on my scabs, but it's a good pain—it's waking me up. I splash toward the wormhole till I'm up to my knees.

"Gottie!" Sof shrieks as I step into a dip and plummet up to my waist. The sudden cold takes my breath away, and the only way to stand it is to go all in—I duck until it's over my shoulders, my lungs screaming, and swim the last couple of lengths to the wormhole. The sand grazes my knees as I kick through the water, and seaweed slimes about my feet. And then I'm there.

I can't see the water; I can only see the television fuzz, but the sea *feels* deep here, up to my neck. I can hear Sof shouting something, but I'm too far away to work out what. There's a tug at my ankle, the underwater current pulling me down—

And I swim through the universe.

"Am I adopted?"

I'm helping Grey after he re-repainted the Book Barn. Instead of cleaning, last month he painted over the dirt in bright dandelion yellow. I didn't help that time, because my hand was still in a bandage from Thomas. The color lasted two weeks, till he blasted through the kitchen door a few days ago: "Balls and buggery to the flames of hell! It's like a bloody cupcake café!"

So yesterday we re-repainted it off-white, the kind that looks dirty even when it's fresh. I helped. And now we're putting everything back. Again.

"You're not adopted, dude," says Grey from the top of the ladder. "Pass me that box?"

I heave it up to him, then sit back down and look at the photo album I've found. The Book Barn is like that: a million paperbacks, half of them the shop's, half of them ours. Sometimes Grey will be writing a receipt and he'll suddenly grab the book back, saying it's not for sale.

"But there are no pictures of me." There are hundreds of Ned, tiny and wrinkled, Mum and Papa staring at him in surprise. Then blank pages until I suddenly appear, the photos loose and not even glued into the album, and I'm a year old, sprung from nowhere. Adopted.

When the pictures return, not as many now, Papa's face is a thousand years older. He looks faded. No more photos of Mum.

Grey sighs, looking down from his pulp fiction. I don't tell him the spines are upside down. "Gottie, man. Sometimes . . . you're too busy living to take a photo. You don't have time to stop and freeze the moment, because you're in it."

"What about Ned?" Ned got a Polaroid for his thirteenth birthday, and now he's always freezing the moment. I flip back to the beginning, to Papa and Mum getting married. A yellow dress, stretched tight across her beach ball stomach. A ribbon round her forehead instead of a veil. Her hair is short and mullety, the same as mine when I was little—like Ned, she's to-tally out of step with fashion, but somehow still cool. Papa half in and half out of every photo, Grey with flowers braided through his plaits.

"Here," Grey adds, climbing down the creaky ladder. He holds out a crumpled photo from his wallet, one I've never seen before. It's Mum, and as usual I try to find my face in hers—we're both all nose, the same olive skin dark eyes, dark hair, and I don't know why I stopped cutting mine—before I notice she's holding a baby. It's small, pink, not Ned . . .

"Me?"

"You," says Grey.

Until then, I'd thought it all happened at the same time: I was born/she died. No one had ever told me there'd been a moment, in between, when I'd had a mami.

I blink and I'm sitting in the kitchen, holding the house phone to my ear. It rings far away, already dialed, except I don't remember doing that. The last thing I remember, pre-wormhole, is being at the beach with everyone and swimming in the cold, cold sea.

In my other hand is the photograph Grey gave me in the Book Barn, almost five years ago. The one of Mum. I'd lost it almost immediately afterwards, and I never told him. Now it's here, in my hand.

When am I?

I put my head between my knees, trying to breathe. I can cope with the collapse of spacetime. Seeing my grandfather again, I can't. My whole body hurts. I don't understand how I'm supposed to get through this. I don't understand how anyone is. I'm counting to ten and still hanging on to the phone when a boy's voice answers with a, "Yeah?"

I stare across the kitchen. Outside the window, peach roses; beyond them, the lawn is shaggy. Ned's fur coat is slung on a chair, and there's a trifle on the table. Next to it is a pile of party paraphernalia—piñatas, packs of balloons. Yet another message for Thomas on the blackboard, to call his mum when he gets back from the bookshop. This is now.

It's not exactly a stab in the dark when I croak: "Jason?"

"Yeah . . ." he says. "Who's this?"

"Aaargh," I cough. "Aaargot. Margot. I mean . . . me. Hey," I finish up, smooth as a cucumber (Papa's phrase).

"Gottie?" he says in his teasing voice, as though he knows more than one Margot and needs to clarify with the nickname he never used to use. "What's up?"

I remember what I need to ask—what happened when I disappeared into the wormhole. All my split-screen theories collapse if it turns out I disappeared in a puff of smoke. But I can't form the question. My brain's still catching up with my body, and the complexity of what I have to say is beyond me right now.

"Can we meet up? It's important," I say instead. "Sorry."

"Maaaybe," he drawls, and then adds, "You sound kind of strange. You okay?"

I lean my head on the wall, drowning in his question. In all the things I want it to mean. That I can find my way home.

"It's about the party," I lie. "I want to surprise Ned."

I hate myself for using this stupid party as an excuse. But perhaps I can persuade Jason to persuade Ned to cancel.

"What about a coffee at the café, a week from Saturday? Ned's busy that day," he adds. "I'll text a time."

Ned chooses this moment to strut in from the garden. I garble, "Okayseeyouthengottagobye," and yank the receiver away from my head before I can mention that my mobile isn't working.

"You're meant to put it up to your ear," Ned says, demonstrating with his hand. Then, because he's Ned, he adds a phone gesture with his other hand, segues into devil's horns, then flashes a Vulcan salute. At least *he's* acting normal.

"Fixed your bike, by the way," he adds. "Want to go for a ride this weekend?"

"Ned—what day is it? The date, I mean."

"The phone?" he reminds me, shimmying across to the fridge and peering inside, bottom waggling in purple paisley Lycra. "Tuesday. Fifteenth of July in the year of Our Satan two thousand and—"

"*Thank you,*" I say. Then, "Oh." And slam the receiver down.

Ned kicks the fridge door shut and hops up to sit on the windowsill, swigging milk straight from the carton.

"Wrong number?" he asks.

"Heavy breather," I lie. The amount that Ned knows about me and Jason is zero, and I want to keep it that way. "What you up to, Freddie Mercury?"

Ned wipes off his milk mustache before answering.

"Garage. Did your bike, then planned my set for the party. My guitar solo's going to be like"—air guitar, tongue between teeth—"*whoa.*"

I smile, despite the party reference and the photograph in my hand, despite seeing Grey in the wormhole and the way Ned seems back to normal while I'm anything but. Because making that phone call, Jason agreeing to see me—it means I'm going to get some answers. It means something. Doesn't it?

Thursday 17 July

[Minus three hundred and nineteen]

Fick dich ins Knie, H. G. Wells!

It might be a sci-fi classic, but *The Time Machine* turns out to be all fi and no sci—sphinxes and troglodytes, rather than equations and mechanics. I throw the book on my bed and look up to the wall where I've scribbled my notes. My room is starting to take on a serial killer's lair Wall O' Crazy appeal.

This is the first chance all evening I've had to be alone. Fingerband was in the kitchen, brainstorming "something major" for the summer's-end shindig, while Papa flitted in and out. Newly minted groupies Sof and Meg tagged along, and when Thomas came back from his Book Barn shift, all three of them launched into a furious comic-book debate. ("Graphic novels," Sof corrected me.) I lurked, cradling the warmth that Jason and I had a secret again.

Now it's past midnight. I'm hypothesizing, trying to narrow down what the wormholes have in common.

Meow. On my desk, Umlaut is hopping around atop the stack of diaries. I get up, grabbing them—kitten and all—and carry them back to the bed. As I move around the room, I notice the kitchen light through the garden, still on.

The diaries. Grey wrote about the day I first kissed Jason. There was DRUNK ON PEONIES, the same day we met at the beach. If I can find some of the other wormholes, I could plot the dates. Establish a pattern.

I let myself fall into the pages, ripping my heart wide open with how the world once was.

Umlaut paws at the duvet as I find the day at the Book Barn, how Grey wrote RESHELVING WITH CARO before scribbling it out and writing my name. In last year's diary, I find more of those asterisked *Rs, confettied on the pages. There are no *Rs in the earlier diaries, but I do find an entry about me and Thomas going on a school trip to the Science Museum, which ended in disgrace when he got trapped inside the space probe.

Seeing the words on the page reminds me that before we got in trouble, there was a projection of the galaxy on the ceiling. Lying on the floor, staring up, it was like . . .

Like being in the Milky Way.

It's not just one diary entry that corresponds to a vortex. All the wormholes are here.

Are the diaries what's causing everything? It can't be a coincidence—even if it doesn't explain the screenwipes, or the way the stars went out in the garden. This means I can only wormhole to days Grey wrote about. I don't have to revisit his funeral.

I don't have to see the day he died.

I grab the nearest textbook and flip through the index. *Causality . . . Einstein . . . String theory . . . Weltschmerzian Exception . . .* The words catch my eye, faintly familiar and already highlighted yellow. When I turn to the page, there's just a brief description:

The Weltschmerzian Exception manifests itself between two points, where the rules of spacetime no longer apply. As well as vortex violations, observers would witness stop-start effects, something like a "visual reboot" as they passed between different timelines. Based on theories of negative energy or dark matter and developed by Nobel-winning physicist

The next page is torn out, cutting off the entry.

The rules of spacetime no longer apply . . .

Vortex violations—that has to mean wormholes, which shouldn't be real. But I've witnessed them.

The Gottie H. Oppenheimer Principle, v2.0. The world has "visually rebooted" twice now, both times when Thomas mentioned an email. An email I never received. What if that's because it doesn't exist in my reality? Thomas and I share a timeline in common except for this, so every time he mentions it, the world reboots? Is that even possible?

As I put the diaries back on my desk, I notice the kitchen light is still on. Cursing Ned, I yank on my sneakers. *The earth's not getting anywhere near my toes,* I think, stomping out into the night.

———————

When I open the kitchen door, I discover Thomas. Baking.

While I'm still half out of my skin in surprise, he smiles, then goes back to painting something warm and golden-scented onto dough.

The past week clicks into place: the wonky bread, his first morning. The cinnamon muffin in my book bag. The mess in the pantry, which I've been blaming on Ned. And he never once came out and said, "It's me." He's as secretive as I am.

"You've been making the bread. You *bake*," I accuse.

"I bake, I stir, I cook, I roll!" He flips the brush in the air like a baton. We watch as it lands on the floor with a clatter, splattering honey on the tiles. "Oops."

"Papa used that brush to varnish the table," I tell him, and he stops trying to pick it up. "But why do you bake *now*? It's almost one in the morning."

"Jet lag."

I point at the dough. "What's that?"

"It's when you travel through different time zones and it takes your body clock a while to adjust." Thomas manages about two seconds of straight-facedness before his mouth wobbles and he cracks up at his own joke.

"Funny." My mouth twitches. "I meant *that*."

"Lavender bread. Here, smell." He lifts the baking tray up and starts towards me. I shake my head and he shrugs, spinning on his heel to the oven instead, talking over his shoulder as he slides the loaf in. "Good with cheese—normal stuff, not your weird German ones."

"Rauchkäse is normal," I reply automatically, surprising myself. Thomas keeps shaking words out of me. Perhaps it's friendship muscle memory. "You honestly bake now? This is what you do?"

"Where did you think the food was coming from?" Thomas cocks his head, sitting down sideways in a chair. I sit the same way next to him, and our knees bump awkwardly; we're both too tall. I still don't know what to think of him.

"I thought Ned was going shopping," I explain. "He's a foodie—well, he lives in London." We're probably keeping Ned awake—his bedroom is off the kitchen. Then again, he might have gone out after the Fingerband meeting. He mostly gets in at dawn, dry-heaves in the garden, then sleeps all morning. A blur of glitter, guitar, gotta-go-bye out the door every afternoon.

"You think anyone who can bake more than a potato is a foodie," Thomas points out, then leaps up with a stop-hand and a "Wait there!"

I sit, confused, till he returns from the pantry, piling ingredients on the table: flour, butter, eggs, as well as things I didn't even know we had, like bags of fancy nuts and bars of dark, bitter chocolate wrapped in green paper. It reminds me of that first morning, a week ago, when he made me toast and jam and got Grey's Marmite jars out of their shrine.

"The best way to learn what's so great about baking," Thomas says, not sitting back down, "is to do it. I want to open a pastry shop."

He beams down at me, and I resist the unexpected urge to reach up and poke the resulting dimple.

"A pastry shop," I repeat, in the tone I'd use if he suggested casual larceny. I can't imagine the Thomas *I* knew in charge of hot ovens and knives and edible foodstuffs. Well, I can, but it would end in disaster.

"Ouch. Yes, a bakery. You've eaten my muffins—don't even try to tell me I'm not Lord of the Sugar."

. . .

"King of the Muffin."

. . .

"Impresario of Flapjacks."

I pinch my mouth into a hard line. He's not funny. He's a hobgoblin. We stare-off, and Thomas gives in first, cracking a smile and an egg into a bowl.

"Honestly? It's fun, and against all odds, I'm good at it," he explains. "You know how rare it is to find something that combines those two things? Actually, you probably don't, you're good at everything."

Ugh. I hate that—as though an A in math means I'm figured out. Not everything comes easily. I don't know the names of any bands. I can't dance, or do liquid eyeliner, or conjugate verbs. I baked more than one hundred potatoes this past year, and I still can't get the skin to crisp up. And I don't have a plan.

Ned was born a seventies glam rocker, has wanted to be a photographer since he got his first camera. Sof's been a lesbian since she could talk and a painter from not long after that. Jason's going to be a lawyer, and now even Thomas—chaos theory incarnate—is opening a freaking bakery? All I've ever wanted was to stay in Holksea and learn about the world from inside a book. It isn't enough.

"I'm not good at everything. You know *The Wurst*?" I tell Thomas, to prove it. "The painting above Grey's—your—bed."

"G, for the love of"—he bat-grabs the air, no, pterodactyl-grabs it—"why would you WANT to paint like that?" In a church-library-funeral whisper, he adds: "I can't believe you never told me Grey did *erotic art*."

"No, I—" The laughter comes so suddenly I can't get the words out. Thomas must think I'm a complete loon, doubled over and wheezing, flapping my hands in front of my face.

"Wait, wait," I squeak, before I'm gone again. This laugh is a burst of relief. Briefly, tantalizingly, reminding me of what it can be like—to be happy to the tips of your toes.

Thomas starts laughing too, saying, "G, it's not funny! I have to sleep under that thing. I think it's *watching* me."

Which only makes me laugh harder, sucking in shallow breaths as I begin to verge on the manic. A kind of happy hysteria that threatens to overflow, spilling into something worse.

I suck in air, pushing the laughter and everything else down. Then explain, "No, *I* painted it. That got me a D."

"G. You are joking." He sits down opposite me again, astonished. And no wonder, if he thinks it's a six-foot blue penis! Maybe it is, maybe I've got boy parts on the brain and that's been my problem all along. I wonder if the Boner Barn has anything on Freud.

"Told you I was terrible," I say cheerfully. I'd faked my laughter at the school exhibition, pretending to make fun of myself, but somehow with Thomas, it's real. I'm terrible and it's okay. "Your turn. Why baking, really?"

"Everyone says you have to be superprecise to bake—like your extra-credit thing, the time travel project. One calculation out of place and the whole thing would go wrong, right?"

"Yeah . . ."

"It's hogwash!" Thomas announces gleefully. I'm charmed by his use of the word *hogwash*—it reminds me of the pigs at the fair. He points at the bowl. "Look at this—bit of eggshell in there, scoop it out with a finger, what the hell. Too much flour, forget the butter, drop the pan—it doesn't matter how many mistakes you make, it mostly turns out okay. And when it doesn't, you cover it with icing."

"Is that true?" I'm suspicious of Thomas's grasp of commercial health and safety.

"Probably. It's mostly metaphorical, but I suspect you missed that part. Here." He holds out the green-paper-wrapped chocolate and I break off a chunk. "Okay, so that's me—wannabe pâtissier and upside-down apple cake of my father's eye. Which is another terrible metaphor for saying my dad's not exactly thrilled by my career ambitions. Or, outside of home ec, my grades."

"You're failing?" I ask.

After confessing *The Wurst*, I feel full of questions. The Great Thomas Althorpe Quiz! We've got five years to fill, and I've been wordless for so long. Wanting to use my mouth, to ask-talk-laugh—it feels as good as a thunderstorm when it begins to break.

"I'm majoring in biscuits—hey, look at that, I said biscuits not cookies. Canada's wearing off. My grades are okay, but cookies-not-college *is* failing, according to my dad." He says it lightly, but there's an edge. I can imagine Mr. Althorpe's response to a harebrained bakery scheme.

"Is that why your parents split up?" I nibble on my chocolate.

"Bloody hell, G," Thomas says, suddenly as full English as breakfast. "This is what I like about you—that Teutonic sensitivity. It's a chicken/egg thing." He stares at the mixing bowl unhappily, flicks a bag of flour with his finger. "They were fighting nonstop anyway; my one-man detention parade probably didn't help. It was a conduit—do I mean catalyst? Anyway, Dad was fuming when Mom took a pro-bakery stance. I won her over with my *chocolatines*."

"And she wanted you to live with her in Holksea? Your dad didn't try to get you to stay in Toronto?"

"Living in Holksea . . ." he trails off.

Silence blooms, expanding to fill the room. My mouth has rocks in it again, and I shove the remaining chocolate in to take the taste away.

"Canada wasn't awful," he allows. "It wasn't wonderful either. It was somewhere in between. The baby bear's porridge. Just fine, you know? Mom was planning to move back to England, then I got the chance to come back minus all the awkward years. And I'll admit: I was curious."

"About?"

He holds his fist straight out at me, little finger aloft. Our childhood signal, promise, salute, whatever. I gulp my chocolate down, but don't raise my own hand. I can't. Not yet. Neither of us moves, then he says:

"You."

This time, the stare-off goes on and on. I'm sure Thomas has a hundred reasons for coming back to Holksea. I'm only part of it. But it's a confession, so I match it with one of my own, in the form of a question.

"Thomas. When you left . . . why did you never write? And please don't turn it round to me, because I need to know. I mean . . . you disappeared."

"I know you want one big, earth-shattering reason," he says at last, flopping back in his chair, his hands in his lap. "The boring truth is, it's lots of little ones. I didn't know your email or your number—if I wanted to talk to you, I always crawled through the hedge. The next reason was I didn't know where to get stamps. It took eight hours to get to New York, then we stayed in a hotel and my parents watched me like a hawk because of the blood pact. When we got to Toronto, my dad gave me a million chores around the new house, then I had to register at school, then Mom made me get a haircut, because what you need on your first day at a new school is to rock the medieval monk look."

Thomas picks up steam, waving his hands in the air.

"My dad kept his study locked, and when we fiiinally got a kitchen drawer filled with paper clips and stamps and a rubber band ball and a pencil with a little troll on the end, I was all set to write, when you know what I noticed? It'd been over a month, and *you* hadn't written to *me*."

I can't believe that's all it was. All this time I thought he'd Not Written as a unilateral decision, some grand sense of betrayal. It never occurred to me it was Thomas being Thomas—twelve, disorganized, and stubborn. It was geography. How different would the past five years have been if I'd just written to him?

How different this year might have been.

"Even Stevens?" Thomas holds out his hand for me to shake.

"A détente," I agree, and take his hand.

There's a crackle of static, then Umlaut appears, suddenly curling round my ankle. I hadn't even known he was in the kitchen. Thomas and I disengage as the kitten springs up into my lap.

I wait while Umlaut turns figures-of-eight on my legs, revving like an engine.

"I looked for your email . . ." I admit. "I couldn't find it. Did you use the Book Barn address? Because it's not there—maybe Papa deleted it."

"No—I used yours."

Um. One of us is confused here, and it isn't me. I don't *have* an email address.

There was a point in the autumn when I couldn't stop going online, watching Jason's status updates, talking to everybody but me. I knew I had to wait till I saw him, and seeing his life flicker by in real time was lemon on a paper cut, so I stopped going on the Internet completely, turned off my notifications, deleted all my accounts. Waited.

I'm about to tell Thomas I don't have email, that whoever he sent it to isn't in this reality, when

time

reboots

again.

Umlaut's gone. Thomas is no longer in the chair opposite me, but sliding something in the oven and asking over his shoulder, "Want to watch some TV or something?"

"It's late. I got up to turn out the light," I mumble, standing up. I like my string theory theoretical, not in my kitchen in the middle of the night. The spell is broken. I'm looking for a do-over on last summer, not five years ago. "Maybe another time . . ."

I expect Thomas to make a fuss or a chicken noise as I start backing out the door, but he yawns and stretches, pulling his cardigan tight against his arms.

"You're right. We've got all summer," he says, leaning against the oven as I wave goodnight from the garden. "There's plenty of time."

Outside, it's getting light. Somehow, Thomas and I have talked till dawn. I pass Ned as I trudge back to my room.

"Grots." He nods formally before serenely throwing up in the bushes.

Back on my bed, I think about what Thomas said. That there's plenty of time. It's not true, but it's a comforting lie. I write it on the wall, then I finally fall asleep. Dreaming of chocolate and lavender.

Friday 18 July

[Minus three hundred and twenty]

I wake a couple of hours later to sunshine and a piece of chocolate cake on my doorstep. Actually, there's a plate between it and the step, the difference between Thomas-now and Thomas-then. What other midnight baker would be leaving cake outside my room—Umlaut? He's sniffing round my ankles. Tucked underneath the plate, to stop it from flying away, there's a folded scrap of paper. In Thomas's blocky print, it reads:

BEAT BUTTER AND SUGAR TILL CREAMED. STIR IN WHISKED EGGS, THEN FOLD IN SELF-RAISING FLOUR. USE 4 OZ OF EACH INGREDIENT PER TWO EGGS. ADD 2 TBSP COCOA POWDER WITH THE FLOUR FOR CHOCOLATE. BAKE AT 150°C FOR AN HOUR. EVEN YOU CAN DO THIS. TRUST ME.

There are hydrangeas in bloom, the sun is shining, and I've finally slept. *Alles ist gut.* Confessing *The Wurst*, if not the worst, has left me somehow able to close my eyes. Are Thomas and I friends? Age twelve, if someone had asked me that, I'd have punched them in the nose. Our friendship just *was*, like gravity, or daffodils in spring.

I stand on the step with the cake, the note, the kitten, and this thought: we talked till the sun came up. And it only makes me want to say more. Next to me, Umlaut does flips in the sunshine.

I scoop him up and head to the kitchen, where I get my second surprise of the day—a new phone. This comes with a note, too, a more enlightening one: *Sie sind verantwortlich für die Zahlung der Rechnung. Dein, Papa.* (You're in charge of paying the bill. Love, Papa).

I abandon my cake on the windowsill and tear open the phone like it's Christmas morning, plugging it in to charge. Papa has Scotch-taped my old SIM onto the box. I'll be able to see if Jason's texted a time for us to meet. I'll be able to ask him: what happened in Grey's room—did I disappear?

And the real question: what happened, with us?

"Goog 'ake."

I look up from my phone-charging vigil to see that a pajama-bottomed Ned, his hair wild, has emerged from his nest. Wednesdays and Fridays are his bookshop shifts, which means he's up early-ish. And he's eating my cake for breakfast.

" 'Eckon." He swallows in one gulp, like a snake, and tries again. "Think Thomas would make a massive one for the party?"

This is the first time he's spoken to me directly about the party—but he still hasn't asked me if I'm okay with it. For all the hydrangeas and sleep in the world, *alles ist* not *gut*. I grab my satchel and my partially charged phone and run out of the house.

My phone chimes along with the church bells. I've been hiding out in the churchyard for hours, folded like origami between the yew tree and the wall. The text is from Jason. We're meeting at lunchtime, a week from tomorrow.

Notebooks and diaries are spread out around me on the yellowing grass. It's out of sight of the church, the graves, the road. We came here once.

It was the beginning of August, about seven weeks after our first kiss. We hadn't slept together yet, but suddenly I could see it on the horizon. Every day, everything—the air, the sunshine, the blood in my veins—was pulsing hot and urgent. The minute we were alone, our words and clothes would disappear. Grey's diary for that day says: *LOBSTER WITH WILD GARLIC BUTTER ON THE BARBECUE.* Behind the tree, Jason's hand slipped between my legs, and I bit his neck. I wanted to eat him.

Where did all that love go? Where did that girl go, who was so alive?

My phone emits a rapid flurry of beeps, and I swoop on it. But it turns out to be old messages from Sof, arriving all at once. A couple checking if I'm okay, after our beach spat, but mostly chattering about the party I don't want to happen. There's no way to answer those, so I throw the phone onto the grass instead and pick up a notebook.

The Weltschmerzian Exception.

It started the day I saw Jason again. I'm writing his name down when a shadow falls across the page. Thomas is peering round the tree.

"I'd say you're avoiding me," he remarks, flopping down opposite me, against the wall, "but I know you know *I* know all our hiding places."

He stretches out his legs, putting his feet up on the trunk next to me, making himself practically horizontal. Whatever landscape he's in, he folds himself into. I parse my way through his sentence, come up with: "So you'd say I'm . . . waiting for you?"

"If *you* say so." A laugh bursts across his face.

Well, I walked into that one.

"You liked the cake?" he asks.

"Delicious," I lie.

"Funny, Ned thought so too."

Twelve years of stare-offs between us, and my impassive face is perfect. Finally Thomas blinks and says, "Okay, subject change. Is this your extra-credit project?"

He makes a "may I?" gesture and reaches for the notebook, which is balanced on my bare legs. His fingers graze my knees as he takes it, glancing at the pages and saying, "Senior year here must be intense."

I peer over at what he's reading. A page of impenetrable numbers, and standing out like a big red flag, Jason's name. For some reason it seems important that Thomas not know this particular secret. Time for my own subject change.

"How's the jet lag?"

"I think my time zones are still cuckoo." Thomas yawns.

"As in the clock? They're actually very efficient." It's this sort of fact-based fun, Sof informs me, that doesn't get me invited to the parties I don't want to go to.

"For real? Okay. Wackadoodle, then." Thomas closes his eyes. There's no cardigan today, he's wearing a T-shirt with a pocket, which he tucks his glasses into. He looks less artfully constructed without them. More like someone I would be friends with. "I stayed up too late. Don't lemme sleep, though," he mumbles. "Keep talking."

"I need a topic. Unless you're interested in Copernicus."

"Not Copper Knickers," he says. "Umlaut. What's up with that?"

"Papa brought him home in April." I lean forward, lifting the notebook off Thomas's knees as gently as I dare. But he opens his eyes and squints at me. In the sunshine, his flawed iris looks like a starburst nebula.

"G. That's not talking. That's information. I need details."

"Okay. Um. I was doing homework in the kitchen after school, when this orange *thing* shoots out from under the fridge, scuttles across the room past the stove and into the woodpile. So I picked up a ladle—"

"A ladle?" mumbles Thomas, closing his eyes again.

"You know—for soup?" Maybe they call it something else in Canada. A ladle*eh*.

He chuckles. "I know what a ladle is. I wanna know *why* you got a ladle."

"I thought there was a mouse."

"What were you gonna do, scoop it up?"

I rap him on the knee with my pencil, and he shuts up, smiling.

"Woodpile, scuttly thing, ladle, me," I recap. As I name each thing, the picture in my head clarifies, and I suddenly remember what happened right before the ginger streak across the floor: the kitchen *screenwiped*. At the time I put it down to a headache. Has time been going round the twist since then? That's three months ago.

"G?" Thomas murmurs sleepily, tapping me on the shoulder with his foot.

"Oh! Right. Then this kitten pops up from behind a log and it's Umlaut."

"That's it?"

"Then I put him in my jumper and rang the bookshop, because I thought maybe Papa could put a sign up. And he answers and goes,

'*Guten tag, liebling*. Did you get my note?' I look around and he's written on the blackboard, but it just says 'Gottie? Cat.'"

When Thomas laughs at my story, his mouth crinkling, my brain bolt-from-the-blue redelivers the thought from the bookshop: *I don't remember you being this gorgeous.*

I start reciting pi to one hundred decimal places. Except my brain won't play along, because it ends up going like this:

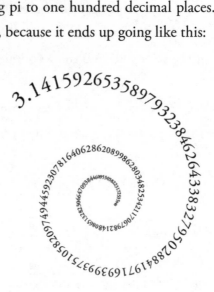

And I start to wonder: what would have happened if Thomas had kissed me five years ago? If he'd never left? Would I still have fallen in love with Jason, or would it have been Thomas I was behind this tree with last summer? When I let myself think this, the churchyard around us gradually fills with the numbers I was reciting in my head. They hang in the air like Christmas baubles, suspended on nothing. We're flying through the galaxy, up in the stars. And it's beautiful.

It's Grey's string theory: a giant cosmic harp. What would my grandfather say to me now? I imagine him stealing my notebook, peering at the Weltschmerzian Exception. "The rules of spacetime are buggered, are they? Make your own rules."

"Thomas?" I ask. "That email you sent me. What was it?"

"Email? It's a form of communication, sent through the In-ter-net." Thomas pulls himself upright and does a cute little typey-typey motion with his hands to demonstrate. He's oblivious to the mathematical weather phenomenon, to the thought that sparked it—a version of the world where we'd once kissed.

"Ha." I prod him in the leg with my trainer, and he catches my ankle for an imperceptible moment, smiling, his face mirror-balled with light from the numbers.

"G, it's no big deal," he says. "I wrote you that, yeah, I was coming over. It was just a reply to yours."

K   7

8

I

1   S

S

6

I

4

N

0

G

6

The numbers fall from the air, raining silver on the grass, where they fade away. We're back to normal.

Normal—except there's a timeline where I wrote Thomas an email!

"I guess I didn't get what yours meant till I arrived," he continues.

"Your dad explained when he drove me from the airport. About Grey."

A record scratch, a squeal of tires. I can pretend that life goes on, in stories of kittens and emails, but death brings it all to a screeching halt. My face slams shut and Thomas must know why, because he waves at the notebook and very carefully says, "Talk to me about timespace."

"Spacetime," I correct, awkwardly bum-shuffling around on the grass to sit next to him, grabbing hold of the latest subject change like a life raft. Our shoulders align. "Time travel. I'm still figuring out the rules. How it would work, if it were real."

"Cool. Where would you go? I'm thinking dinosaurs. Or maybe the Age of Enlightenment, hang out with ol' Copper Knickers." He leans forward, his arm brushing against mine as he gestures out to the churchyard, almost snowy under its blanket of daisies. "Or stay here in Holksea, get some medieval times happening. Get my head stuck in the stocks again."

"Last August," I interrupt. "That's where I'd go."

"Boring," he sing-songs. "What's last August?"

Jason. Grey. Everything.

"Shit," he says, realizing. "Sorry."

"It's okay." I yank up a clump of dry grass and start shredding it. I don't want to . . . Talking to Thomas last night, today—these have been the first conversations in forever where I haven't felt brain-locked, searching for words to say . . .

Scheisse! I can't even finish a sentence in my own head!

Next to me, Thomas puts his hand over my frantic ones, shushing them. The church bells ring out for six o'clock. A funeral chime.

"We should go," I say. "Umlaut needs feeding."

I scramble up, stuffing books haphazardly into my bag. Thomas scoops up half of them. As we pick our way through the grass, I see he's holding Grey's diaries.

"Is this where . . ." he trails off, obviously infected by the Gottie H. Oppenheimer disease of Never Being Able to Talk About the Worst Thing, looking round. "Is this . . . is Grey . . . ?"

Oh, God. I'm übercreep. Reading a dead man's diaries, surrounded by graves. This was always one of our hiding places, even though Mum's buried on the other side of the church. But that's different—she doesn't belong to me in the same way that Grey did. She's a stranger.

"No," I say, too sharply. "He, we didn't . . ." Deep breath. "There was a cremation."

We shuffle along the path around the church in silence, leaving yew needle footprints behind. We pass Mum's grave. It's never not a shock, seeing the date covered in moss: my birthday. Her death. Carved in stone is the stark reality: that we only ever had a few hours together, before a blood clot, her brain, a collapse. And nothing anyone could do. Thomas leans down and scoops up a pebble in one fluid movement, placing it on top of the stone, keeps walking.

Another ritual. A new one. I like him.

"It's nice that you have these," Thomas says, gesturing with the diaries. "Like he's still around. An idea I'm far more comfortable with now I know *you* painted *The Wurst*."

I laugh. Sometimes it's so easy to. Other times, it feels like I'm going to implode. And it can be totally at random, when I'm doing something irrelevant—showering. Eating a garlic pickle. Sharpening a pencil and suddenly, I'll want to cry. I don't get it. Denial, anger, bargaining, depression, acceptance. That's what the books promised. What I've got instead is an uncertainty principle—I never know where my emotions are going to end up.

"I wish Mr. Tuttle had left diaries when he died." Thomas elbows me. I laugh, again. "Mr. Tuttle finally died? I thought he was everlasting."

"He was actually six hamsters. My dad vetoed the endless resurrection last year. I think he was worried he'd get custody."

We've reached the gate. Thomas turns around so quickly it makes me wobble. I end up standing way too close to him. But even though we're inches apart, he's in the blazing sunshine, and I'm in the shade.

"G. I wanted to say—back then. I haven't told you, I really am sorry. About Grey."

And he hugs me. At first, I don't know what to do with my arms. It's the first time someone's hugged me since Oma and Opa, at Christmas. I stand there, made out of elbows, while he bear-tackles me. But after a moment, I wrap myself around him. It's a hug like warm cinnamon cake, and I sink into it.

And as I do, I sense that something deep inside me—something I didn't even know existed anymore, after Jason—has woken up.

Saturday 26 July

A week later, it starts to rain.

It's biblical, thrumming on the roof at the Book Barn, sending the shelves shaking. Exactly like the day Thomas left. Midmorning, I climb up to the attic, where Papa is a sprite on a camping stool, tapping his red sneakers to the radio and deliberately misalphabetizing poetry. Maintaining his shrine to Grey. He and Ned are in cahoots.

He waves a copy of *The Waste Land* at me.

"*Hallo.* No customers?"

"I turned the sign off," I tell him, drifting over to the skylight. The rain is horizontal, not tourist-browsing weather or even determined-to-buy-an-obscure-first-edition weather. When I peer outside, the whole world is bruised. Across the fens, the sea shows up in frosted waves. It's 11 a.m., but it looks midnight—all the lamps are on inside. Tucked inside the heart of the bookshop, light in the darkness, is like being on a spaceship.

And I want to take off. The last time I was here was with Grey, in a wormhole.

I still have no concrete clue about what's happening. I thought I was clear on the wormholes—they're just high-definition memories—but then I came back from one with the photo of Mum.

There's this principle called Occam's razor that says when you have lots of different theories and no facts, the simplest explanation—which requires the fewest leaps of faith to believe—is right. And the simplest explanation for all this is 1) I was reading a diary and the picture was tucked in the pages. Which means 2) I'm making the wormholes up, mad-crazy with grief.

Is that it? I'm nuts?

It's not a thought I want to pursue. Even if it's all inside my head, even if I'm making it all up—I want it to be real. Every vortex I fall into, I kiss Jason. I see Grey. I find me.

"You think should I shelve Ted and Sylvia together?" Papa asks.

"If you want Sof to organize a protest," I say, turning away from the window.

"It's romantic, *nein*?" He lines them up next to each other on the shelf, making a note on his list, then looks at me. "Like you and Thomas coming back. You know, I was a bit older than you when I met your mami?"

I blink at him in astonishment.

"You know there's a book for you on the desk?" he adds. "I think it's maybe from Grey."

"Oh." I linger in the doorway, waiting for him to elaborate. Talk more about Mami, about Grey. When he doesn't say anything, I add, "I'm meeting a friend for lunch at the café. Want me to bring you back a sandwich?"

"Ja." He half waves me off. I bet he won't look up for hours—if I don't put a sandwich in front of him, he won't remember to eat. I grieve in wormholes. He grieves inside his head—always has. Would things be different if Mum were alive? Ned and I might not have even grown up here, with Grey.

Back downstairs, I rummage through the desk chaos and unearth a biography of Cecilia Payne-Gaposchki, the PhD student who discovered what the universe was made of. The sun, the stars, everything— it's all hydrogen.

FOR GOTTIE, it's inscribed, in Grey's handwriting. MAY YOU ALSO DISCOVER THE UNIVERSE.

It was my seventeenth birthday the October after he died. This was my present? A book? Grey never gave books. He said it was lazy. Ned, Sof, Papa—they gave me things like T-shirts, lavender nail polish, gift vouchers. Grey gave me a telescope. Bugs preserved in resin. Goggles for chemistry lab with my initials monogrammed on the lanyard. A subscription to *New Scientist*. Silver square root stud earrings.

I don't know what to think about a book.

When my phone beeps, I want-assume-hope it's Jason—but it's Thomas. Against all odds, he and Sof and Meg have bonded over comics and are on a trip to London. They've gone to a signing at Forbidden Planet, and he's texted me a picture of *The West Coast Avengers: Lost in Space-Time*. I recognise Sof's paint-stained fingers holding it up to the camera. And there's a message: I assume you're the one in the green spandex?

There's a text from Sof, too. I ignore both messages and flip back to the inscription Grey left for me in the book. Picking up a pen, I write inside the cover: *The Gottie H. Oppenheimer Principle, v 3.0.*

Most everything in the universe is made of hydrogen—what 5 percent we can see, anyway. The rest is dark energy, and dark matter. The stuff we haven't figured out yet.

What if it's all the other possibilities?

More than just two timelines. Schrödinger the shagger says every time an atom decays—or doesn't—every decision we make, it splits the universe. Starting from the Big Bang onwards, until the world spreads out like the branches of a tree. And that's what we mean by infinity.

I label the branches:

A world where I never kissed Jason
or a world where we weren't a secret
A world where it's still last summer
A world where wormholes are real
A world where they're not

The question is, which is the right one?

The ancient computer whirs loudly when I switch it on. Three minutes after the Internet connects, I have a new email address: gottie.h .oppenheimer@gmail.com.

I glance down at my notes, typing rapidly about timelines, and I send it to Ms. Adewunmi. I'm not saying I'm taking her deal—writing the essay in exchange for university help. Let's just call it . . . a possibility.

It's time to meet Jason.

"Papa, I'm going to the café," I bellow up the stairs. No reply.

I don't waste time standing in the rain locking the door, or wrestling with an umbrella, just scurry the few yards across the grass. The café's empty, the windows fogged up as I pick my way through the Formica tables and order a herring on rye for Papa and a tuna melt for me. I'm going to be blasé as hell when Jason arrives—hanging out with my sandwich, no big deal. Even though my stomach is turning flips.

"Fifteen minutes for the tuna melt," the man grunts from behind the counter. Great. "I haven't turned the grill on yet."

"Can I use your restroom?" I ask, and he jerks his thumb.

The toilet is rickety, with overhead Victorian plumbing, but it's a palace compared to the Book Barn. I sit down and shiver in the draught, then see the rusty streak of blood. Oh. I don't have anything with me. I've got money, but the café isn't exactly fancy-tampon-machine territory.

In the end, I wedge cheap, shiny toilet paper into my underwear, then waddle out to the sink, rustling. When I got my first period, I marched to the pharmacy with my legs clamped at the thigh, not wanting to tell anyone. Grey would've tried to throw a pagan ritual. I ended up buying giant winged mattresses that scraped at my thighs and gave me diaper rash, till Sof gave me a crash course in vaginacrobatics. I'd just turned thirteen, and she'd got hers at twelve—apparently this was light-years ahead of me. She forced me to write tampons on the shopping list we kept on the blackboard. "Otherwise I'm starting a performance art band called Are You There, Gottie? It's Me, Menses."

I stare at myself in the mirror as I wash my hands with gritty liquid soap and cold water. I haven't seen Sof in any real way since that day at the beach two weeks ago. We've nodded when she and Meg trail in Fingerband's wake. I dry my hands on my jeans and reply to her texts. Kind of. I ignore her questions about the party and write the performance art band name, and—remember? Maybe we can all go to the beach tomorrow, if the rain clears. If she replies.

I wish I didn't feel sick.

He's standing by the till when I come out, laughing with the man behind the counter and ordering a black coffee. Black coffee. Black leather jacket. Blond hair dark from the rain, swept back into what Grey called a duck's arse. *Jason.* He's shorter than Thomas, I notice for the first time.

I'm glad his back is turned so I can stare at him. I itch with not knowing whether I'm allowed to hug him yet, or even touch him. Last summer, I knew I could reach out and brush straw from his shoulder, sand from his stomach, grass from his legs. Even when the others were around, I'd find a thousand excuses to touch him. And I knew he wanted me to.

I'm falling to pieces when the man calls out, "Tuna melt girl!"

Jason turns around. "Margot. Been. Swimming?"

"No." I finger-comb my topknot. "It's raining. The sea will be cold."

"It was a joke," he drawls. "Your hair's wet."

"Tuna *melt*," Counter-man grunts irritably.

"Oh. Yes. Ha-ha-ha," I say to Jason, then fumble in my pocket for change, swapping a handful of coins for two greasy paper bags. The combined smell of Papa's herring and my melted cheese hits my anxious stomach with a hurl.

"You okay?" Jason tilts his head. But he's still leaning against the

[124]

counter, not reaching out to me. I wish I believed he was as nervous as I am. I want to believe it so, so much.

"I'm fine," I say queasily as he pays for his coffee, and we sit down.

"You going to eat that?" My sandwich is still in its bag. Jason's building a tower out of the sugar cubes.

I lift it up, mechanically take a bite. It takes an hour to chew and longer to swallow around the moon-sized lump in my throat. My ankles twitch, wanting to wrap themselves around his, make both our bodies a pretzel. We were in this café once before. Everyone else was at the beach that day, so we came here instead of the food stand, even though the chips aren't as good. We barely ate anyway, just smiled goofily at each other while they got cold and congealed. That was the day he asked, "Do you love me?" That was the day—

Get it together, Gottie. You have to ask about the wormhole.

"Jason, when you came by the house the other week—when we were in Grey's room, packing his things. What happened?"

His sugar cubes tumble down onto the table. This is it. This is where he tells me I disappeared.

"Ouch. Hot," he says after a slurp of coffee. "Yeah, it was awkward, wasn't it? It's been a while. We're out of practice."

He smiles at me, and I try to smile back.

"But," I persist, "I was, um. I was there?"

"Yeah, I see what you mean." He frowns. "You were a bit daydreamy."

I fumble for a neat way of asking, *I didn't disappear like a magic trick?* There isn't one. Jason's rearranging the sugar, unconcerned. He'd mention it, if I'd vanished. But I have to ask.

"Sorry, so, what was awkward?" I imagine watching me sucked into a cardboard box would fall into that category.

"Oh, I was trying to tell you about college—how busy it is, all the work. How it wasn't fair to you, me being distracted. Then Ned inter-rupted us talking, and like I said—we're out of practice. You need to work on your subterfuge." He winks.

I should be relieved. I'm not disappearing. I'm right about the split screen—my brain wanders off down memory lane, but at the same time, I'm still walking and talking in this reality.

But all I can think about is how last time we were here, he said, *Margot. Forget the chips. Let's go to my house.* That was the day we had sex for the first time.

"But we're cool, right? We're friends," Jason assures me now. He reminds me of Sof, telling me what my opinion should be.

"Tuna melt! Coffee!" Counter-man interrupts. "Sorry, folks, I'm going to close up. If this is the lunchtime rush, I'm going home."

Our chairs scrape the floor as we stand up. In the doorway, I hesi-tate, my fingers tightening round the greasy sandwich bags.

"Have a good swim," Jason says, nodding at the rain. "Shit—you were going to tell me something about Ned's party."

"You want to come to the bookshop? Papa's upstairs, but it's warm. You can share my sandwich . . ."

I will him one last time to follow me outside, across the grass, onto my spaceship. Fly away through the rain, kiss me like it's last summer. But he just crumples his coffee cup and throws it in the trash.

"Can't. Sorry. This is like a whatdyacallit?" He snaps his hands into a finger gun, an echo of Fingerband's fratty vibe, when he finds the word he wants: "Halfway. It's halfway. I can catch the bus from here—my girlfriend lives in Brancaster. You know Meg."

He keeps talking but my ears are roaring with that word—*girlfriend, girlfriend, girlfriend*—and of course it's Meg, perfect pretty Meg. I was a secret but not her, and I'm running out the door: outside, across the grass, through the rain, the storm roaring too. The Book Barn door has blown open but inside it's not the bookshop, it's not my spaceship. It's nothing, it's television fuzz, it's a wormhole, it's a rip in the fucking spacetime continuum.

And this time, I choose to run right into it.

. . . we tumble into the kitchen, laughing and kissing. I don't even care if someone sees us. But Jason lets go of my hand.

There's a note on the blackboard. It's in Papa's handwriting, but it doesn't make sense. The words swim in front of my eyes, I have to spell the letters out one by one and even then it can't be right because they spell

G-R-E-Y-'-S-I-N-H-O-S-P-I-T-A-L

I can't deal. I want to be back in the field with Jason, sun on his skin. I try to grab his hand, to show him.

"Shit," he says, running both hands through his hair. "Shit."

I look at him, wanting him to get it, to say: let's pretend we didn't read this, let's pretend it's not true, let's have a few more hours. We never came into the kitchen. We're still in the fort in the field, in the sunshine.

But he doesn't read my mind. He says, "Dude, you should go. You need to—shit. My mum could give you a lift. Or if you bike to Brancaster, you can get the bus to the hospital."

He keeps talking but I can't hear him, like I couldn't read the note: the sea is rushing in my ears, there's not enough gravity in the room. Where did all the oxygen go?

"Gottie? You go. I'll text Ned and say you're on your way."

Finally, I find my voice: "You're not coming with me?"

"I can't, I've got work." Jason works at the pub. Sometimes I sit out back behind the kitchens, and he sneaks me crisps.

"But—" I point to the note on the blackboard again. Maybe he doesn't understand it either. "Grey's in the hospital."

"Yeah, shit. I know. But it'll be fine—they wouldn't have left a note unless it was fine." He's steering me out of the kitchen, shutting the door behind us, holding my hand, leading me to my bike. It's on its side on the grass where I'd left it. For some reason, I look across to the hole in the hedge and think of Thomas Althorpe. Who put me in this same hospital, long ago.

It takes me two goes to climb on the bike. I want to be back in the field.

I want to call Sof and tell her everything: me and Jason!

I want to hold hands under a blanket, and talk in whispers.

I want to go back in time. Just ten minutes. If we'd gone straight to my room instead of the kitchen, we wouldn't have found the note. Grey wouldn't be in the hospital, and I'd be naked with Jason.

These are the wrong thoughts to be having. I'm a bad person.

"Text me later, okay?" Jason says, squinting at me. I can't see the blue of his blue, blue eyes. And then the world is folding in on itself, blinding white pain, I'm being squeezed, my heart hurts—

———

—and then I'm doubled over on the kitchen doorstep, spitting bile in the grass between my feet. It's night, and raining. A hand is rubbing small circles on my back. Thomas's voice murmuring, asking if I'm okay. The wormhole ache hasn't even worn off when the truth hits me like a meteor: Jason never loved me. There's no universe where he wasn't going to break my heart.

I can solve $f(x) = \int_{-\infty}^{\infty}$ in my head, so it's easy enough to calculate the time I've wasted on him since 9 October last year: 293 days, 7,032 hours, 421,920 minutes.

This boy, who wouldn't even hold my hand at the funeral!

Enough. That's enough.

"Thomas." I straighten up. His hand stays on my back, his face half-lit from the kitchen behind us, as he searches mine to find what's wrong. "Do you want to open the time capsule?"

{3}
FRACTALS

---

*Fractals are never-ending, repetitive patterns
found in nature—rivers, lightning, galaxies, blood
vessels. Mistakes.*

*A tree trunk splits three ways. Each way splits into
three branches. Each branch carries three twigs. And so
on to infinity.*

Simplicity leads to complexity.

Complexity leads to chaos.

Wednesday 30 July

[Minus three hundred and thirty-two]

It rains for the next four days. Thomas skips off his Book Barn shifts, and by wordless agreement, we hole up in my room, playing Connect Four and eating wonky *Schneeballs*. I unroll my Marie Curie poster and stick it back on the wall. Dust my telescope. Think about wormholes, flip through Grey's diaries, ignore Sof's texts. Thomas reads comics, graffitis notes on cookbooks, and drops his socks all over my floor like he lives here. Which, I'm getting used to the idea that he does.

It's as if he never left. And, ever since that hug in the churchyard, there's something else, too. An occasional, unspoken wondering . . .

When it finally stops raining, we emerge and go looking for the time capsule. It's only three weeks since the apple-twisting incident, but it could be years: the ivy is out of control, there's a wasp orgy over the rotting fruit on the ground, and the grass is beyond "needs cutting" and into "Ned's hair" territory.

Grey would murder us. He liked the garden untrammeled, so there's no distinction between "grass" and "flowerbed" and "tree." Most years, it's impossible to lie straight on the lawn because he plants yellow tulip bulbs willy-nilly. But this is neglected. It's a mess. As though without him, we don't give a shit.

"I missed this," Thomas beams, taking off his Windbreaker. "That after-rain smell. I swear it smells different in Canada."

Bentley's paradox says that all matter is pulled to a single point by gravity. Apparently for me and Thomas, that single point is this tree. He stretches up, up, up, revealing a sliver of stomach, as he flings the coat onto a high branch, showering us in rain.

"Oops," says Thomas, twisting back around towards me. "There's something about this tree, isn't there?"

We're both rain-damp now, silver droplets lacing our hair like dew. He watches me as I dry my face with the edge of my sleeve.

"Petrichor," I blurt.

"Is that Klingon?"

"The after-rain smell. That's the name for it. It's wet bacteria."

Congratulations, Gottie. Last time you were under this tree with Thomas, the stars went out. Now you're talking about *wet bacteria*.

"Petrichor, really," says Thomas. "Sounds like one of Sof's bands. Or your dad when he talks German."

"That reminds me—Papa said I had to tell you to phone your mum back, and stop wiping her messages off the blackboard and pretending you've called." I prod at the wet earth with my shoe. "Whatever you've done, you have to talk to her sometime. Like, when you're back next door in a month?"

"Right," says Thomas. He leans back against the tree trunk. "Next door."

There's a pause. I know he and his dad don't get along—and actually, none of the messages on the blackboard have been from him. But should I not have mentioned his mum either?

Then he smiles, wickedly. "Why do you assume *I've* done something?"

"Instinct." The word flies out of my mouth automatically, and Thomas cracks up. "Prior experience. Fundamental knowledge of you. History. That time with the pigs. Mr. Tuttle. A big, doomy sense of foreboding."

As I list our past, my mind jumps to the future—Thomas next door, clambering through the hedge, biking to school, eating cereal together, hanging out at the Book Barn. He's home, and it will be a year so different from the one I've just had.

Thomas smiles, pushing himself off the tree trunk.

"Race you," he says, his leg already swinging onto a low branch. Next thing I know, he's a few feet above me—I can see the bottom of his Adidas. "It's still here!"

"*What's* here?" I thought we were going to dig up the time capsule?

"Come up and I'll show you!" He pokes his head through the leaves, offering me his hand.

When I'm sitting on a nice, sturdy branch next to him, I open my mouth, but he puts a finger to his lips, then points. Tucked inside the tree is a rusty metal tin, one of those beige petty-cash ones, with a handle on top and a loop to use for a padlock. Our names are written in marker pen on the lid, and sitting on top of it is a frog.

"Oh," I say, not recognizing it. The box, I mean, not the frog. Though I'm pretty sure I haven't seen that before either. "This is the time capsule? We didn't bury it?"

Thomas shakes his head. "We found it."

I turn my head to look at him, his face leaf-dappled in the sunshine.

We used to climb up here all the time, but now we're both too big for the tree, crammed into the branches.

"Oh. You really don't remember this?" he asks.

I have to hold on to his shoulder with one hand, so I can show him my left without losing my balance.

"All I know is we talked about the blood pact at the Book Barn," I say, waving my palm, "then waking up in the hospital with this."

"Right. That makes sense. Hold on." Carefully, he leans forward and lifts the frog onto his finger, then stands up on the wonky branch and reaches over to put it on a cluster of leaves.

I'd swoon right out of the tree if it wasn't a totally Isaac Newtonian thing to do. Then Thomas does it for me.

"Whoa!" As he turns to sit back down, his foot slips on the wet branch. Without anything to hold on to, he windmills his arms for a second, one foot hanging off the edge. I freeze, already watching a future where he falls in slow motion.

Time speeds up when he regains his balance with a "Phew" and grins at me. "Think I just won Canada the gymnastics gold for that, eh?"

"Graceful," I say to cover my panic, grabbing his arm at the elbow to steady him as he sits down. It's not entirely necessary—his center of gravity seems fine. But then he grabs my arm back, in a strict violation of the Spaghetti Arms Principle.

"Thank you." He settles next to me. We're still holding arms. Not hands. *Arms.* I'm holding elbows with Thomas Althorpe, and it's ridiculous.

And I don't want to let go.

"Ready?" He looks at me. His eyes aren't muddy—they're hazel.

I chew on my lip, considering. I like holding elbows with Thomas, eating cake and joking about *The Wurst.* Against all odds and expectations,

I like him bouncing into my room uninvited, lounging on my bed and tickling Umlaut's ears. I like re-becoming friends—and the something else there is between us, building like electricity in the air.

But inside this box is everything that happened, on the day he abandoned me. Am I ready to remember?

"It's just a box," says Thomas. "Bawk, bawk, bawk . . ."

Before I can think about it, I grab the lid and yank it, hard.

It's empty. There's a brackenish black smear as though slugs have been nesting in it, and the inside of the lid is sort of sooty and covered in illegible Sharpie scribbles, but otherwise, nothing. What an anticlimax.

"G, did you open this already?"

"I told you—I didn't even know this was . . . whatever this is. What is it?"

I feel Thomas shrug next to me. "It's nothing now, I guess."

"What did you think was going to be in there?"

"I don't know!" He sounds completely frustrated, like he wants to shake the tree so all the apples fall out, bonking us on the head till we get some answers. "We found a bunch of junk, then we did the blood pact. I left you here to get Grey, and when we came back the lid was closed. I always wondered . . ."

"What?"

"Nothing." He shakes his head like a dog coming out of the sea. "Nothing. Maybe we opened it too soon, I don't know."

I twist to look at him, sliding one arm behind his back so I don't fall out of the tree. With the other, I take his elbow again.

A month ago I didn't want any memories of this summer. Now, I'm not so sure. I'm starting to remember that there are two sides to every equation.

"Thomas. Listen. It's empty. So what? We can put something new in there. A time capsule of you and me. Who we are now."

He turns to take my elbow. The shift means now neither of us can move without totally losing our balance. My face must be as serious as his as we look at each other. I want to ask, *Who are you, really? Why are you back?*

"So who are we now?" we both ask at the same time.

"Telepathy," Thomas says. And his smile could light the whole fucking tree on fire.

The sky turns from sun to rain in an instant. Within seconds, it's pouring.

Lightning flashes through the leaves, bouncing off Thomas's glasses. Followed fast by a long, low rumble of thunder.

"G!" Thomas has to raise his voice over the noise even though we're inches apart. "We have to get out of this tree."

Lightning flashes again. I can barely see through the water in my eyes, but I nod. My arm is still tucked around his waist, his hand still on my elbow. If either of us moves, we'll both fall.

"I'm going to let you go," Thomas shouts. "Jump backwards. On three?"

Instinct says don't wait, jump—I slide down the trunk, scraping my stomach on the bark. My topknot snags on a twig, tugging at my scalp with a sharp wince. There's thunder again, then Thomas, tumbling down from above me, grabbing my elbow the minute he's on the ground.

"You didn't wait for three," he yells, his other hand pushing back his soaking-wet hair.

"Neither did you!"

We turn, laughing, jostling, grabbing at each other's hands in a race to my bedroom. Where Ned's standing sentry in the doorway, arms folded, his fur coat bedraggled from the rain. He looks like Umlaut after losing a fight with a squirrel.

"Althorpe." He scowls at Thomas, who drops my hand, which makes Ned scowl more. What's his problem? "Just had a nice chat with your mum—she's on the phone, wants to talk to you."

After Ned practically frog-marches Thomas across the garden, I curl up on my bed with Grey's diary from five years ago. Turn to the autumn, the winter, after Thomas left. I'm not sure what I'm looking for—clues, mentions of a time capsule, *something*. What I find is:

THE POND FROZE OVER, ICE-SKATING DUCKS
G'S HAIR IS GETTING AS LONG AS NED'S. SHE STILL LOOKS LIKE CARO.

I drop the diary on my bed, go and sit on the floor in front of my mirror. The photo of me and my mum is taped to its corner. My hair's still wet from the rain, scrolled up in its topknot—and when I take out the elastic, it falls in damp waves all the way to my waist. A stranger looks back at me.

"What do you think, Umlaut?"

Meow?

I consider my reflection, my mum's face in the photo. Who am I?

I was someone so afraid of making a choice, I held on nine months for Jason. I waited five years for Thomas, silently. I painted *The Wurst* and never told Sof I was quitting art. I drift, I don't decide. I let my hair grow long.

I twist it in a wet rope around my hand. This doesn't feel like me anymore. I opened the time capsule and jumped before the count of three—that's someone who gets drunk on peonies and dries her underwear in a tree. I think I might want to write Ms. Adewunmi's essay.

I want to come out of mourning.

Cutting my hair is suddenly a planetary necessity. I high-paw Umlaut, then jump up and tear out into the rain forest, immediately tripping over a bramble and ripping a chunk out of my ankle. *Scheisse!* I'm going to take a flamethrower to this mess.

Wet-haired and wild-hearted, I burst into the kitchen, where Jason and Ned are sitting round the table. Ned is playing acoustic guitar, half a hot cross bun dangling from his mouth like a cigarette.

"Rock 'n' roll," I say, giving Ned double thumbs. The gesture falters when it comes to Jason. I chose to be over him. He told me we were friends. We've never been that, I don't know how. I turn back to my brother and say, "Hot cross buns are for Easter, it's July."

Actually, July's nearly over. Ned's party's in two weeks, and then two weeks after that—a year since Grey died. Term will start and time will slip away. It already is.

"Hangovers yield to no season," Ned mumbles round the bun, even though it's seven in the evening. All the joy I felt moments ago is draining away.

"If you're looking for lover boy, he's in his room," says Ned, as though I were rummaging for Thomas in the cutlery drawer. I assume Jason's staring at the back of my neck while I all-over blush at Ned's foot-in-mouth comment, or maybe he isn't and hasn't noticed and, God, how hard is it to put spoons back in the right place, anyway?

"I've commissioned him for the party," Ned adds. "We're thinking a giant croquembouche."

"Hey, Gottie, did you see the Facebook invitation?" Jason calls over as I turn around, drawing me into their circle. "Meg drew this cool—"

I walk out while he's still talking—I've found the scissors, and I'm hacking my way back through the soaked garden to my room, jabbing at random shrubs as I go. I want it all gone. Hair, party, garden, Jason, wormholes, time, diaries, death—especially death, I've had a lifetime of it.

My room feels like a coffin.

CHOP.

That's how I imagine it—one swift, clean slice of the blades and I'll be able to stuff all my sadness in the trash. Jason's hands in my hair, his mouth on my neck, the girl I was and am and will be—whoever she is. Gone.

Reality: I ponytail my hair, reach behind me to cut, there's a crunch—then the scissors stop. Even yanking as hard as I can with both hands . . . Nothing. They're stuck.

Patting around the back of my head with my fingers, my pulse fluttering, I can tell I'm only about a third of the way through my hair—but it's enough that I have to keep going. Except I can't. Open. The. Scissors.

A chunk of chin-length hair swings loose.

Umlaut turns in circles on the diaries, yowling.

"Not helping," I sing-song to him.

My face burns even though there's no one but the cat to witness my embarrassment. There's no Sof to call like when I shaved my unibrow instead of plucking it—I've shut her out. Why did I do that? The scissors hang off my hair, bouncing against my back as I throw myself across the room to my phone and text her back, reply to everything, rapidly, urgently, immediately.

Pick a color, pick a number—meet me at the beach on Sunday. Please?

A world where Sof and I are friends.

Then I grab my nail scissors and start hacking away in tiny blunt snips, not caring about the strands that are falling to the floor, how it's going to look. I'm so ready to be—

Free. The kitchen scissors hit the floor.

I run my hand over my head–it feels *really* short. In places. There are also long lengths that I've missed. When I was a kid, Grey would cut the food out of my hair instead of washing it. I suspect I've accidentally re-created toddler chic.

Umlaut pads over to the mirror with me.

My eyes flick between my reflection and the photograph. Olive-skin-dark-eyes-*so*-much-nose-out-of-time-eighties-mullet-hair: yes, I do look like Mum. But it's nice. Because also, for maybe the first time in forever, I look like me.

A mirror ball of light ripples across the room. I look up, catching the end of a screenwipe—and on the other side of it, my ceiling is starred with phosphorescent plastic constellations. Like I used to have when I was little and shared a bedroom with Ned. He always hated them.

Did I stick these up there? Or did Thomas?

Under their fluorescent glow, my phone beeps with an alert for gottie.h.oppenheimer. Thomas's email has arrived. Even though it's impossible, even though this is a brand-new address: this is the email he sent a month ago. The timelines are converging.

Thursday 31 July

[Minus three hundred and thirty-three]

Delivered-To: gottie.h.oppenheimer@gmail.com
Received: by 10.55.141.129 with SMTP id p123csp1805138qkd;
       4/7/2015, 17:36:27 X-Received: by 10.50.45.8 with SMTP
idi8mr5770927igm.47.1447183047627;
Return-Path: <thomasalthorpe@yahoo.ca>
Received: from nm42.bullet.mail.ne1.yahoo.ca
(nm42.bullet.mail.ne1.yahoo.ca. [98.138.120.49])
       by mx.google.com with ESMTPS id
       s85si6481364ios.153.2015.11.10.11.17.27
       for gottie.h.oppenheimer@gmail.com

b=G9e8uJO59jG58LGKeSc0H4+9NN0Xa2jzmCf+rBK+JUtnv96EI5tHIAGXXah8avMuvw96p
43H20g/6u1Gnlsk58mtvZeN84ae35D2ZVWwq1AAKrHxlkj6AI1d6YPeuq3chEmU0HahPfde
WDeY4JzCMTsMSo9W8AvVCueo9PXbwGfFTc3ZMKVjYX30DsoxUxTXojhue+Dg1tWFTYY1vHe
cd4/ntp6GfZv30iHB1jal7vUs15anRAIM1YMjTSwYqyZV0tjaY30i8gNCWvKGkpwpL30kG1
Ubzy1M5UH5CPCDbYDTN4X9zMwLkCjo2YHyJ10P33WtIiRqJqZxRkeIyYroLw

I've deleted and reinstalled my email app, climbed the apple tree and waved my phone around for 4G, and boinked it with my fist— but, aside from our addresses and the date at the top, Thomas's email refuses to be anything but this gibberish.

It shouldn't even exist! I hadn't even set up this account when he sent this. Did he guess hundreds of addresses, sending out emails like messages in bottles?

v 4.0—opening Schrödinger's box determines whether the cat is dead or alive.

But what if the cat isn't in there yet?

When dawn arrives, I shove my new hair into a facsimile of normal and change out of my planet-print PJs into a vest and shorts. At my bedroom door, I pause, looking out at the damp grass—and kick off my tennis shoes. If I'm going to discover the universe, I'll start with my feet.

When I enter the kitchen, muddy up to my ankles, Thomas and Ned and Papa are already at the table. There's a plate of cinnamon rugelach between them.

Papa's eyes go wide, while Thomas swallows in a choking sort of way, then says, "Whoa. Your *hair*." I can't tell from his tone if it's good or bad.

I reach up and prod it. "Scale of one to eleventy million, how awful?"

Thomas shakes his head, his own tousled hair bouncing. "Nah, you look awesome. It's exactly how it's supposed to be."

We stare at each other for a moment, something unspoken passing between us.

Then Ned whispers in Papa's ear, and he harrumphs, muttering in German. I think I catch the word *Büstenhalter. Bra.*

I fold my arms across my chest, and Thomas leaps up, launching himself round the kitchen, putting a rugelach on a plate for me, flipping the kettle on, bat-grabbing and babbling a mile a minute about Ned's croquembouche commission.

I eat the pastry, licking sticky sugar from my fingers, and let myself laugh at Thomas's antics. Ignore the way Ned's scowling at us both.

After nearly a year of mourning, I feel like the Victorians when

Edison came along—all those years in the darkness, and then *electric light*.

I've got the earth between my toes.

———————

On Sunday, I dodge Ned's weird policeman act and walk inland out of Holksea, along the canal to Sof's. It's a scalding day, and she's already sunbathing when I get to the boat, barely visible through the jungle of pot plants her mum keeps on the deck.

I stand on the towpath for a couple of seconds, watching as Mrs. Petrakis goes from watering the plants to sprinkling Sof, who shrieks with laughter. Grey used to do that to us in the garden. Did he do that to my mum? Would she have done it for me? The thought is a wormhole yank to my heart.

"Sof!" I bellow, to stop thinking about it.

She sits up, peering over the ferns, and her mouth forms a perfectly lipsticked, perfectly gobsmacked O.

As in, *oh*, my hair. I'd forgotten about the makeover.

While Sof stares at me, I clamber on, rocking the boat—my movement makes all the leaves sway, even though there's no breeze. Sof shakes her head, maybe in disbelief.

"Hi, Mrs. Petrakis." I wave, awkwardly.

"Hello, stranger." Her mum's smile is warm, sending lines radiating out from her eyes. She puts the watering can down. "Darling, I'd give you a hug, but my hands are covered in compost. It's only been four days since all the rain, but everything's totally dried out. I expect your garden's much the same?"

She and Grey used to bond over mulch and leaf mold and compost, oh my. Her ideas are all throughout the diaries. It's how Sof and I first became friends. Sof, who still hasn't spoken.

"It's okay," I fib. Has Sof told her how neglected the garden has become? I should invite her round to say hello to the plants. Ask her what we need to do to restore the garden to its former glory.

"Let me get you a drink—coconut water?" Mrs. Petrakis smiles again, turning away and taking off her gardening gloves. She touches the back of her hand to Sof's shoulder. "Don't forget sunscreen."

Sof follows her inside to get it, and I try not to hate her for having a mum who remembers about sunscreen.

"Wow," Sof finally says when she returns, carrying bottles of water and a bag of dried apple slices.

"You think it was a mistake?"

"No, no . . ." Sof *looks* like she thinks it was a mistake. Her own hair is done up in giant Princess Leia buns as she stares at mine. "Turn around, let me get a better look at it."

I do a three-hundred-and-sixty-degree spin, then sit down on the towel next to hers, sweating from the small exertion.

It's blazing hot. The air is still and smells of salt and sea lavender, with the kind of endless sky you only get here on the fens, where the land is so flat it could prove Ptolemy wrong, and the blue goes all the way to the edges. Not that I've been anywhere else to compare. Perhaps Ned sees similar skies all the time in London. Perhaps Thomas left behind a Canadian sky as big as this one.

I want to see all the skies, not only the one I know. *This is how you discover the universe.*

"Do you hate it?" I rub my hand over the bristles on my neck, still not used to it.

Sof adjusts her lime sunglasses—they match her bikini—not looking at me as she croaks, "I don't hate it. But I wish you'd told me about it first."

"So you could tell me not to do it?" I half joke. "I know it's wonky, I think Thomas got peanut butter on our scissors . . ."

Sof doesn't answer, just stares out at the canal. The surface is a mirror: all that blue sky is underneath us too. We're at the center of everything.

"You and Thomas. I haven't seen you in weeks, but he's cutting your hair with you—"

"*I* cut my hair. Thomas had nothing to do with it."

"He's in your house. He's getting peanut butter on your scissors, working at the Book Barn . . . You barely reply to my texts, you never said you cut your hair."

This isn't fair. Sof's abandoned me before to spend hours on the phone with girls she's never met, going googoo-eyed over an Internet crush. Can't she just be happy I'm happy? I don't want to wade into a quagmire of conversation. I want to fast-forward through all the awkward like coming out of a wormhole, and emerge with us as friends and have everything be normal.

"It looks like it did when I first met you," Sof mutters. "How it would have been when Thomas lived here before."

"Thomas lives with us," I say. "I can't not see him. And didn't you guys hang out in London with Meg?"

"You and Thomas are friends," she says, finally looking at me—or at least, pointing her sunglasses in my direction. "Me and Thomas are friendly. Where are you and me?"

I stuff an apple slice in my mouth—it's the texture of sea sponge—for something to do. When Grey died, Sof visited me every day, bringing magazines and chocolate and wide eyes full of question marks: are you okay, are you okay, are you okay? I started dreading the tap-tap-tap of her knock because I could *feel* her wanting—wanting me to talk to her, wanting me to let her in, wanting me to come to her. Wanting me to act a certain way. It was exhausting.

What if friendship has a best-before date, and ours has gone off?

"Bet they'd be a novelty one-hit band," I say, nudging her. "Peanut Butter Scissors."

No response.

"Surprise Haircut—quirky singer and a couple of nerds on keyboards."

Nothing from Sof.

"Your Best Friend's A Moron And She's Sorry—me on Niall's drums, scatting a song of apology."

Sof smirks. Only a little. And she quickly pretends she didn't. But it's a start.

"My *maybe*-best-friend's a dick. And it's uneven at the back."

"Hey, Sof." I nudge her. "Do you want to come over this Friday? You could help me even it up. And Thomas makes really good cake . . ."

There's a pause, then she asks "Gluten-free?" and I know I have her.

"Certified fun-free, I promise." I give it a second, then make my next offer. "Want to know a secret? Something Thomas doesn't know."

"Depends." She takes off her sunglasses and squints at me. Fondness fills me up as I think: *I'm not ready for this friendship to be over.* "Is it a good secret?"

"I had sex with Jason."

Ned should be here to photograph the look on her face.

This is how it would go if things were normal between us:

"Wooowww." Sof would scramble upright and wolf-howl into the air. She'd use up the world's supply of vowels. I'd tell her about me and

Jason, how he'd done it before and I, very obviously, hadn't. But how quickly that turns out not to matter. We'd talk and eat licorice till our tongues turned black, go over every detail.

There would be a thousand questions. Is that why you were reading *Forever*? Are you on the pill? Did I need her to talk me through the options? And *Jason*? Did he strike a pose halfway through? Sof's head would go *Exorcist*, and I'd love her for all the reasons I couldn't last summer: her enthusiasm, her exuberance, her nosiness, her put-on air of worldly wisdom. She'd peer at me over her poseur sunglasses and explain that there was no such thing as virginity and have I read Naomi Wolf and penetration is just a myth anyway and I know that, right?

What actually happens: Sof picks her jaw off the floor and a piece of nail varnish from her toe before croaking, "When was this? He's going out with Meg."

"This was before that."

I can't tell her how *long* before. This is the trouble with secrets—you can't just reveal them and hope for normality. Even when exposed, they leave ripples in the universe, like a stone skimmed on the canal.

"You know he and Meg are going to be at Ned's party."

Even though it's happening at my house, there's no question—it's Ned's party, not mine. Thirteen days and counting down.

"I'm sorry I didn't tell you before," I say. "About Jason."

"Yeah, well." Sof jams her sunglasses back on. "I don't tell you all my secrets."

"About Jason," I say, not any lighter for telling her. "You're the only one who knows . . ."

"And you want me not to tell Ned," she says, standing up. Ever since the time capsule, Ned's been popping up between me and Thomas like a jack-in-the-box. Lurking in front of the bathroom door and in

[149]

the kitchen like a Roman centurion. Never leaving us alone. "Shall we swim?"

The ferns sway as we walk silently to the prow of the boat. At the edge, we stand side by side, together but not.

"Best summer ever?" I ask Sof. It's so, so far from that, but that's what I always used to say.

And she always used to say the same thing back: *Nah—next year will be better.*

This time, she doesn't bother to answer. Instead, ahead of me in everything like always, she dive-bombs into the mirror-smooth canal, shattering all that blue into a thousand pieces.

Swimming with Sof—that was the plan. But by the time I jump in after her, the canal's a wormhole.

I let myself sink into the cool, clear water.

After I come bursting up for air, I turn onto my back, and float. Earlier, when we were kissing, Jason persuaded me to take my hair out of its topknot. Now it's drifting out around me in the water. I'm a mermaid.

I close my eyes as the sun washes over me, enjoying the contrast of warm on my stomach and cool underneath. When Jason calls my name, it sounds far away, as though we're in two different places.

It's only after he says "Margot" for the third or fourth (hundredth) time, I bother opening my eyes. He's upside down above me, leaning over the prow of Sof's boat. Her whole family's on vacation, and I'm on plant-watering duty. The canal is the perfect Ned-free and everyone-free zone.

"Hi." I crinkle my nose, wishing I could reach up and topple him into the water.

"Hi, daydreamer." He smiles down at me, love and sunglasses. "Are you ever planning to get out?"

"Nope." I splash with my hands a little, and he laughs. "You could get in . . ."

"I didn't bring my bikini," he jokes.

I close my eyes, because I don't dare say this with them open: "So swim naked."

Shortly afterwards, there's a splash. I tip myself upright, treading water, and Jason's beside me. Wet hair flopping into his eyes, bare chest, warm eyes inky blue. And as he looks at me, I suddenly get it. This isn't the Big Bang. It's just summer. But it's still love. It's still something.

"Now you," he says, cocky. His arm slides around my waist, holding me steady, and we half swim to the side of the boat. Our gazes don't break as I reach behind me to unhook my bikini top and fling it over the boat-rail, where it drips cool and steady into the canal next to us.

When I shuffle off my bikini bottoms, they sink away from me. I don't bother diving down to find them. Instead, I say to Jason: "Race you." And kick my feet off the side of the boat, slicing through the water, turning circles, living in 3D.

Every inch of me is electric. Without that polyester layer, I feel the water differently against my skin. The sun is hotter on my shoulders, Jason's mouth when he catches up to me and kisses the back of my neck, it's all just so much more. This is the most alive I've ever been.

Monday 4 August

It's midnight, or thereabouts. A Cinderella time. The witching hour. The mood is magical: dark and starry, hot and close. And I'm wide awake. Ever since I burst out of the past, back into the canal, I've got superhero hypersense. It's like someone cranked the world's volume up and it's all blazing color. No more wormholes—I'm *here*.

It feels both better and worse than before: intense and alive, but farther from my grandfather than ever. Being here means letting him fade away. The diaries are just words on a page.

The kitchen door is open, and the night jasmine drifting in from the garden mingles with the lemon drizzle cake Thomas has just put in the oven. It's his first practice run for the gluten-free promise I made to Sof. Papa went to bed hours ago. Ned's finally given up and left us alone. And every inch of my skin is alive. Tingling.

"Here. It's the best bit." Thomas hands me a wooden spoon, the air stirring as he passes me on his way to the sink, our fingers fumbling.

I lick the cake mixture from the spoon and try to focus on the paper in front of me. I'm plotting the wormholes. Each time and place I've gone back to, and each origin point, gets a dot. If the timelines are converging—I want to know what they're converging *on*. It's ten days till Ned's party. Twenty-eight till the anniversary of Grey's death. And a week after that, Ms. Adewunmi is expecting an essay in her inbox.

Behind me, Thomas is washing up, the sink overflowing with bubbles. He hums over the rumble of our creaky plumbing, the ancient tap that I have to constantly tighten with a wrench. Bare feet tapping on tiles.

I smile and turn back to my work, choosing a new felt-tip and charting all those Thomas anomalies, too. The numbers in the churchyard, the way the stars went out in the garden and the rainstorm in the tree. After a moment, I pick up an orange pen and add one last dot— April, in the kitchen. Umlaut.

"Astronomy homework?" Thomas puts his chin on my shoulder.

I look again. He's right: the dots do look like stars. And not just any constellation—the one Thomas stuck to my ceiling that matches nothing in the galaxy.

Where else will I find this pattern—the sprinkles on top of Thomas's cupcakes? His freckles? The *Rs scattered in Grey's diaries?

"Come on," I say, pushing back my chair. I don't wait for him as I run out into the garden.

Outside, the moon mingles with the light from the kitchen—illuminating the dandelions on the lawn. It's the same pattern.

I lie on the grass and look at the apple tree—imagine its branches twisting round each other like ribbons on a maypole, all the timelines coming together. Is the world converging on something, or laying everything to rest? Earth to earth, ashes to ashes. I don't know that I'm ready to say goodbye.

"Okay, G." Thomas has finally followed me outside. He lies down next to me, scooching his arm so I can rest my head on his chest. "What are we looking at? The same stars you drew?"

"Sure." I burrow into him and let him point out constellations to me—"That right there is Big Burrito. Over here we have Ned on Guitar"—till his voice begins to blur.

Then he yawns. It's huge and Umlaut-y and breaks us apart. I want to wriggle back to how we were, tucked up for bed on the lawn. Then it dawns on me:

"Wait." I roll onto my side, grass tickling my cheek. "I thought you were jet-lagged?"

"I was—a *month* ago," he teases, rolling towards me. Sleepily. "Baking was a distraction. After the chocolate cake, I noticed your light was always on late. I figured, if you were awake, maybe you'd come back to the kitchen. I've been setting my alarm."

He yawns again, squeakily. Shakes it away and looks at me.

"But why?" I whisper. All the creepy-crawlies in the garden hold their breath for the answer as Thomas's hand finds mine.

"I like you," Thomas whispers. "I liked you when you were twelve and you told me to kiss you, all scientific about it. I liked you when I walked off the plane and into the Book Barn, and you were passed out and covered in blood. I like you then, and now, and probably forever."

We move slowly in the dark, finding each other. His hand moves up to touch my face; mine finds his heart. I feel its beat, steady underneath my palm, as he says, "Gottie."

When Thomas says my name, it sounds like a promise. And for that, and for the frog in the tree and the whiskey on the carpet, for the baking lesson, and for the stars on my ceiling, I take a quantum leap.

I close the last atoms of space between us, and I kiss him.

It's late, almost dawn. Witches and ghosts and goblins.

We're outside on the lawn again, the following night. Side by side under the apple tree. Thomas has his head on my shoulder, his watch balanced on his knee—inside, a new gluten-free cake is in the oven, hopefully less disastrous. The minutes are ticking away and, somehow, we're talking about Grey.

"This will sound stupid," I whisper.

"You're talking to me, remember?" His blinks take longer and

longer, slow-motion eyelashes, and his usual frenetic dialogue is playing at 33 rpm.

I should be in my room, working on a telescope theory. Thomas
should be asleep in Grey's room, dreaming of superheroes. We have to
wait for the cake. We could have baked it much earlier. But we did it
like this, because some secrets are easier to tell in the dark.

"I don't think I did it right," I confess. "When Grey died."

"What do you mean?"

"You know they give you a leaflet, at the hospital? When somebody
dies. A to-do list. Ned was getting ready to move to London, and Papa
was—he sort of tuned out." Papa drifted into rooms and stood there not
moving for ten minutes at a time. He locked the keys in the car. He cried
doing up his shoelaces and forgot how to be my daddy. "So I read it."

I pause. This is the most I've spoken about how it was, when my
grandfather died. It's the most I've spoken about *anything*. All those times
Sof came tap-tap-tapping, and I told her I had homework. All those silent baked-potato-and dinners after Papa tuned back in, but I didn't,
till he stopped trying.

When we went to Munich at Christmas, Oma and Opa gave us *Glüh-
wein* and sang carols and quietly suggested to Papa that he could move
back. Unspoken was their real meaning: there was no reason to stay in
Norfolk, now that Grey was gone. There was no connection to my mum
anymore. In response, I don't think Ned knew what to do except get
drunk. He smashed a glass in his hand and left blood in the sink, and
I cleaned it up and didn't mention it.

"I did the things it said to do. I called the registry office and I wrote
an announcement for the paper. I ordered flowers." I tick off items on
my fingers as I whisper the list. "I recorded a new message for the answering machine. I canceled his subscriptions. I cleaned his room. But

Papa kept buying Marmite." My whisper reaches hysteria pitch, and I take a deep breath. "Grey's the only one who likes it. And Papa kept buying it. It's not as though we'd ever run out—no one's eating it—but every few weeks, I see it on the list on the blackboard and wipe it off. And he buys it anyway. We have thirty jars of Marmite."

"I'll eat the Marmite."

"Thank you." I sigh. "But it's not that . . . It's—I did everything the leaflet said! I talked to the funeral director. I chose the hymns."

"You did the rituals," says Thomas. "You poured the whiskey."

My throat aches with uncried tears. Papa buys Marmite and Ned's throwing a party, but I follow the instructions. I do the rituals. So how come I'm the one who's haunted by wormholes?

"I didn't cry at the funeral," I confess. There was a wake afterwards, in the village pub—all Grey's friends, beards and corduroy. We drank ale and ate quiche, and people told funny stories that they didn't finish, breaking off halfway through, upset. But I didn't cry then, either. I didn't deserve to. The first time I cried wasn't till October, the day Jason finally texted me back. What kind of a person cries over a boy, but not their grandfather?

I don't tell Thomas that part.

"It doesn't make any sense," I say.

I'm lost. After remembering swimming with Jason in the canal, how it was its own kind of love—I thought I was okay. I came back to the world, and it dazzled. But this morning, I wasn't even doing anything memorable, just writing on the blackboard that we needed washing-up liquid—and a black hole of emptiness hit. It's as though every time there's a moment like that, where I think I'm better, there has to be something sad to balance it out.

"I don't think it's meant to make sense."

We're shoulder-to-shoulder, arm-to-arm, leg-to-leg, all the way down to our toes. His sock has a hole in it. Even though he's so clean, his socks always have holes. And I think, from nowhere: *I'm going to buy Thomas a new pair of socks.*

I turn to look at him, and he's already looking at me.

"Thank you—"

His kiss interrupts me, sudden-short-sweet. Unquestionable. It feels like reading a favorite book, and falling for the ending even though you already know what happens.

It's different from last night. That was a few giddy, unbelieving seconds before we sprang apart, wondering. This is a squash of his glasses against my cheekbone and a tentative warmth of his mouth on mine. This is my hands curled tight around the neck of his T-shirt, twisting it in my fingers, tugging him closer. This is noses and faces and chins bumping, tongues not sure whether to talk or kiss or all at once, hands on faces, hands everywhere, clumsy and new.

Then it's suddenly floodlights and noise blaring. The oven timer, shrieking through the garden.

We jump apart, looking at each other wildly, then squinting towards the kitchen.

Ned's leaning out the window, lights blazing.

"All right, children," he calls over to us. "Say bye-bye."

"You're sending me to bed?" Unbelievable.

"Thomas and I have things to discuss." Ned beckons him from the window. "Let the menfolk talk cake."

I glance at Thomas, who looks like he's swallowed a bee. I kiss him on the cheek and whisper, "Ignore him."

Ned harrumphs—a Papa impression at Grey volume—and Thomas quickly unfolds himself, sloping away across the garden.

"Sorry," he mumbles over his shoulder to me. *Sorry* isn't in our vocabulary.

In my room, Umlaut hops up onto my pillow, chirruping as he paws in circles. I change into my pajamas, glancing at the email still pinned to my bulletin board.

It's changed.

It's now a string of mathematical code. It doesn't make any sense, but it's closer to a language than the gobbledygook that was there before. In Schrödinger's universe—Grey's "mad shagger," he of the cat that is neither living nor dead—there are an infinite number of possibilities. But I think there are only a few now. I think I'm getting closer to peeking inside the box.

The change in the constellation on the bulletin board is so tiny I almost don't see it. I'm half turning away from my desk when I notice that the little orange dot, the Umlaut dot, has moved.

And when I look back at my bed, the real Umlaut, the one naughtily clawing my pillow, vanishes with a pop.

Friday 8 August

"Do you believe in heaven?"

The afternoon air is drenched in pollen, and everyone's soporific in the garden.

Seriously, everyone. Worlds converged. Inviting Sof begat Meg begat Jason begat a panicked silent sorry-no-wait-I-can't-reveal-this-help-aaargh flail behind his back from Sof. The three of them are in the grass, ignoring the promised gluten-free cupcakes, playing a card game that doesn't appear to have any rules.

Ned's in sequins, skipping his bookshop shift in favor of taking photos and swigging from a water bottle I suspect isn't filled with H_2O.

By mutual, silent consent, Thomas and I retreated under the apple tree. Grey's last diary is in the grass next to me. Above us, beyond the leaves, the sky is bright, bright blue, and I wonder if that's why Thomas is asking about heaven. If he thinks Grey's up there, looking down at us.

But Grey didn't believe in heaven—he was all about the re-incarnation.

"Gottie," he'd tell me now, "I've come back as a beetle. That's me climbing the stalk of grass near your foot. You want to know where Umlaut is? The answer's everywhere around you, dude. You're so close to figuring it all out."

I watch the beetle as it reaches the very top of the meadowsweet, which bends under its tiny weight. From its perspective, this garden is the whole universe. I want to tell it what I've discovered, that there's so much more. For a moment, I let myself believe it's true. That it's Grey, and he's thinking beetle-y thoughts: "I hope there's ants for dinner." But I don't think he can see us from the grass, or the sky, or heaven. I don't think that's how it works.

"No. Heaven is too easy."

Heaven lets me off the hook. Heaven is warm and happy and a big cosmic harp. It's not waiting for wormholes and counting down the days to Ned's party, powerless.

"G—" Thomas sneezes, interrupting himself. "Gah, pollen. I didn't say heaven. I asked if you believed in fate. You and me. This summer." He peers at me over his glasses, solemn. "Us."

"Like it's destiny that you came back?" I don't know if I like that idea. I want to think I have some choice in any of this.

"I mean that it doesn't make a difference whether or not I'd fallen off the books and chinned you that day at the bookshop," Thomas says. "You're not my first kiss. But you're the one that counts."

Whoa. I glance over at our self-appointed chaperone. Ned's got his back turned so I dart in fast, kiss Thomas smash boom on the mouth. Intending it quickly, but it's like the Big Bang—a kiss that keeps expanding.

"Children," Ned interrupts us, striding over, and we break apart. I glance across the garden—Sof's watching, her eyebrow cocked. I'd had the sense to text her about me and Thomas before she came over.

"Say *Käse*." Ned tilts the camera. A drop from his bottle falls onto my leg, followed by the Polaroid fluttering down. Minutes drift by while the picture fades in: Thomas and me side by side, our fingers linked between us in the grass. His head is turned towards me, smiling. I want to reach inside the picture and turn my face to his.

Ned keeps on idly playing paparazzo. Sof makes him take three or four shots on her phone with a poppy in her hair, until she gets one she's happy with—"New profile pic," she says to Meg. "There's a girl I want to invite to the party . . ."

Time passes in a sleepy way. It could be any summer from the past few years—ours was the house people congregated at. Except there's no Grey to play conductor, and there never will be ever again. Ned's party is in a week. Summer's last hurrah. I turn the diary to a blank page and write, *Why aren't you here?*

"We should do something," someone murmurs.

"Definitely," comes another voice.

"Think we should throw the party open to the whole village?" Ned's asking. "Or bequeath it to the next generation?"

"What, like *Star Trek*?" Thomas whispers.

I lie on my stomach, resting my chin on my hands. I want to stay this way forever, drowsy in the heat, where nothing matters. Not wormholes and a grave with my birthday on it, not willow coffins and ashes in a box. Disappearing cats. I want my biggest concern right now to be the effort required to stand up, go to the kitchen, and root around in the freezer for Popsicles. I want it to be like last year, the endless summer when I fell in love and imagined a future and lied to Sof and didn't care.

Before my world fell apart.

Across from me, Meg's making Jason a daisy chain, one end already draped around his leather jacket collar. I watch as though they're strangers on a cinema screen.

And I can brush away the hurt just like it's rain.

"G." Thomas's whisper makes its way dozily through the flowers. "Why do you keep staring at him?"

"Hmmm?"

Jason's laughing, Meg's foot now in his lap. He's playing mine and Sof's game: writing on the sole of her shoe with a felt-tip, while she pretends to hate it, giggling. My own feet are bare, twitching in the grass. I still have a pair of shoes with Jason's name on them.

A nudge at my side. I look away from Jason, laughing in the daisies. Thomas has rolled over and he's shoulder-to-shoulder with me—the way Jason and I once were, next to each other on a blanket, a long time ago. Or was it yesterday? That's the trouble with revisiting the past—it makes it hard to live in the now, and the future, impossible.

"Sorry, what?"

"Jason. Whenever he's around, you always stare at him."

"I wasn't staring at him," I lie. Then add in a lofty voice, "If you must know, I was gazing into the middle distance and thinking important thoughts. Jason's stupid hair was just in the way of my eyeline."

"Important thoughts." Thomas snorts. "Like what to plonk on your baked potato for tea?"

First kisses, second chances. If Thomas hadn't fallen off the books, he would have been my first kiss. I don't care that it was Jason instead.

I only regret keeping it a secret. What would Grey say? Sing a booming chorus of "My Way," probably, then tell me love is something to shout out loud. But maybe there are a hundred different types of love, and ours was never meant to be more than a summer.

I want an endless summer and to fall in love a new way, with a future.

"Hey, Thomas . . ." I press the reset button. "You were my first kiss—at least, the first that counts. I think you'll be my first everything."

I mean first love. A little white lie. But Thomas's whole face is wide-open wondering, eyes warm on mine as he says, "Your first everything. You've never . . . ?"

I don't get the chance to clarify, because Sof interrupts.

"What are you guys whispering about?" she drawls from across the garden. She's half asleep in Grey's deck chair, a beer dangling from her fingers, her feet curled underneath her.

"Fate," replies Thomas, looking at me. Then he turns away, grinning at Sof. "First single by Deck-Chair Girl—you look like a pop star."

She smiles and toasts us, saying "C'mere" to Thomas. "C'mere and tell me more about Canada."

As he clambers to his feet to go over to her, he whispers to me, "Phew. For a while, I wondered if you'd based *The Wurst* on personal experience."

I laugh again and turn onto my back, closing my eyes and letting the sun wash over me, dancing red patterns through my eyelids as I tumble through half sleep. The lie I just told flickers at the edges of my consciousness. It's a misunderstanding, I tell myself, shutting it away in a corner of my mind. I'll clear it up tomorrow—the sex part, anyway. I've no intention of telling Thomas I've already been in love.

Because, Thomas-and-Gottie. Somehow we're managing friends, and something more too. I don't know yet whether we'll be like or love and I don't care. Growing up, coming of age, bildungsroman, whatever— this time around, I'm growing up right. It's *fate*.

A bug tickles my arm and I brush it off. I hear Ned's window creak open, and music spills out over us.

"I'm bored." Sof's voice comes from far away. *Only boring people get bored, Sofia.* Grey's voice in my head.

Another tickle, a midge or a ladybug or an ant or something. The sun goes behind a cloud and I shiver.

A butterfly on my arm. A cool breeze, the first of the day.

"Gerroff," I murmur, but another bug lands on me, another and another—cold and wet and hundreds of them, and when I open my eyes, it's not bugs. It's raining.

I'm alone in the garden.

Did I fall asleep? Not waking me up when it started to rain, and per-suading everyone to go inside without me, that's a typical Ned prank.

"Ned! Edzard Harry Oppenheimer," I yell, spluttering on a mouth-ful of rain as I sit and scramble up, slipping and sliding through the wet grass to the kitchen. It's absolutely pouring, dark as a winter's eve-ning, the rain sluicing in great sheets as I burst through the door.

"Thanks a lot, you b—"

No one's here. It's dark. There's no sound but the hum of the fridge and the steady drip of my wet clothes onto the floor.

"Hello?" I call out, flicking on the lights. Maybe they're all hiding. "Here I come, ready or not."

The rain pounds the windows as I grab a tea towel, rubbing my hair into a static frizz. A trail of damp footprints follows me through the kitchen. I tiptoe towards Ned's half-open door and fling it wide: "Found you!"

It's empty. Just records and Ned's huge stereo system, a collection of cameras, and a dank dirty-laundry smell. The sheets are the same ones Papa put on at the beginning of the summer. I wrinkle my nose: gross.

I close the door and squelch back through the kitchen, then into the sitting room, peeking up the staircase to Papa's bedroom and even check the bathroom. No one's home.

Huh. Maybe they're at the pub or went to the beach before it started raining—maybe I was asleep for ages. But when I wander back to the kitchen, the clock says it's only half past three. Even with the lights on, it's Addams-family spooky. I pinch my arm and tell myself I'm being silly, flick the kettle on to follow the ritual: tea bags, mug, milk.

But when I open the fridge, normality falls apart.

This morning there were trays of Thomas's fudge, a plate of brownies covered in cling wrap, leftovers in bowls and Tupperware, and a door crammed with jars of pickles. Now, there's nothing but a moldy hunk of cheese and a milk bottle that—ugh. It fails the sniff test. Unease blooms like algae. This isn't right.

Still holding the milk, I shut the fridge. There are no photos on the door, no magnets.

I can't shake the idea that I'm not supposed to be here.

Lightning flashes through the gloom, and I run to the window as the thunder follows fast, stare out through the rain. Where *is* everyone?

Another flash makes me reel: the entire sky is television fuzz. The whole world's a wormhole.

I stumble away from the window, colliding with the table. Pain shoots through my hip bone. My breath comes in gulps, my lungs won't fill. This is a nightmare. I spin round, taking in the details I should have noticed before. The blackboard is blank. It's been marked all summer with notes for Thomas to call his mum—and somehow he never does, and it occurs too late that I've never asked him why not, or why his dad never calls. In the sink, there are three dirty cereal bowls, hard corn-flakes barnacled to the sides.

The calendar on the wall has the days marked off in pen as Grey used to do and Ned insists on still doing—it's Friday the eighth. The newspaper on the table concurs. A glance at the gone-off milk says it passed its sell-by date last week.

It is Friday, it is the eighth of August. It is the right *time*.

But I think it's the wrong branch.

My heart collapses like a dying star. I don't want to be here, in this lonely house. Three cereal bowls—Papa, Ned, me. This is a world where Thomas isn't. A timeline of how this summer coulda-woulda-shoulda gone, if he'd never come home.

I drop the milk onto the floor with a sour splash and hurtle towards the door, running out through the garden, under the rain. Ignoring the nothing sky until I'm safe in my room, the door shut, and I'm crying into my pillow, gasping, please, please. I don't want to be here. I want to go home. I want this all to just *stop*. Please.

I'm inside a wormhole, but this is no memory of mine. It's some other timeline, some other place. But what did I do to cause this? Think, Gottie. What did you do? What did you do? *What did you do?*

{4}
WELTSCHMERZ

---

*Inside the Exception, remember: the rules
no longer apply.*

*Don't assume that when you enter a wormhole from one
timeline, that's where you come out. Don't assume all
timelines last forever, or are going in the same direction.*

*The universe is made of hydrogen. The Weltschmerzian
Exception is made of dark matter.*

*And the longer it goes on, the more time gets twisted.
The harder it becomes to untangle.*

But how does it start?

And how do you make it stop?

Saturday 9 August

[Minus three hundred and forty-two]

The page is blank.

It's past midnight. Outside, the storm rages on. I'm still on my bed, but now I'm wrapped in an old jumper of Grey's. Staring at his diary.

The day Jason and I tumbled into the kitchen, the day Grey died—that was early afternoon. He always wrote his diaries in the evening. The page in front of me, the first of September—he hasn't written anything.

The Gottie H. Oppenheimer Principle, v5.0.

The diaries may have been navigating me at first, but they're not anymore. The rules don't apply—I could go anywhere. The funeral. The hospital. The world could show me all the things about myself that I don't want to see.

And I know now where this will all end up if I don't stop it. Ned's party. A wormhole. Grey's death.

For the third time, I write a list of all the wormholes. But now, I admit what truly happened.

Grey's bedroom. The first time I'd been alone with Jason since he dumped me.

Outside the Book Barn. The first time I'd been there since Grey died.

Grey's chair. I'd just crashed my bike and I wanted my grandfather and I hurt.

The library. Seeing my relationship with Jason in Grey's diary. He'd called it love.

The beach. Watching Jason talk to everyone but me. As though I didn't exist.

With Jason. Deciding he'd never loved me.

The canal. Arguing with Sof.

And—

In the garden. I lied to Thomas. I told him I'd never been in love.

I can't believe I didn't see it before. The Weltschmerzian Exception. *Weltschmerz* is a German word for melancholy. It translates to *world pain.*

At their most basic level, wormholes are time machines, powered by dark matter and negative energy. And what's darker than heartbreak? Here's a theory: the twin hurts of Jason and Grey rocked me so much, time broke down. The rules no longer apply.

Every single one of the wormholes has opened when I've been sad, or angry, or grieving, or lost. Or lying.

That's the Gottie H. Oppenheimer Principle. It's nothing to do with particles or fractals or diaries. It's to do with me, and what I did on the day Grey died. I'm a bad person. And this wormhole I'm in now? It's punishment.

I want to rest my head on all these books and go to sleep, wake up to the world as it should be. Tell Thomas everything and see where time takes us. But the only way to get there is to do something about it. I force myself to pick up one of my many notebooks again and start reading it through. Third (hundredth) time's the charm.

The very first thing I see is a diagram I printed out that day in the library, weeks ago.

The Schwarzschild metric. If you stand a billion light-years away from one, a Schwarzschild black hole looks like a wormhole. They're the same thing.

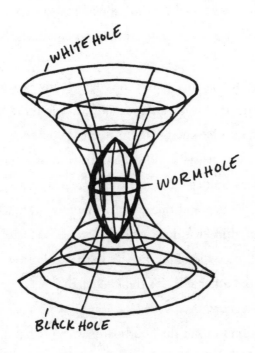

It doesn't flip the TV channel to a new timeline or show you something that's already happened. If you can find a way to keep it open without a gravitational collapse, you could walk through it.

The way to keep it open is to use dark exotic matter—like jamming your shoe in a doorway. If you went through it, you'd have to cross that darkness.

Even so, I find myself "walking" my fingers across the diagram. Through the door.

And however dangerous it would be, I would go in a heartbeat. Because, oh, here I am. Under a rainstorm that shouldn't be. This can't be reality; this can't be how the summer is supposed to be—without Thomas. Fate. The thought of not seeing him again makes me ache with loneliness.

At the exact same time that I start to cry, the rain stops. The pounding on the roof, the howling wind, the noise—it's gone. It's too sudden to be a coincidence. I wipe my running nose with the back of my hand and sit up. Alert.

There's light, creeping round the edges of my bedroom door. Shining through its little wavy-glass window. I switch my lamp off, plunging my room into darkness—there are no Thomas ceiling stars in this reality. But there it is—a glow, coming from the garden. My heart pounds, but my Spidey senses are tingle-free.

I slide off the bed and tiptoe across the room. I'm a little apprehensive of what's behind the door, wormhole-wise, so instead of opening it, I kneel down. But when I put my eye to the keyhole, it's not the garden I can see on the other side. It's the kitchen.

What the *scheisse*?

I look behind me. Pat the floorboards with my hand. Yup, definitely my bedroom. Turn back to the door, look through the keyhole again.

Yup, still the kitchen. The lights are on and there are herbs on the windowsill, magnets on the fridge. And then there's Thomas coming out of the pantry, striding across to the hob and I'm on my feet, yanking open my door, *Gott sei Dank*, calling his name—

"Thomas!"

It's not the kitchen on the other side of the door. Of course it can't be that easy. It's not the garden either. I teeter-totter on my toes, almost falling into it. The doorway is filled with darkness. Not television fuzz. Not the see-through film of a screenwipe. But the dense, inky infinity of a black hole.

Dark matter. Negative energy. Pure heartbreak.

What happens if I step through it? On the other side is the kitchen, is Thomas. But this is darkness. This is grief and graves. By walking through this, I'm asking for trouble, somewhere down the line. I'm volunteering to revisit the day he died.

But where I am, there's no Thomas, no Umlaut. It's worth it. I walk right into the dark.

I emerge, gasping, in the kitchen.

It's nighttime. The air is hot and close, heady with jasmine and lemons, and I'm sweating in Grey's jumper. And I'm here. Somehow, I'm here. Wherever, whenever it is. I'm home. I'm safe. The tide has come in.

Thomas hasn't noticed me yet. Instinct stops me racing over and bear-tackling him to the ground. The pain I just felt, tearing me apart as I stepped through the dark, that can't be leading anywhere good.

I lean in the doorway, catching my breath, and watch him whisk. His muscles tense as he beats air into the saucepan, a small frown of concentration on his face. He's wearing the T-shirt he wore last week, when he baked lemon drizzle cake. When he stood whisking at the hob. When the air smelled of jasmine. When . . . When . . .

The tide retreats.

Holy long division. Last Monday. Thomas stood over a saucepan on a hot, still night. He wore that same T-shirt, and he baked gluten-free lemon drizzle cake for Sof. Thomas never makes the same thing twice. *Ach mein Gott*—I haven't come back to the right timeline. I've come back to last week!

Ms. Adewunmi's warning roars in my ears: *Do I need to worry about Norfolk getting sucked into the fourth dimension?*

This isn't home, this isn't safe—this is the past. I'm going to throw up. I'm going to win the Nobel Prize. Water. I need it. Sitting down, that too. Dizzy and delirious, I stagger away from the doorway, into the room.

"G." Thomas looks up, noticing me at last. When he smiles, it's all for me: an explosion of dimples and his tongue poking between his teeth with delight. And suddenly I don't care if I've destroyed the whole fucking solar system.

But I can't speak yet. I manage to make it to the table and sit down, no thanks to my legs. Thomas nods at my outfit and asks, "Aren't you baking?"

I flush, guiltily, even though there's no way he can know why I'm dressed for a freezing, rainy night. For another night altogether.

"Aren't *you* baking?" I counter, pointing to the saucepan. My tongue is dry.

"Ha. Seriously," he says, turning down the hob and sitting next to me. Knees bumping again. This time, he sandwiches mine between his. "You look cute in that jumper, but it's ninety degrees out."

Flustered by *cute*, I yank off the jumper without unbuttoning it. It gets stuck over my head and takes my T-shirt with it, the static cling sending out sparks from my hair. "Help," I say from inside the jumper, and feel Thomas's hands on my waist, holding my T-shirt down. When I eventually emerge, he's considering me. A smile twitching at the corner of his mouth.

"Stop throwing yourself at me," he says. "It's embarrassing."

"Are you jet-lagged?" I croak. My brain rapid-fires memories of last Monday at me and I grasp for them, trying to make sure we do things the same way. Because if I change the smallest thing . . . This is messing with time on a *Back to the Future* scale. This is Marvin, your cousin Marvin Berry!

"Are you feeling all right?" Thomas asks. He puts his hand to my forehead, pretending to take my temperature. I'm so tired, it's all I can do not to lean into it. Fall and let him catch me. "Nope, normal—yet asking me about jet lag."

"Jet lag, it's, um," I stammer, "when you change time zones and end up all weird."

"I know what it is. It's just a funny thing to ask—I left Canada a month ago. And it's not any later than we're usually up. What are you, seventeen or seventy?" Thomas tilts his head, considering me. "Sure you're okay? There's something strange about you tonight."

I freeze. Why did I step through the doorway? From wearing different clothes to saying things before Thomas should, I've already made a hundred tiny tweaks that could affect the future. I'm an enormous butterfly, flapping stupidly around the kitchen and triggering intergalactic tsunamis, and it's going to end in disaster—

"Aha!" He snaps his fingers. "No homework. I barely recognized you without a giant calculator hanging off your arm."

My shoulders slump in relief.

"Your nose in a book, scribbling things," Thomas continues. "Stand back, sire. I'm away to the library! There's math to be solved!"

He's right. I don't have my constellations chart. I don't have the diaries, or my notebook. How do we end up outside, kissing? How do I get home again? I'm utterly, totally lost.

Thomas mistakes my silence, nudging me gently.

"Sorry," he says. "Look, you are always reading something off-the-charts clever with a scary title, but to be honest . . . I'm jealous of your homework ethic, especially compared to my own." He does the breathless half chuckle of someone who's not entirely joking. Maybe whose dad tells him so.

"You work hard," I tell him. "You *do*. I've seen you at the Book Barn, you're the only one who bothers inputting the receipts. And you literally bake our breakfast every day."

Without warning, Thomas pushes his chair back with a Ned-bothering squeak and darts into the pantry. He emerges, arms laden, and starts flinging ingredients on the table, like that first night. Rosewater, sugar, unsalted butter, and bags of pistachios.

"Forget Sof's cake," he says. "Let's make baklava for breakfast. No project, so . . . You're going to help me, right?"

A do-over. The universe is giving me a second chance. It wants me to be bold. It wants me to say: "Yes."

Baking turns out to be surprisingly easy—or Thomas is a good teacher. A few minutes later, we're standing side by side at the stove, me on idiot duty, melting butter, while he does something exceedingly complicated with the sugar and rosewater. And all the while I'm thinking: *This is how it's supposed to be. This is how it should have been all my life.*

"Store-bought?" I tease as Thomas opens a packet of filo pastry, pretending to sound aghast.

"Shush, you." He elbows me back.

Thomas starts folding layers of pastry into a cake tin, instructing me to brush them with my melted butter. Tutting when I keep brushing his hand instead. "Ztoppit. Now you sprinkle on the pistachios and—or, no, one giant, clumping heap like that is fine too. I think that's what they call 'artisan.' A D in art, was it?"

I steal a pistachio. Thomas bats my hand away.

"Tell you what," he says, "I'll do the cooking, you tell me about time travel."

I nearly choke on the pistachios I've crammed in my mouth. It's not that I'd forgotten what's going on here—absentmindedly discarding the knowledge that I've *time-traveled*, like it's an old sock. But the universe has twisted back on itself, in order to make things right. And for a second, it seems like Thomas has figured it out.

"Your extra-credit project?" He raises his eyebrows at me, and I wonder where Ms. Adewunmi's essay would take me. Far away from Holksea, she said. Far away from Thomas too. "It's about time travel, right? Easy on the math, obviously—are we talking forwards or backwards?"

"A little of both, actually," I say, stealing another pistachio.

"'Splain more."

"Okay . . . If you and I went back to a point in time, like to—"

"Summer eleven years ago, after I was banned from the fair," Thomas interrupts. "What? I'm still *incensed*. Those pigs were asking to be set free."

I laugh. Sixteen racing pigs chased by Grey and Thomas's dad, while Thomas watched gleefully from under the cake table.

"Fine. We write an equation factoring in you, and me, and our coordinates. And we need power, like ten stars' worth, and we use it to open a Krasnikov tube . . ." I glance at Thomas to see if he's following. "Erm, we bake a cannoli. One end is in the present, and we go through it to the other end—to the past."

"G, I got what you meant," he says gently. "I understand the word *tube*."

I blush. "Then we go through the tube, tunnel, cannoli, whatever, and, er, that's it. I mean it's mathematically complex, but what we're talking about is making a tunnel through spacetime."

"Two questions," says Thomas, as he picks up a knife and starts slicing the baklava into little diamond shapes. I keep waiting for the knife to slip, but it doesn't. "What happens when we run into our past selves—a 'Shoot us both, Spock!' situation? And can you get the saucepan? That's not the second question, by the way."

I hand him the saucepan, peeking in. The sugar has melted and it's pink syrup, which Thomas pours over the pastry layers as I explain, "You can't ever meet your past self."

He raises an eyebrow. "You sure about that?"

"*Ja*, because of cosmic censorship."

"Let's assume every time you talk science, I eye-roll till you explain it, okay?"

"Ha, ha. Space law. There are rules. If you ever got close enough to see what was inside a black hole, you'd get sucked in. The universe keeps its secrets in there. When you go back, six-year-old you temporarily doesn't exist—the universe hides you in a little time loop until it's safe to come out. Like a mini cannoli."

"Otherwise—*kaboom*?"

"There can only be one of you." I nod.

"Huh," says Thomas, gazing at me like he's trying to memorize my face. "I wonder."

I resist the urge to prove my science credentials by pointing out: *There aren't two of me here right now, for instance.* Instead, I dip my finger into the syrup and sketch a sticky diagram on the table to demonstrate. "And then vacuum fluctuations, because in algebraic terms—"

"La, la, la, la, la," he sings, off key. "No algebra. More cake metaphors! Who knew you knew so much about patisserie? That's also not the second question. Which is: Then what? How do you get home again?"

"That's the interesting part." I stand back while Thomas transfers the tin of baklava to the oven, setting the timer. "We could stay, live linearly. Wait for time to pass naturally and end up back here anyway, eleven years later. But by doing that, we'd change the universe."

"Don't we want to change the universe? Fight to clear my name?"

"But six-year-old you isn't there to release the pigs, remember? You're in a little cannoli, floating around in space until the universe is sure it's safe."

"So if we stayed . . . our younger selves wouldn't exist?" Thomas asks. He makes a head-exploding gesture with his hands.

"And eventually, teenage us would disappear too, because we're not meant to be there," I confirm. "That, or it'd be your basic end-of-the-world-type situation."

As I explain it, I understand: I can't stay. I'm not supposed to be here. Five days from now, I'm missing. Whatever happens between us tonight—I'll have to go back. Find a new wormhole to the future, and leave this Monday unchanged. Thomas will have no memory of this conversation—it won't ever have happened.

I can't undo my lie. Even if I told Thomas right now, about Jason, it wouldn't make any difference. So what's the point in any of this?

"What, then, if we don't do that?" He tilts his head at me, waiting carefully for the explanation. "If we don't stay?"

It's still hot, but the air smells of roses now. And it takes me a minute to answer him.

"We bake a second cannoli," I say, "and we leave the past as it was, and return to the present, and nothing will have changed at all."

"Holy cannoli," says Thomas. "As it were. Look at that, I understand science. Don't tell my dad; it'll only make him happy."

We go quiet, looking at each other.

"G. Why would you go back at all, then? If in the end, you couldn't change anything?"

"You could learn something," I say. "Find out things about yourself."

"Where would you go?" he asks. "What do you want to learn? And please don't say 'How to paint better,' because I've grown to love you at your *Wurst*."

I take a deep breath, bunching up my hand, sticking my little finger straight out. I point it at Thomas and he curls his into mine.

"I'd go back five years," I say, pulling him towards me. I want to make sure we do this in every reality. "And I'd make a really stable pile of books, and I'd find out what it was like to kiss a boy. And even though it wouldn't change the future—I'd always know what it was like."

One hand clasps Thomas's, drawing him close. With the other, I reach up and do what I've secretly wanted to do all summer: poke his dimple. And when he laughs, I kiss him.

It's electricity. It's light. It's a shot of liquid silver.

When I said I believe in the Big Bang theory of love, I never thought it could be like this. We fit together like Lego. It's overwhelming. Thomas's mouth moves to my neck, and I open my eyes to take in this moment, take in everything—

The kitchen is changing.

A row of spices on the far wall Mexican-waves itself into a new order. Over Thomas's shoulder, the basil on the sideboard splits and blossoms and flourishes into parsley. The clock spins around; suddenly it's sunrise. And the roses outside the window, which have always been peach—my whole life they've been peach—are now yellow in the pale dawn.

This kiss is changing the universe. I have butterflies, the earthquake-in-Brazil kind, as I pull away.

"Wow," says Thomas, fake-staggering. Then he pulls me back towards him, pressing our foreheads together, his hands on my face. His glasses squish against my cheek. "Sorry," he whispers. I don't know what for. He doesn't say anything about the spices, the roses, the basil. He doesn't know anything is different. For him, it's always been this way.

Every instinct tells me that behind me, on the other side of the kitchen door, is my bedroom. A week from now. The universe's safety exit.

He trails a finger down my arm, whispering into my mouth. "We should probably go to bed."

I squeak in surprise.

"Separately, to clarify, you perv," he laughs. "Before Ned storms out here and murders me."

"I should . . ." I turn and gesture to the open kitchen door. I'm right: I can step through it into my bedroom. My ceiling glows with stars, and no storm rattles the window. The books I left scattered on my bed are stacked neatly on my desk, and—oh! Umlaut is there, sleeping on my pillow. I'm going back to a different world than the one I left.

But not necessarily a better one.

On my wall, among the equations, there's a pool of dark matter. Waiting.

There's a week to go to the party. And I walked through the worst aspects of the universe to come back here. I don't believe the Welt-schmerzian Exception will let me get away with that.

And I can't take Thomas with me to hold my hand. If this version of him jumps five days forward, he'll displace his future self—time will still be twisted. He belongs here. I belong in the future. Only I can go through the wormhole.

These are my choices: Path A. I take this chance to tell Thomas about Jason. I stay in the kitchen, with the truth. And the universe would gradually implode.

Or Path B. I go through the doorway. The universe stays safe but my lie still stands.

Either way, it's the end of the world.

Quickly, before I can change my mind, I turn around and kiss him. Hard and fast on the mouth, sucking on his bottom lip, clinging on for desperate seconds before I have to let go, before I have to—

I pull away and step backwards, away from him, and then I'm standing in my room. My lungs burst with just those few steps.

Across the doorway, the garden glimmers in the dawn.

"Goodnight," I say, even though no one is there.

Sunday 10 August

[Minus three hundred and forty-three]

A shaft of sunshine wakes me. My clock says it's Sunday. My head aches. I swim slowly up through sleep, staring into the window-ivy, which is laced with dark matter, thinking about that universe-changing kiss. It was on my lips a few hours ago, but to Thomas, it never happened.

The past is permanent.

I roll over, struggling with philosophy and the weighed-down duvet.

Thomas is on the bed next to me. Whoa! I go from sleepy to wide awake at warp speed.

He's still asleep, his breathing warm and heavy and metronome-even, and I watch him, watch the mouth that I've kissed. Multiple times now. Thomas Althorpe. Who said he liked me. Who I changed the universe with. Who's in bed with me. Kind of.

He may have spent the night, but he's fully dressed on top of the duvet. Even so, I'm alarmed: I stepped through negative energy to come back here. What world have I fast-forwarded us into?

I run my tongue round my mouth and huff a little air at Umlaut to check for morning breath. The kitten is a good sign. How can a universe where he's back be bad? Then I put my hand on Thomas's arm and shake him.

"Thomas," I hiss. "Thomas, wake up."

He blinks awake, his face half-mushed into my pillow. Seeing him without his glasses it's like sharing a secret.

"Hey." Sleepily, he wriggles, closing his eyes again. A heavy arm is draped over me and I'm a bear tucked up for autumn.

"Hi," I whisper, snuggling myself into his warmth. It's fine. There's an entire duvet between us. "Do you, um, do you remember what happened?"

"Mmm, must've fallen asleep," Thomas mumbles into the pillow.

"Yes. But. *When*."

"Was up early." He yawns. "Choux pastry practice. Saw your light on and thought"—rawr, another yawn—"I'd say hello. But you were asleep and then Ned came home and passed out on the grass right outside the kitchen door. Didn't want to risk climbing over him. Bed looked comfortable."

"It's okay," I squeak, trying to talk out of the corner of my mouth so I don't breathe on him. Jason and I never spent the night, or even fell asleep together. I've never woken up with anyone before, what if I'm a wildebeest? I shouldn't speak. But I want to find out what happened between hanging out in the garden on Friday, and him falling asleep in my room just now. I've hopped about in spacetime, skipped an entire day.

"Did I see you at the Book Barn yesterday? My mind's gone blank."

"Mmmm," Thomas says noncommittally, and shivers.

"Are you cold? Get in," I say, without thinking.

"I smell like a monkey cage." But he's already rolling off the bed and clambering under the duvet with me.

Uh-oh.

Serious uh-oh, because Thomas on my bed is one thing. It's safe. It's friends. We've been here a million times before. But underneath the duvet is arms and legs, skin on skin, warm sleepiness. I'm only wearing a T-shirt and underwear.

Atomic particles, on high alert.

"Hi," he whispers into my mouth, his lips brushing against mine with each word. "I think we've got about fifteen minutes before Ned goes on the rampage."

There's no morning breath, just warmth and cinnamon cake, his mouth against mine.

And then it's his hands underneath my T-shirt, cold on my warm back. Then it's my legs tangled with his. Then it's our bodies pressed together. Our mouths, pressed together.

My heart hammers, and I break away. Back and forth, up and down, happy and sad. I can't keep track of where we are, how far I want to go. Last night was crazy intense, and now we're here, a week later from a kiss that doesn't exist—kissing like we've done a lot more than that. I want to live my life in the right order.

"Hi," Thomas says again, pushing towards my mouth.

"Hello," I respond formally, tucking my chin down like Umlaut, which makes him laugh.

"Okay. Back to sleep for you," he says, lifting his arm and letting me burrow into him. I curl up, staring at the ceiling stars. The pattern is different.

When I stepped through the doorway, I changed something.

Above me, the stars start moving, spiraling open. Television fuzz. I'm not upset right now. I'm not lost, or sad, or lying. There's no diary nearby. A glance at Thomas tells me he's asleep. I clamber out from underneath the duvet, and Superman my hand to the stars. It's going to hurt. But beam me up anyway, Scotty.

My body bursts apart, scattering particles across the sky.

"You made a fort?" Jason looks from the hay bales to me, and back again. He shakes his head, smiling. "I forget you're younger than me."

It was a solid-gold idea this morning. I regretted it a little when it took me an hour to move one bale, sweating in the sun. But when I came back with a blanket to go inside and an umbrella propped up at the top for shade, it was brilliant again. A little three-sided hideaway. But Jason's looking at me like I'm nuts.

"Not just any fort, party pooper." I grab his hand and drag him inside, sort of half push him to sit before plonking myself next to him. It's August and the wheat's been harvested—the cut-off stalks prickle up through the blanket like leg hair underneath tights. "Look."

"All right." Smirking, Jason aims his sunglasses in the direction I'm pointing. Golden fields, stretching out forever and fading into blue sky. Nothing in sight but birds. "What am I looking at?"

"The universe," I point. "The whole, wide world. Isn't this great?"

"Margot," he says. "Holksea's hardly the whole world. Wait till I get to college . . ."

I tune him out and turn away to rummage for all the stuff I brought: books, apples and packs of biscuits, bottles of fancy fizzy water in a little picnic cooler. I haven't quite figured out what we're going to do when we need to have a wee, but otherwise we could hang out here all day.

He's leaving in three weeks. We haven't talked about what will happen after that. But I think, nothing, very much. A fizzle and a fade and a forgetting. I almost don't mind. We've had a whole summer. And he's still talking, but I'm not listening.

"I got ice cream," I interrupt. "You have to eat it now, before it melts."

I hold out a Creamsicle and an ice-cream sandwich, and, annoyingly, he reaches for the Creamsicle, my favorite—then takes my wrist instead, and pulls me into his lap.

"I've got to be at work pretty soon," he says. I've still got both ice creams in my hand as Jason slowly lies down. I shriek, but his hands are on my waist, holding me steady. I end up in this weird position with my elbows beyond his shoulders, fists clenched round the ice creams, face in his neck, laughing.

"Margot," Jason says into my neck, "put the ice cream down, yeah?"

"Oh." I drop them. We only have a few more weeks, so I remember what else you can do in a fort with your secret boyfriend, on the last day of summer.

My skin feels flayed raw—traveling through time, it's not like before. It's starting to hurt. But I'm back in bed, face-to-face with Thomas. He has his glasses on now, and Umlaut is snuggled between us, making little kitteny snores.

My heart is still half in the field fort. How had I forgotten what I'd known back then, that Jason and I weren't going to be forever? How had I forgotten that I hadn't minded? It's like Grey's death was a tornado, wiping out everything that came before it. Leaving me clueless.

"Shall we do it on Wednesday?" Thomas asks me. For a moment, I think he's asking me about *it*, sex. Put a condom on a banana and never eat fruit again. And I blush from my head to my cherry-red toenails.

Across the pillow, Thomas matches me blood cell for blood cell.

"G." He smiles, reading my mind. "I wasn't asking you to do *it*. Although . . ."

He bats his lashes, slowly. Reaches out, pushes my hair back from my face. Between us, Umlaut purrs in his sleep. I lean over the kitten and poke Thomas in the chest.

"Shuddup." I grin back, leaving my hand where it is. No dark matter in sight. I didn't need a do-over after all. My lie doesn't even matter— aren't I right back where I should be? "Don't make me paint *The Wurst No. Zwei*."

"How do you make German sound so cute? It's so terrifying when Ned does it." Thomas stuffs his face into the pillow for a second, then pops up again. "Never mind—so, Wednesday night is go? You, me, the finest fish and chips Holksea beach has to offer."

I think he asked me out. I think I missed me saying yes.

I wish I was here for the big moments in my life.

Thomas clambers out of bed, stretching down and putting his shoes on. When he straightens up, he's looking over at my corkboard. "Aw, you kept my email! Cool. And you've . . . done math all over it. Okay, rawr."

He bounces to the door, back again to kiss me, and out into the garden before I can react.

"Hello, Ned," I hear from outside. My brother's voice growls in reply, but I can't make out the words. "It's not what . . ."

I wait for their voices to fade before climbing out of bed and fetching the email. It's transformed again, but as meaningless to me as ever—though it obviously made sense to Thomas. And he's right: I *have* done math all over it. At least, it's my handwriting. But I don't recognize the equation.

Wednesday 13 August

[Minus three hundred and forty-six]

The evening we go to the beach, a daytime full moon looms giant on the horizon. The world's biggest optical illusion. Huge and heavy, it follows Thomas and me as we cycle along the marsh path, past the hedge—my crash a hundred years ago now. The hole in the leaves is filled with dark matter, waiting for me, reminding me.

The car park is half empty when we get there, small kids carrying buckets and shovels, trailing their parents as they head home through the dusk. We chain our bikes to a railing and run to the food hut just before its shutters close.

"Fries, please," says Thomas, just as I say, "Chips."

They grumble, it's the end of the day, they've turned the fryer off; but Thomas charms them and soon we're on a blanket in a hollow in the dunes, warm vinegar steam rising up between us into the dusk. His satchel spills open when we sit down. He has my copy of *Forever*, two postcards keeping each of our places in the pages.

"Thomas!" I blurt.

He turns to me, holding down his hair against the wind, a smile as wide as the sky. I wish I could tell him: *I don't want to time-travel anymore. I want to stay here, and discover the universe with you.* But I can't make the words come out of my mouth.

"You okay?" he asks.

I nod and rescue a chip from his ketchup overkill. All day, our *us* has stalled—replaced by stutters, long pauses, and then both of us speaking at the same time. No, you go, no, you say. I know what's wrong with me: I'm waiting for a wormhole to drag me away. I'm not sure what Thomas's problem is; he's been antsy since leaving my room on Sunday. We eat in silence till a gust of wind sends hot vinegar straight up my nose, and I start spluttering. I catch Thomas's eye.

"All right, clever clogs," he says, standing up. "Wait here."

He scrunches the empty Styrofoam container, dripping vinegar all over the blanket, then runs off with it through the dunes.

"Where are you going?" I call after him, leaning over to see him jog down to the path that leads to the beach.

"It's a surprise," I hear. Just before he rounds the corner and disappears out of sight, he slam-dunks the carton into the bin, with a little heel-click in the air and a "Yesssssss!"

While I sit and wait, I watch the sea. Or rather, its absence—over the top of our hollow, there's nothing but flat, wet sands, stretching into the distance. Somewhere, invisible beyond it, is the North Sea. When I was little, the tide going this far out made me sad. I'd want to run for miles, right into the horizon, until I was invisible too. If I ran and ran and ran into the emptiness now, would I leave all this behind? Grey. Wormholes. Myself.

Then Thomas pops into sight, walking backwards across the flats and waving his arms in the air. It makes me want to stay right where I am. When he sees I've noticed him, he puts his hands to his mouth and shouts something.

"What? I can't hear you," I yell.

He shrugs dramatically, then he's off, jogging farther on, not stopping till he's about fifty yards away. I sit with knees up to my chin, arms around my legs, watching as he drags his foot through the wet sand. After a few seconds, I work out what he's writing. I grin and grab our bags and blanket, running down the dune to join him. By the time I reach him, breathless, he's written the best equation I've ever seen:

$$X2$$

It's what Grey said about us when we were little. "Uh-oh," when I walked into a room. Then, if Thomas was following me, "Uh-oh, trouble times two." After a while we said it ourselves, a little chant when we were up to no good. Water is already pooling inside the letters. Thomas still has one foot in the tail of the 2—his jeans are soaked up the knees, his hair is crazy-curly from the salt and humidity, his glasses sea-flecked.

I stumble through the wet sand to him, but he shrinks back—barely perceptibly—shoving his hands in his pockets so his shoulders hunch.

"Very mature," I settle for saying, pointing at the letters. "Thank you."

"You're so welcome," he says with exaggerated formality.

"There's seaweed on your foot," I tell him.

He flicks his trainer and the samphire jumps into the air—he catches it, then stares at his hand, amazed. "Let's pretend I'm truly that dexterous on purpose," he says, and reaches over to tie it to my bag strap. "There. Now you're a mermaid."

There's a pause. I'm missing something.

"What do you—" I start, and at the same time Thomas says, "Listen. Hey, we keep doing that, don't we?"

"You go."

"Before I say this . . ." he begins. Then circles his foot in the air, gesturing to the *X2*. "We've always been friends, right? And I promise this time, we always will be. I won't let that go. I don't go silent on you, you don't go silent on me. Deal?"

"Um, okay." I prod the sand with my trainer, squelching it underfoot. Obviously, I've misunderstood something about Thomas and me, about tonight.

"Ned made me say that bit. It's true. But I can't believe he did the whole 'protective big brother' thing." Thomas does his air quotes extra jazzily to make me laugh, but I don't. For all the hot chips I've eaten, there's still an ice block in my stomach.

"What do you mean? What about Ned?" My voice sounds small and thin.

"He found out . . . Look . . . There's something I didn't mention, about this summer. Ned found out a few days ago, and when he caught me coming out of your room the other morning, he said I had to tell you, before anything happened."

"What?"

"I'm not staying in Holksea. When my mom moves back to England, we're not going to be next door."

"Where are you going to be? Brancaster?" It's a stupid question.

Thomas wouldn't be acting this squirrelly if he was moving ten minutes up the road.

"Manchester." He shoves his hands in his pockets and looks at me. Between us, the *X2* is melting back into wet sand. Soon, the marks will disappear, as though they were never there at all. "You know, it's not so far. We could get the train."

"It's five hours," I guess. Manchester's the other side of the country, and Holksea's not exactly well connected. It takes a bike ride and a bus and a train just to get to London.

"Four and a half," he says. "Three changes. I checked."

"You were checking train times, but you weren't going to tell me?" I don't understand. "Is that why your mum keeps calling? To let you know the plan had changed?"

"Shit." Thomas hunches his shoulders, blows air up through his curls. "Shit. Look, that was never my plan, okay? Mom got a job at the university in Manchester, it was all arranged for her to get there in September. Then I got your email and thought maybe I could come here first. This—" He gestures round to encompass everything, the moon, the sea, the sand. Me and my airless lungs. "This was only ever the summer."

"You lied to me?" I take the little voice in my head that's reminding me I've lied to him, and I squish it down. That was a misunderstanding, a one-off. It's not the same thing. "All those times I said about starting school, or you being back next door? You didn't think to mention it?"

"Also not my plan." He shuffles in the sand. "Look, I'm not proud of myself, okay? But things were so awkward between us when I arrived, and I knew if I told you I wasn't here for long, you'd never talk to me. We wouldn't have the chance to become friends again."

He thinks this is friendship? This is five years ago, all over again.

"When?" I ask.

"When what?"

"When everything. When were you going to tell me? When do you go to Manchester?"

"Three weeks."

Stars swim in front of my eyes. All this time, all this time I've spent trying to understand the past, and it goes and repeats itself. Thomas is *leaving*. And he never even said.

I want to scream the clouds away, punch the moon back out into the sky. I can't *do* this. Time is moving too fast. I turned around and it was winter, closed my eyes and it was spring. Summer hot on its heels and it's already half over, and Thomas is leaving, *again*, everybody leaves, Mum, Grey, Ned, Jason, Thomas. Grey, Grey, Grey. I'm on my knees and I can't breathe, I need a wormhole, *now*—

"Gottie." Thomas's voice is soft. "G. I honestly thought, for the first couple of weeks, that you knew."

I stay on my knees and shake my head miserably: no.

"I guess I thought your dad would've explained. My mom called him, when I was on the plane. I'd left her a note. She told him the plan. He's talked to me about it." He sounds confused, frustrated. I don't turn around. "Then I figured out you had no idea, and I just . . . I didn't know what to do. It took weeks to get you to be my friend again. You were so sad about Grey . . . I don't get why he didn't tell you."

"So it's my fault for supposedly sending you an email," I say, hunching up my shoulders, staring at the water pooling by my feet. "And Papa's fault for expecting you to tell me yourself. Who else should we blame? Ned? Sof? *Umlaut*?"

"I think you needed me to be here this summer," he says. "And I am. Doesn't that count for anything?"

"Nope." It comes out in two sulky syllables, my throat tight. I know I'm not being fair, and I don't care. If I say another word, I'll cry. Next to me, I can see Thomas's feet shuffle forward. He stoops and grabs a stone, skimming it across a tidal pool.

"We can visit each other. Take trains. I'll buy a car. Get another bakery job and meet you halfway across the country with home-baked iced buns." His voice is cajoling, and I'm not in the mood to be cajoled. Just for once, I want things to go my way. I stand up, and I kick my way through his stupid equation, stomping all over the X.

"I hate iced buns . . ." I turn to tell him, viciously, and the words disappear in my mouth when I see what I've done.

The sand I sent flying through the air is hanging there. It won't ever fall. The white foam waves hover over the dark sea, forever cresting and not crashing down. Everything is still. Everything is silent. And Thomas is frozen, midplea.

The geometry of spacetime is a manifestation of gravity. And the geometry of heartbreak is a manifestation of a stopped clock. Time stands still.

I speed-cycle the three miles home through the gathering dusk, and it never gets dark. The world is as broken as my smashed watch. The sun isn't setting. It stays right where I left it at the beach, hovering just under the horizon, as the moon fails to climb the sky. It's beautiful and awesome, in the old-fashioned sense. Daunting.

Pedaling fast, I take the shortcut through the field and straight through the nettle patch, not caring. I need my books, I need to figure out what's going on—mathematically speaking. It may not make a difference. But for all that the universe is in charge, I want to at least try to take control.

I ditch my bike in the driveway, out of breath, and jog-walk-wheeze into the garden. And stop dead. Ned and his bandmates are—were?—having a bonfire. A prelude to the party, which I realize with a jolt is this Saturday. Where did the summer go? In nineteen days, my grand-father will be dead forever. No more diaries. And I've spent this whole time chasing myself down wormholes, without ever thinking I could be finding my way back to Grey.

The flames are frozen, sparks painted on the air. Ned stands near the Buddha, mid-beer-chug, while Sof is a tableau of worry-tinged admiration as she watches him. It's a momentary glimpse of her private face.

I'm an interloper. I tiptoe past, trying not to look, Edmund creep-ing through the White Witch's lair. Then I think, *screw it*, and dou-ble back to tie Jason's shoelaces together. His lucky lighter's in his hand and I pocket it, planning to drop it down a drain later or some-thing.

The trees are as still and silent as gravestones. It's spectacular and eerie—I'm already writing equations in my head to describe it all, the frozen antigravity. This is what I've wanted all year, isn't it? To stop the inexorable forward motion.

As I pass under the apple tree, I see Umlaut. He's midprowl along a branch, towards a moth he'll never catch. I fetch Thomas's email from my room, along with my A-level physics textbook, then I climb the tree and grab Umlaut onto my lap. If I can restart the clock, I don't want him falling off the branch in surprise. He's warm, which is reassuring, and taxidermy-stiff, which isn't.

"Okay, Umlaut," I say. I don't think he can hear me, but talking helps me swallow the incipient panic. This is Halloween levels of creepy. "How do we fix this?"

The Friedmann equations describe the Big Bang. Maybe time could be jump-started like our crappy old car in winter. I know what Grey would do: read them aloud as if from a spell book, the origins of the universe. Perhaps he's right. Perhaps I should enact them, create a Little Bang—heat from Jason's lighter and a vacuum inside the time capsule. Tweak the math and make it smaller. It's a start.

I get comfortable, flipping the time capsule shut so I can stretch my legs out.

The lid is blank.

When Thomas and I climbed up here to open it, the day of the frog, our names were on the lid. He's disappearing. *Himmeldonnerwetter!* Time hasn't just stopped. The branches are unraveling. We're reverting to a world where Thomas isn't here. For all that he's lied, I don't want that.

I want the forward motion.

I want to see summer dwindle into autumn. For school to start, university applications, mock exams, and A-level results. I want to kiss Thomas again, and kill him for not telling me he was leaving. Tell him about Jason, everything, and all about the day Grey died—a truth I don't even admit myself. I want to see what happens with him and me, even after he leaves. Even if it all goes wrong.

Because I want the chance to cry when it hurts.

Faced with a choice between this—stopping time, making my world so small I can wrap my life up in a blanket—and smashing my heart to pieces, well. Pass me the hammer.

I scrawl the first equation underneath the lid of the tin, then crumple up some pages from my physics textbook, put them inside, flick Jason's lighter—thankfully, it wasn't lit when time stopped, and it catches flame—and drop it in. Then I shut the tin and write *THOMAS & GOTTIE* on top.

I cross my fingers. The inside of the time capsule was black and sooty when we opened it, clean just now. I'm lighting the fire we found a few weeks ago. Actions have consequences—it just so happens that I do mine the wrong way round.

I'm right. Gradually, the world begins to turn. Slow and creaking at first, like a carousel at a funfair, the first ride of the day. A *meow* as Umlaut starts clawing through my jeans. Wind begins to rustle through the tree. Nettle stings finally blossom on my ankles.

Faster now, the moth flutters through the branches, there's a whoop from the garden. Faster and faster, the crackle of the fire, the world going dark as the sun dips away.

I stay in the tree, and curl myself up like a caterpillar.

I'm not sure how much time passes, how long I wait until I hear Thomas calling my name. I know that I'm cold and that there's a pool of dark matter in the hollow of the tree. And I'm afraid of what's happening. How things that started off as beautiful, cosmic occurrences—stuttering stars and pi, floating in the air—have turned ugly and intense. The world is spiraling out of control.

And I don't think time restarting has anything to do with what I've done, mathematically.

"I'm up here," I yell.

A few seconds later, his face pokes through the leaves. It's a question. Our eyes meet, and I nod.

"I'm really pissed off at you," I tell him.

"Fair enough."

"But I've got nettle stings. And I'm cold. So I'm coming out of the tree."

"Okay."

After I climb down, I let Thomas take my hand.

"I don't forgive you, or anything," I say.

As we walk through the garden, Ned and Sof have their heads together, hair mingling as they whisper. She looks up as we go by. "You okay?" she mouths. I nod.

Thomas holds my hand as he leads me inside, into the kitchen. He holds my hand as we detour into the pantry, as he rummages one-handed past the Marmite tower to grab something I can't see. He holds my hand all the way to the bathroom, and then he holds my hand as I sit on the edge of the bath, and he cranks on the taps. He did promise me friends. He did promise me he wouldn't let go.

The water is Niagara Falls loud, and we don't speak as he lets go to undo the jar he grabbed from the kitchen, dumping the entire thing in the water. Bicarbonate of soda.

I look a question at him.

"Grey," Thomas shouts over the water. "He taught my mom to do this when I had chicken pox. I guess it'll work for nettles."

Mutely, I nod, staring at the water as it turns milky white, filling up to the brim. I'm shivering as I stand up and yank off my jeans, and Thomas turns away. I climb into the bath in my T-shirt. The warmth and the relief of the water on the stings is so good I actually growl.

Thomas laughs, sitting down on the floor, his back against the bath.

"You sound like Umlaut."

"It's good." Two-word sentences are all I can manage.

The water's hot and deep, up to my neck, and opaque. When was the last time I had a bath? The day after Thomas arrived, when I crashed my bike, and all I wanted was for him to go away. Now I'm back in the tub, and he's leaving. Ironic.

Also ironic: there's a wormhole in the bath. Life moves forwards and I go backwards. What is it I'm missing? What more does the world want from me? It's already so fucked up.

"Aren't I a total gentleman?" asks Thomas, not turning round.

"You are." I splosh the water with my hands. I could fall asleep in here. "I feel like I'm in a science experiment."

"Dropping you into a bathful of fizzing chemical compounds?" There's a smirk in his voice. "Are you . . . in your element?"

Thomas jazz-hands over his head at me. I want to clamber out of the bath, and kiss him. I want to clamber out of the bath, and clobber him. How can he be going away again? How could he lie to me?

I laugh, at his stupid joke, at his stupid hands. It mutates into a sob.

"G, please don't—" Thomas breaks off. "Can I turn around?"

I nod, my face buried in my hands, my hands buried in my knees. I don't care.

"I'm taking that as a yes," he says, and then his arms are around me as I go into full meltdown, crying into his shoulder. "I'm sorry. For a while, I really did think you knew. Then when I realized you had no idea . . . I didn't know what to do. I don't want you to hate me."

"I don't want you to go," I say, my face hot. I'm falling apart in Thomas's arms.

There's a wormhole reaching for me, and I'm bruises and hurt as I hold on to him. I don't want to disappear. I don't want to do this any-more, but I don't know how to stop it. I'm here. I want to exist.

I'm ready to live in the world again, but the world won't let me.

He's warm and safe and cinnamon as he promises me, "I have to go. But you remember my promise, right? I'll always—"

Before I hear the rest, I spin away down the drain.

Thursday 5 September (Last Year)

[Minus four]

I'm sweating hot. Autumn, and the air is glossy with sunshine. It's the wrong day to be wearing a black wool dress. Any day is the wrong day for what we're doing.

We've been standing, singing hymns I don't know, for ten minutes. I'm not used to wearing heels; Sof got the bus to town and bought me these. They've rubbed all the skin off the back of my feet—I can feel my tights sticking to the blood. I sway in the heat, shifting my weight from one foot to another. I want to sit down, *I think. Then immediately try to unthink it.*

Ned grips my elbow as I sway, and I look up at him. His hair is tied back in a neat bun.

"You okay?" he mouths. I nod as the hymn finishes and we sit down *with a murmur, a clatter of pews, a rustle of paper. There's a pause while the pastor climbs back up to the lectern. I glance over my shoulder, searching*

for Jason. He's looking at Ned, not me. Sof catches my eye. I turn back to the front.

"Grots," Ned hisses at me, nodding at the coffin. "It kind of looks like a picnic basket."

A giggle forms in the back of my throat. I chose it—one of those woven, willow branch ones. Grey would have been pushed out to sea and shot at with burning arrows if he could. Instead, after this, there's—

Don't think about it, don't think about it, don't.

We stand up again.

Papa gets the words of the next hymn wrong, confidently launching into a second chorus. Ned snorts.

It's been like this all day, lurching from ordinary to horror, a binary rhythm.

Washing my hair with mint-flavor shampoo, eating a piece of toast. Putting Marmite on the table before I remembered. Pulling on black tights even though it's twenty-nine degrees outside and Grey would want us all barefoot anyway. I took them on and off a thousand times and I was still ready too early. Ned's arm around me on the sofa, flicking through the channels. Waiting for the motorcade to arrive, even though the church is a five-minute walk from our house.

Traveling in a hearse. Feeling hungry. Trying to remember what food I asked the pub to prepare for afterwards. Papa red-eyed. Ned asking me to tie his tie.

The word eulogy.

Listening to the pastor talk about James Montella. Thinking, who's that? Why aren't you calling him Grey? Everybody laughing at a story the pastor tells about him trying to jump across the canal to prove something, and his daughter asking him to at least hand over the keys to the Book Barn first. I

try to remember, then understand he's talking about something that happened before I was born. He's talking about Mum.

We're standing up again, another hymn. I wince, my feet aching.

"Take them off." It's Ned, his hand steady on my shoulder. "It's okay,
Grotbags. Take them off."

It's what Grey would do. But I can't, I don't deserve to be comfortable,
and I sway in the heat and I'm falling—

Saturday 16 August

[Minus three hundred and forty-nine
and Minus three]

"No, like—forsythia, or heather. That color yellow."

The florist shows me more lilies, creamy ones, and I want to shout at her because she's not getting it. She won't give me yellow tulips and it has to be right; it has to be yellow tulips at the funeral! I'm practically scream-ing it, and she's looking at me blankly, saying, "It's September . . ."—

[Minus two]

I yank the dress over my head. It gets caught around my bra. I'm sweating already, huffing and puffing as I tug on the zip. Sof's outside the changing room curtain and she needs to shut UP, everything comes up too short around my thighs and stretches tight round my armpits, I'm too tall. I'd never choose this dress anyway, this color. It's black, but then, it's supposed to be—

[Minus one]

The phone in the kitchen rings and none of us move to answer it, just carry on staring at nothing like we have been all evening. After a second, the machine cuts in. "This is James, Jeurgen, Edzard, and Margot," Grey's voice booms out and then he starts chuckling at our ridiculous names and he's laughing fit to burst, it fills the room, like his death is just a big cosmic joke the universe is playing on us. Ha, ha, ha—

It's obvious what's coming next. Since the funeral, I've been lurching in and out of time, closer and closer to Grey's death. Four wormholes in three days, their intensity and frequency leaving me dizzy. I only know it's Saturday, the day of the party, because this morning Ned was staggering round the kitchen, haphazardly assembling a bacon sandwich and asking me if I wanted to borrow his eyeliner for tonight.

I have time-travel jet lag and a sick, sour headache. There's a stale taste in my mouth as I sit in the Book Barn, a pool of darkness waiting in the shadows. Papa is harrumphing. He's prowling around the shelves near the desk, while I painstakingly type. The computer is so slow, it clicks and whirs between each keystroke.

In between each click and each whir, there's a harrumph.

It's setting my teeth on edge. Especially as I'm not actually inputting the receipts, like I'm supposed to be—all those clicks and whirs are another email to Ms. Adewunmi. She hasn't replied to the first one I sent. What is it with me and emails?

I want my fingers to fly across the keyboard, minding their own business, spilling out everything that's happened, from split screens to apple trees, how the Weltschmerzian Exception is out of control. I know exactly what the next wormhole will be, and when it's coming out of the shadows—it will be at the party tonight.

Isn't that what this whole summer has been about? Inevitability.

I need to know how to stop it. I've got five hours. And, essay or not, I need to do this without clicks, and whirs, and winces.

Click.

Whir.

Ow.

"Harrumph. Harrumph. Gottie."

I look up to see Papa itching from one foot to another in front of the desk. Automatically, I cover my notebook with my hand.

"Nearly done. I'm just waiting for the computer to catch up," I lie, nodding at the list on the other side of the keyboard.

"Ah, so." He nods. Then pulls out the other chair and sits down opposite me, tweaking his trousers upwards. He's wearing red Converse again, and his serious face—the one he had when he announced Thomas's arrival. The one he had when he came out into the corridor at the hospital last September, and told us we could go home.

"Margot," Papa begins, formally. Then he clears his throat and picks up Umlaut, fussing him on his knee. He's brought the kitten to work? "Gottie. *Liebling.*"

I wait, fiddling obsessively with my pen and trying to arrange my face into the nonguilty expression of a teenager who isn't half destroying the fabric of reality.

"Ned saw Thomas coming out of your room last Sunday. Morning."

Oh. Unbelievable. *And* Papa's waited nearly a week to talk to me! Grey would have marched in there and dragged us both out by our ears.

"Do I need to have a talk with you"—a series of harrumphs—"*du Spinner*, I *do* need to have a talk, about you and Thomas."

I'm relieved as I realize Papa's talk is *that* talk, the sex talk. Then shudder as I realize, ugh, it's *that* talk. I can't listen to this. I want to lie down in a dark room for several hours and vomit repeatedly. That sounds restful.

"It's—fine—we're not—" I babble, grinning brightly.

We're really not—I don't think. The wormholes have me lurching in and out of time, so I don't know exactly what's happened since the beach, the tree, the bath. He's leaving, and he lied.

LIGHT BLUE TOUCH PAPER AND LEAVE, Grey wrote about me in his diaries. My temper isn't as quick as his was—a fireworks show that faded after the first *ooh*. I stick to mine, stubborn and unforgiving. Resenting Sof for not understanding me anymore, resenting Ned for being happy, resenting my mother for dying. I don't want to resent Thomas for leaving. But I don't know what we are to each other either.

"We're not . . ." I repeat to Papa. "And if we are, it's new, brand-new in fact. And I know all the stuff. So, um."

"Ah." Papa nods. I'm hoping he'll harrumph his way *anywhere else* so I can die of mortification, but he just sits there. I'm bracing myself for a rare telling off—the sort where he puffs up and starts hissing, like an angry goose—when he adds, "It's good to make sure, because we—me, your mami—we didn't know. *Empfängnisverhütung.*"

I nod warily. *Obviously* they didn't know. Ned is empirical evidence of the not-knowing.

"And," continues Papa, beaming, "we're running out of bedrooms to put babies in!"

[211]

I make a harrumph noise of my own. "Papa, was that a joke? Because we're still wrapping our heads round the duck one."

"One of its legs is the same," Papa chuckles, wiping his eyes at his favorite punch line. I roll mine (it hurts). Seventeen years of "What's the difference between a duck?" and I still don't get it, but it always has Papa—and Grey—rolling on the floor in stitches.

I make a little shooing motion with my pen, hoping he'll go away so I can commune with my headache, but he just carries on giggling. I haven't seen Papa laugh in months. It's nice.

"We didn't know with Ned, I mean. We knew the second time, obviously—when you were to arrive," Papa carries on, oblivious to my grimacing. Maybe this is his plan: gross me out with *conception* talk so I'll spend my time with Thomas crossing my legs. "But still."

"Papa, I know," I say, to hurry him along. I've already gone off the thought of the banana cake in my bag.

"Maybe you don't," he says contrarily. "I saw in your room, you'd put the picture of you and your mami. This is where the hair is from?"

I prod my hair self-consciously and one-shoulder-shrug, neither *ja* nor *nein*.

Papa looks down at Umlaut in his lap as he sucks air in round his teeth. "You know, you always were such a surprise."

"A surprise?"

"Mmmm. I was deferred, you know? And Mami too, with her Saint Martins place. We were thinking to go back to London with Ned, then"—he makes a funny little whoosh noise, an explosion with his hands, sending Umlaut's fur on end—"things changed. There was going to be a Gottie. So even though we *knew*," he harrumphs, "knowing isn't always enough. Which is why, maybe better that Thomas sleeps in his own room."

I'm going from *a* surprise to *being* surprised. My whole life, every-one's behaved as though this is the way it always was—that after Ned arrived and life veered off course, Papa and Mum decided: why not have a teenage wedding and another baby? Work for Grey at the Book Barn. Stay in Holksea. Forever. The only accidental thing was her death.

No one ever told me this wasn't the plan. No one ever told me they had wanted more.

They never told me I'm what stopped them.

"What is it called—a carthorse?" Papa asks.

"Huh?"

"Your mami, she throws the stick over her shoulder and carthorsed, when she found out about you." He nods to himself, remembering. I'm not the only one lost in the past. But Papa doesn't need wormholes.

"Cartwheel," I correct, thinking of a theory Thomas told me the other day, about why Papa's English is still so loopy. He says Papa delib-erately tries to sound foreign, so he can hold on to something of home. Now that I know that they were planning to leave this life, I think it's for a different reason. It's so he doesn't have to admit that this is all real.

That he's truly here, two blue lines and seventeen years later. I know Oma and Opa ask him to move back to Germany. Live with them, even. There was that fight about it, at Christmas, raised voices and closed doors. Maybe he will, now. I'll be eighteen in six weeks—this time next year, I'll be packing up to go to university. And Papa will be free.

As if he's reading my mind, Papa says, "*Nein*. Not in ten million years. I never regret it, ever."

He's looking at me so fondly, so seriously, it's embarrassing. And I wish he hadn't told me this. Mum's dead and Grey's dead; Papa's trapped here and it's my fault. I was never meant to be part of this family at all. It's so obvious I don't belong.

Surely, somewhere, there's a timeline where I don't even exist.

I'm a wormhole away from losing it completely. I close my ears with a lurch of nausea: the pounding in my head is overwhelming.

"Have fun tonight," Papa says. "I'm going to hide here. I don't know what happened with you this year, *Liebling*, but now—it's very happy. To see you in love. It's *gut*. How can this not be a wonderful thing?"

After all that: it's not a sex talk. It's a love talk. I stare at my fingers, wishing Papa had talked to me last summer. Wishing my mami had still been alive to. I'd known enough to use condoms with Jason. I hadn't known enough not to love him.

How can love not be a wonderful thing?

It's a good question.

The Gottie H. Oppenheimer Principle, v6.0. I'm not supposed to be in this universe. All I've caused is trouble. The next wormhole will show me just how much. Unless I stop it.

Papa stays at the Book Barn after my shift finishes, saying he'll come and check on the party later. The darkness follows me as I dawdle home the long way, through the fields, past the hay bales, thinking about how to fix time. About what the opposite of grief is.

On the way, I text Thomas—Meet me in the churchyard before the party?

He's waiting for me, tucked between the tree and the wall. I watch him for a few seconds, wondering how he won't be here in a couple of weeks. That we'll never see each other again. On what stupid planet is that even possible?

"Couldn't face the chaos alone?" he asks when I sit down next to him. He takes my hand into his lap, holding it between both of his. He's right—whatever else is going on between us, the friendship remains.

"Something like that." I frown. My head still hurts. What happened to the bottle of Grey's hippie remedies? I need a bunch. "How about you?"

"I, uh . . ." He scratches his head, embarrassed. "Prepare to have your mind blown, but I'm not the Michelangelo I once was."

"Huh?"

"A party dude," he clarifies, but I'm still mystified. "I'm cool but rude, like Raphael. Seriously, *Teenage Mutant Ninja Turtles*? Heroes in a half shell? No? We need to get your house hooked up to Wi-Fi. You have pop culture holes that need filling. Then we could Skype, after I move . . ." he adds slyly.

"I'm not the life and soul either," I say in response to this babble, hesitating, then leaning my head on his shoulder. He readjusts, putting his arm around me. My voice sounds sleepy as I add, "Maybe I don't mind the outskirts."

"Sabotaging the balloons, stealing the cake."

"Baking the cake," I correct. My neck cricks when I twist to look up at him. "How did the croquet thing turn out?"

"Croquembouche," Thomas corrects. "I think Ned was a bit over-ambitious. And it's meant to be a party for Grey, right? So I made a Black Forest gâteau."

Schwarzwälder Kirschtorte. Grey's favorite. "The best choice your mother ever made," he always said, "was bringing a piece of Germany home with her." I'd never seen him eat it without needing to be hosed down afterwards.

"Thank you."

Gently, like he can sense my skull is about to burst, or maybe wondering whether I forgive him about Manchester, Thomas kisses me on the head. I could sink into this friendship like a comfortable sofa. But wouldn't that miss the point of this entire summer? And Grey would kill me. It's all through his whole life, all through his diaries, with their explosions of peonies and majestic goats. Take risks. Live boldly. Say yes.

Like a comet, I know: that's how you stop a wormhole, that's the opposite of grief—love.

Before I can think about it, I twist round to kiss Thomas—and boink my head on his. There's a crack like thunder as we connect. Stars everywhere. Nothing spacetimey, just *pain*.

"*Ow.*" He rubs his jaw, looking at me with concern. "Are you okay? Of course you're okay, your skull's made of concrete."

"Me?" I twist around and prod him in the ribs. "That's twice now, you've chinned me."

Then I flatten out my fingers and try to read him like Braille. Scrunch his cardigan underneath my hands. How are you supposed to be best friends with someone when they're a hundred and eighty miles away?

"Third time's the charm?" Thomas offers, jutting his chin.

We're still laughing when we start kissing, messy and clumsy and happy. Dizzy and smiling and tentative, figuring out a way towards each other. I didn't know it could be like this.

"Ready to face the death metal?" I ask, when I can finally speak.

———————————

We kiss-walk-stumble the couple of hundred yards home hand in hand, so by the time we get there, the party is in full swing. We stand in the driveway, hiding behind Grey's Beetle. The hood is vibrating with noise.

My skin vibrates too. I'm pulsating—with Thomas's kiss, with Papa's revelations. With what's to come. My head has started to throb again. I can't let go of Thomas's hand; it's tethering me to the world.

"Is there any way," he yells in my ear, "that we can get to your room without anyone seeing us?"

I wish. From what I can see of the garden, this is *not* Grey's party. No one's in a toga, for starters. And his style of debauchery was much more aren't-tea-lights-everywhere-romantic?-oops-I've-accidentally-set-the-rhododendron-on-fire. The hundreds of different-colored balloons pay lip service to that idea—I half expect to see Papa floating about up there—but ultimately this is Ned and his mates, rocking out.

"C'mon." I lead Thomas into the melee. Immediately, we're in a throng of people. Niall pushes a plastic cup of beer into my free hand and I accept it. He says to someone else, "That's Ned's baby sister."

After that, "Heys" follow us through the garden as we push our way through clumps of people. And out of the corner of my eye, a pool of darkness follows us too. A kiss wasn't enough.

"Heeey." This comes from Sof, a vision in gold who bursts through the crowd to hug me. I let go of Thomas's hand to hug her back, surprised by her warmth. When she peels away, I see her cheeks are flushed and both her beehive and eyeliner are wonky. She's got a beer in each hand.

She peers at my own half-empty cup as someone bumps into us and we stagger sideways. I feel a sudden emptiness. "Gottie! You need to catch up! Where've you been?"

"The bookshop. And Thomas and I—" I break off. I've lost him in the crowd. "Where is everyone?"

"You see all these people?" she stage-whispers. I can smell the beer on her breath. "They are everyone!"

"People *I* know." I only know her and Thomas and the band. "Ned." Talking makes me wince, the headache building up steam with all the noise, and maybe Sof notices, because she says, "Drink."

I follow her instruction, downing my cup like a shot, and she says, "Whoa, actually, slow down. You're not used to it."

Her fussing reminds me of last summer. We were both the same year, weren't we? Both finished with exams, out of school uniform forever. I already don't have a mum; I don't not need another one.

"Seriously, where's Ned?" I drop my empty cup on the grass. Under a nearby shrub, the darkness slides into view. A little bigger than before. I turn away, picking up an unopened can that's sitting on the bench. Someone says "Hey" and not in a "Hello" way, and I shoot a glance at them: "What?"

"That's my beer," says a boy I don't know, gesturing to the can I'm opening.

I stare at him. He has a weird chin and I don't know who he is and I don't care. "I'm the baby sister," I explain.

"Gottie!" says Sof. "What's up with you? Ned's setting up."

"I'm going to find Thomas," I tell her, walking off, pushing my way through all these people I don't know.

Behind me, I can hear her apologizing to the boy whose beer I took. Whatever. I fight my way to the kitchen, then beyond that to the bathroom.

Inside, I lock the door and stuff a couple of aspirin in my mouth, then chug the beer. That's the plan anyway, but I only manage about two gulps. I'm not used to it. Sof's right. How predictably annoying.

My reflection throbs, pale and tired, and my stupid, wonky haircut sticks up in all the wrong places, until I can't see it anymore because the mirror is an untuned television. I turn away and put the toilet seat down and sit on it, closing my eyes, but that just makes my stomach lurch and someone's knocking on the door anyway. I force myself to finish the can, then I go back to the kitchen.

I scour the fridge. Thomas's Black Forest gâteau nestles pristine among six-packs. What would Grey drink? Something effervescent. I find an old bottle of sparkling wine at the back of the pantry and take a mug from the dresser. It's a celebration, isn't it? There should be champagne bubbles and dancing. Every year at this party, Grey would waltz me across the garden on his toes. I want to dance. I want to feel joy. I want to exist.

I go outside and no one's dancing there either, so me and the bottle stomp around on our own for a bit in the flower bed, because it's the only place there's room. The darkness dances with me, hand in hand. We never got the yellow tulips in the end, for the funeral, and it doesn't matter, except it still does.

I top up my mug, and wander round the edges of the garden, looking for Thomas. More people say "hey" as I pass them. Ned's friends, boys in bandanas. When I reach the big stone Buddha, I stop and lean against it, gulping in air. It takes me a couple of seconds to realize I've basically joined Jason and Meg.

Great. Perfect. Unholy long division. Meg's floating dreamily back and forth to the music, wearing ballet flats and generally being petite and adorable and not a great galumphing secret giant. She sees me staring and waves, cautiously. Her other hand is entwined with Jason's.

"Gottie!" she calls out. "Isn't this party insane? Can't wait for later. I'm going to get drinks. You want?"

"Hi. No," I shout, waving my half-empty bottle at her. I lost the mug, somewhere. She nods and moves off through the crowd. Then to Jason I say, "I wish you'd disappear down a wormhole."

"What?"

"Nothing, I said 'Hi.'"

Jason nods warily. I don't think he can hear me, so I say experimentally, "You're a monumental arsehole."

"Yeah!" he shouts back. "Strong tunes!"

It's not quite right, though. I don't want to call him an arsehole. I want him to hear what I have to say, to acknowledge me—to acknowledge us. To admit that we really were something, once. I lean forward to shout it at him, grabbing his shoulder with my bottle hand, a bit more forcefully than I mean to. He staggers and steadies himself on my waist, then I cup my other hand to his ear and say, "We were in love."

"What?" he shouts. Then looks around and leans into my ear, saying quickly, "Yeah. We kinda were. Listen, Margot. After Grey—"

"After Grey, you were awful to me," I interrupt. I'm not sure he hears me. I'm not sure it matters. I kiss him on the cheek and walk away. I'm officially done.

Somehow I make it back inside, fight my way through the kitchen, collect something from the fridge, then carry my bounty through the sitting room, where people are lounging around talking. It's quieter in here. Then somehow I'm outside Grey's door. I haven't been in here since Ned and I cleaned it out.

It's practically silent, inside. I'm on the other side of the house from Ned's stereo and all the people in the garden. I leave the lights off and tiptoe through the mess on the floor—it's like a Thomas bomb exploded, scattering felt-tips and comics and cardigans everywhere. Travel Connect 4 on the piano. It's not quite all the *things* he described in his Toronto bedroom, but it's enough that it doesn't feel like Grey's room anymore.

Which makes it okay to climb onto the bed in my shoes, a piece of Thomas's cake in one hand, the bottle in the other. Somehow, it's almost empty. When did I drink that?

I put the cake on the duvet, then arrange myself cross-legged in front of *The Wurst*. I hold up the bottle, in a toast. That's what Ned's whole party is about, isn't it? A toast to our grandfather. In the corner, darkness slides down the wall.

"What are you doing?"

Thomas is in the doorway.

"Hi!" I yell, then wince. Readjust to nonparty volume. "Sorry. Hello. I know this is your room, sorry."

"That's okay. What's going on?" he asks, shutting the door. "I've been watching you and you seem a little . . ."

Unhinged. Out of control.

"Nothing's going on," I say. "I couldn't find you."

"You didn't look very hard," he says mildly, coming to sit next to me. "Every time I try to cross the garden to talk to you, you run away."

Do I? I haven't even noticed Thomas in the crowd. I've been keeping an eye on the darkness.

"If you're still mad about Manchester, if you didn't want to kiss me . . ."

"I did! I do! I'm running away from the *wormhole*, not you."

Thomas frowns. "Are you drunk?"

The darkness climbs onto the bed, nestling in the shadows between the pillows. And I kiss him, really kiss him. Not like it was in the kitchen. Or sweet, like the churchyard. There's darkness all around us now, so I kiss him like I want the world to stop. At least, I try to.

I launch myself, hands everywhere, pushing him backwards onto the bed. My arms are under his T-shirt, my mouth open and pressed to his closed lips. He's not responding and I try harder, putting his arms under my vest, start fumbling with my own bra strap. The darkness slides closer.

Gently, he pushes me away.

"G," he says, sitting up. "Don't. What's going on with you?"

"Nothing. What? Nothing. It's fate, like you said. Don't you want to?" I throw myself at him again in the half dark, try to put his arms round me. There's so little time left.

"Slow down a second," he says, holding me at arm's length. "Hang on. You're acting strange."

He breaks off, and I fill the silence.

"We're running out of time," I try to explain. "You're leaving, and, and . . ."

"Wait." Thomas holds up a hand, as though I'm a runaway train that he's trying to stop. His other hand digs in his pocket for his inhaler, and he takes two puffs. "Is that the cake?"

In the gloom, we both look at the slice of Black Forest gâteau I stole. It's squashed from where I pushed Thomas into it.

"Sorry," I whisper.

"Let's just go back to the party, okay? I'll get you some water."

He holds out his hand. I take it and let him lead me out into the garden. The darkness follows us.

"Thomas, I . . ."

"We can talk properly, tomorrow," he says, squeezing my hand. Not looking at me.

I nod as I stumble after him. There's cake all over the back of his cardigan. Halfway through the crowd, the music cuts out.

"Weeeiiirrrd."

"Just wait," Thomas says as a guitar chord slices through the silence.

Ned's voice echoes over my head as he yells, "Hello, er, garden! Let's rock!"

"You knew about this?" I say to Thomas as the crowd surges forward, knocking me out of his hand. Ned begins to play. I'm confused—where *is* he? I can see Jason and Niall through a clump of people. This isn't Fingerband. A girl's voice begins to sing and I'm turning around, stumbling into people, trying to work out where Ned is.

Thomas grabs me and steers me through the crowd, spinning me round on the grass and when I stop spinning everything keeps whirling around me, I think I'm going to be sick, and then I'm not going to anymore, I'm just dizzy.

I look up and there, on the shed roof, is Ned, gold jumpsuit and eyes closed, bent over his guitar, hair streaming to the ground. Next to him at the mic, her gold minidress matching his outfit, is Sof. They look like a pair of C-3POs. *Oh.*

My brother has a new band. And everyone knew except me. They must have spent so much time practicing, to be this good. Is this what Ned's been rushing off to all summer? And since when does Sof sing in front of anyone but me?

"Thanyouvermuch." Ned Elvises out of the song. His guitar swings from its strap as he swaps it for his camera, takes a photo of the party. "I'm Ned, this is Sofía, together we are Jurassic Parkas. We're not *The Wurst* band in the world . . ." He winks at the crowd. "I bet you're all just glad it's not Fingerband up here."

Did he really just say that? I can't stop staring at them. They're twins. More brother and sister than he and I are. And I'm the one who made up Jurassic Parkas, last summer.

"Now we're going to play: 'Velocirapture,'" Sof growls into the mic. She doesn't sound shy.

I turn and stumble away, pushing my way through the people cheering. My head is throbbing, I need quiet, I need . . .

"Ermahgahd, ermahgahd, ermahgahd!" Suddenly Sof's croaking at me in the kitchen. I look up from the drink I'm nursing in the corner. My mouth tastes vomity but I don't remember throwing up.

I don't remember how I got here.

"Did you see me?" says Sof. She's extra-raspy, grabbing my arms and bouncing up and down, it's annoying, before jumping past me. "I'm so thirsty, ermahgahd, I might drink straight from the tap."

I trail in her wake. Somewhere near, I'm aware Ned and Thomas have followed her into the kitchen. The half-destroyed cake is on the counter.

"Why didn't you tell me?"

Ned's stereo is blasting Iron Maiden, and I have to yell. It makes me sound angrier than I am—I just want to know why it had to be a secret.

"I'm sorry!" she yells back, reaching into the cupboard for an actual glass, not the plastic cups everyone's drinking from. "What if I'd chickened out, or been terrible? I always told you I wanted to see what it was like to be in a band."

"All your bands are imaginary."

Sof yanks on the tap, which doesn't budge. "I know—but"—she readjusts, shoving aside debris to put her glass on the counter, both hands on the tap—"you'd have wanted to hear us rehearse, and I could only do it if it was me and Ned alone, and—shit, this is annoying—I dunno, what if we were terrible?"

Ned hops onto the counter next to us, even though it's disgusting— broken cups and drink spills, wet cigarette butts and weird sticky stuff. I suppose in spandex it doesn't matter.

"You were brilliant," he says, looking at Sof. There are ten thousand people in the kitchen but it's just the two of them, in a bandmates bubble. Friends, conspirators. Swaps: I get dark matter, you take my friend.

You're being a dog in the manger, says Grey's voice in my head.

Yeah, but Ned's MY brother, I argue back. *And you're dead, and I'm so, so angry at you about that.*

"Who wants what?" says Thomas, catching up to us and plonking down a bunch of bottles, not looking at me. He didn't want to kiss me. How stupid. How embarrassing! I laugh hysterically. Everyone ignores me.

"Is there any water? Even some pop?" croaks Sof. "Your tap is KILL-ING me!" She twists at it again, her knuckles white. The sink is full of darkness and I'm struck by how hugely unfair this is, that I'm the one who'll have to face it.

"Budge over, Sof, it's stuck." She moves aside and Ned puts his full weight and both hands on the tap. "*Scheisse.* Thomas, can you grab me a wrench, or a knife, or something?"

"Wait a second," I say to Thomas, holding him back. He flails, caught between me and Ned. "You couldn't rehearse in front of me? You couldn't even *tell* me? I'm the only one who's heard you sing."

"Sorry we didn't tell you about the band," says Ned, semipatiently, still trying to yank at the tap. Even over the music, I can hear the sarcasm, that he's drunk. "Sof asked me not to. What happens at rehearsal stays at rehearsal—as I've told you a thousand times. You'd remember if you paid attention to anything other than yourself."

He grabs a spoon from the drying rack and starts bashing the tap. I let go of Thomas's arm. Am I selfish? All I've seen Ned do all summer is party, play guitar, and pretend Grey isn't dead. But maybe I've got no idea what he's been up to. Maybe he's got wormholes too.

"I cannot believe you just said that," I say to Ned's back. "Hey! Look at me. You should have told me, you should have . . . She's *my* friend."

It's Sof, not Ned, who turns on me. A hiss so low and furious I can barely hear the words. "I'm your friend? Are you joking? Gottie, you barely want me around! I can see it in your face every time I'm round here, and it sucks. You only reply to my texts half the time, you're always with Thomas, you think the world revolves around you. Even when I was upset about Grey, you wouldn't let me be your friend. Well, guess what? Ned did, and we don't need your permission."

"I'm not giving it!" I shout back, knowing I'm seconds away from being yanked out of time. Thomas is telling Sof to calm down and holding my arm, then Ned is yelling back at me.

"Gottie, shut up. You're driving everybody crazy. You hide in your room for hours and you're always daydreaming, you never listen, I fixed your bike, I try to involve you. And God, his *car*, you cleaned it—that was his STUFF, but you can't deal with his shoes? And you disappear for hours when we need you, you're so selfish, you eat all the cereal and drift around like you're the only one in pain and Jesus, this *fucking* tap—"

Punk is blaring and everyone's still yelling and I'm waiting for the wormhole to yank; it's going to take me right now, surely. None of us notice the tap—the ancient, rusty, creaky kitchen tap, which I've been tightening with a wrench all year because it keeps leaking and Papa won't deal with anything and I don't know what else to do—as it shoots off the sink.

Silently, it rises up and up to hit the ceiling.

Followed by a geyser of water that threatens to drown us all.

"Fuuuck!" hoots Ned, as everything happens at once.

For a few seconds, the water rushes only upwards, as though there's no gravity. Then it comes crashing down over our heads, soaking us, as everyone runs from the kitchen. Now it's spraying every which way as Ned tries to stem the flow with his hand, only making things worse. It sweeps everything before it in a tide, cups and mugs and bottles crash to the floor. Then Thomas's cake.

The four of us watch, drenched.

Frozen.

Then a bedraggled Sof catches my eye. And, unbelievably, she laughs.

After a second, I crack up too—and suddenly we're all hysterical. I'm holding on to Sof and we're staggering about, both of us shrieking as we keep slipping across the floor. The water's still spraying and Ned's still trying to stop it and giggling, "Fuck, fuck, fuck," and this strikes me as the funniest thing ever.

Every time I look at Sof I collapse into giggles. My legs are weak like noodles. And every time she looks at me, she does a startled-donkey snort. Pretty soon we're unable to hold each other up and we hit the floor, taking Thomas down with us—which only sends us into further hysterics as we flap about, beached fishes. I can't see where the wormhole is, and I don't care.

Ned flops down into the water too, even though he doesn't need to, straight onto the cake, which makes Sof cackle even more. Breathlessly, she snorts at me, "Look—at—at—" She's laughing so hard it takes her ten attempts to add, "Ned!"

"Fuck you, Petrakis," Ned says, splashing her with water. "Shit, my camera."

It's Thomas who finally calms us down.

"Ned, Ned," he says, struggling to sit up as the giggles fade out. "Get towels from the bathroom, your bedsheets, laundry—anything, there's a load in my, Grey's, *that* room. G, is the shed locked? Is there a mop or anything? I can't think, um . . . Okay, Sof, can you turn off the music?"

Ned helps Sof to her feet and they head off, following instructions. Thomas nudges me: "The mop?"

"Shed, yes," I say, still faintly delirious.

"Right. Can you handle—this?"

I nod—I don't have a choice—and he runs off, slipping in all the water on the floor and banging against the walls.

There's a saucepan on the drying rack and I grab it, approaching the sink like it's a rat I need to kill. I try holding it down over the tap but it just redirects the spray right in my face. Trying again, both hands now, I manage to use it to sort of deflect the spray back down into the sink. Half of it is still going all over the counter, the windows, but at least not me.

Distantly, I hear the music stop.

A few seconds later, a dripping Sof squelches back out of Ned's room. She comes to stand next to me, tilting her head at the saucepan.

"Clever," she says. I glance at her, my arms shaking with effort. Her beehive has fallen apart, and her eyeliner drips in black streaks down her cheeks.

We stare at each other for a few long seconds, considering. Then she grins.

"You know who'd LOVE this?" She jerks her head at the überdestruction. "Grey."

"Yeah," I agree quietly. "Yeah, he'd think it was hilarious."

"And"—Sof hip-bumps me pointedly—"he'd think *we're* really stupid."

I hip-bump her back.

"I'm sorry I yelled," I tell her.

The kitchen's a disaster. Papa's going to kill us. I sort of don't care. I'm weightless, the same way as when you haven't done your homework and the teacher calls in sick—everything's going to be okay. A reprieve. Wormhole, schmormhole.

"Come on, give us a go," Sof says, putting her hands over mine on the saucepan.

"Okay, hold it tight," I tell her, shifting aside. As soon as I let go, the pan flies out of her grasp, clunking against my wrist and spraying water over both of us again. Sof dissolves in giggles as we slip and slide in the water.

"Stop iiiit," I say, snorting. "Come on, you have to hold it, I need to find a way to stop this."

"Scout's honor," Sof swears, picking the pan up again.

As she braces her arms against the pressure, I kneel down. "Budge over." I crawl past her legs and nudge open the cupboard under the sink. There's got to be a stop button or something. The wrench is on the floor where Ned dropped it. From my hands and knees, I can see how filthy the tiles are—dirty water and discarded drinks, everything that was on the counter has been swept down here by the tidal wave.

"Gross, gross, gross," I mutter as I peer inside the cupboard. I yank at a thingamajig. "Anything?"

"No," Sof bellows.

I hit a whojamewhatsit and tug something else, and the thundering in the sink above me stops. Finally. I crawl out of the cupboard backwards, butt first. Bash my head as I stand up.

"Ow."

While I was in the sink, Ned arrived with armfuls of laundry, sheets, blankets. He's already got a towel turbaned around his head, and he's wrapping Sof in a blanket as I grab a sheet and tie it round myself like a toga. *Now* it's one of Grey's parties.

"No, you—" Thomas comes clattering through the door with a mop and bucket and stops, staring at us all. "Those were for the floor? To soak up the water?"

"Fuck the water," says Ned cheerfully, and I laugh. "We're drowning men anyway—Papa's going to kill us, whatever we do."

"But we should at least . . ." Thomas is goggling at the wreck of the kitchen, and I smile at him. He nods, not unhappily. We're okay, I think.

"Tomorrow!" declares Ned, grabbing a bottle of rum that survived the melee. He tucks it under one arm, and Sof under another. "We'll worry about it then."

"A last drink on death row," says Sof, and he kisses her on the head.

"Yes! You get it." He starts leading us out to the garden. "Let's warm up outside. Grots, did any mugs survive?"

I grab what I can and smile shyly at Thomas. He gathers bottles and mugs with me, meeting my eyes and smiling as we follow them.

Outside, the garden is quiet and inky dark. Pretty much everyone's disappeared. A few entwined couples are melting into the trees, and as we pass a group of Ned's friends in the driveway, there's a sweet smell in the air—a tiny orange firefly is flitting from hand to hand.

Meg and Jason are on the bench outside the house, kissing. I float above them, unbothered.

"We're going to drink rum," I tell her as we walk by, a peace offering. "Come with us."

She gawps at our appearance, then she and Jason follow us through the dark to the apple tree.

Ned and Sof are already cross-legged underneath it, buried in the thick grass, a gold-plated Titania and Oberon.

"A toast," Ned announces, his towel turban wobbling, as we sit down. "Thomas, my man, the glasses."

Among a fuss of mugs and eggcups, rum is poured. I open the bottle of coke I rescued and top everyone's mugs up. It fizzes over the top of Meg's glass, onto her hand. She giggles, trying to lick it off her fingers.

"Ooh," she says. "Wet."

"It's just pop," says Sof. "Have you seen *us*?"

She shakes out her hair, which is drying into the crazy frizz she usually semitames. Ned unwraps his towel to reveal a huge perm, his eyeliner dangerously Alice Cooper. I gaze at them in the half-light. It's not that they look particularly alike underneath all the razzle-dazzle—and Ned and I actually do. But they both have this sense of themselves. They belong. Belong to a band of loons marching to the beat of Gaia-knows-what drum, but still.

But it's okay, because I belong as well. I'm trouble times two. At least for the next couple of weeks. I sip my rum, leaning into Thomas's arm. He's quiet. I squeeze his knee, and he smiles at me, then peers into his glass, fishing out a leaf.

"What happened, anyway?" asks Jason.

"Did you all go skinny dipping?" asks Meg dreamily. "Everyone's wet."

"With my little sister? Gross," says Ned.

"Yes, we're wet," says Sof patiently.

"Did you know Gottie and Jason skinny-dipped?" says Meg, not listening. Too late I see she's stoned, really stoned. In the glow from Jason's cigarette, her eyes are tennis balls. "Jason told me they swam together in the canal. Like mermaids . . ."

Ned is staring at Jason. Sof bites her lip, glancing between me and Thomas—guessing he doesn't know the half of it. He tight-smiles at me, like he's not *thrilled* by this revelation, but he's not quite allowed to be annoyed either. I can't find my tongue; I think I left it in the kitchen.

"Mermaids," Meg giggles, staring at her fingers like they're brand-new. Then she looks up at us all, wide-eyed and full of wonder, and I know what she's going to say before she says it. I can't stop her. Here's where my tiny white lie, a misunderstanding I could have cleared up days ago, comes back and destroys me. "They had sex."

"Fuck," says Jason. He stubs his cigarette out on the grass, then looks at me across the circle. We stare at each other for a long moment, in it together. But not, I suppose, anymore.

"Come on," he says to Meg, starting to help her up. "Time to go home."

"Jason." Ned glowers at him, his hair crackling and huge. "Piss off, would you?"

"Ned," Sof says softly, putting a hand on his arm.

Jason looks around at us all, staring up at him in a circle. In slow motion, he mouths a "sorry" at me, and ambles off into the darkness. Meg wobbles and Sof scrambles to stand up. We all do. I can't look at Thomas. My head throbs.

Meg shakes Sof off and stumbles across to me. She leans right in, looking at my face. "You're pretty," she says, trailing her finger down my cheek. "Isn't she so pretty, Thomas?"

"Come on," says Sof, taking her arm. "Bed."

She starts leading her away, Ned lumbering after them. Sof glances back over her shoulder at me, concerned. Then Thomas and I are alone under the apple tree. I can't not look at him any longer.

"You lied to me?" he asks, his face barely visible in the dark.

"You lied too," I say, and even though it's true, I immediately want to chop off my tongue. I should be pointing out that me and Jason makes no difference—it doesn't make me and Thomas a lie. In the grass, clumsy and new. How we were in the tree, when we held elbows. In the attic in the Book Barn, making promises to each other a long time ago. We can have all that, and I can have my summer with Jason too.

"Seriously? It's hardly the same thing," Thomas scoffs. "And I suppose everyone knows except me and, I'm guessing, Ned?"

"*No one* knew, that's the point—"

"Then what? I don't get it. You didn't have to lie to me. It's fucked up." He runs his hands through his hair, then finger-quotes at me. "'First everything.'"

"That's not even what I meant!"

"Whatever," Thomas says, not listening to me. "You know, I saw you with him earlier at the party? Before I came and found you, you were whispering together, and I knew—"

"Knew *what*?" I hurl my hands in the air, an imitation bat grab of frustration. "I'm allowed to talk to him! I'm allowed to keep it a secret, if I want. And you're right; it's not the same thing—running off to Manchester without telling me? That's actually my business. Me and Jason is none of yours."

I'm picking up steam, ready for a fight—I think I'm in the right here, I think I deserve one—but Thomas interrupts me.

"And when you kissed me earlier—in your grandpa's room," he emphasizes, full of scorn. "When you tried to do more, was it my business then?"

"I didn't lie," I say calmly, thinking back to the kitchen on Thomas's first morning, weeks ago. How I'd tried to pick a fight, and he hadn't let me. "At least, not how you mean. When I said first everything, I meant I'd never been in love before. Except that's not actually true. And I don't even think you're angry I lied. I think you're jealous that I've been in love and you haven't."

When I say that, he turns and disappears into the night.

Ned's right. I am selfish. That's what stops me from running after him.

I go to my room to wait. I know what's coming next. Minus three, minus two, minus one. I strip off my wet clothes, dropping them onto the floor, not bothering with the laundry basket.

Exhaustion sweeps over me as I climb into bed and pull up the covers. I've lived ten lifetimes in one summer. But sleep doesn't come. All the secrets and all the revelations and all the anger—me and Thomas, Ned and Sof—it all crashes over me in waves, smashing me onto the sand again and again. Drowning me.

"Umlaut?" I pat the duvet. Nothing. Even my *cat* wants nothing to do with me.

When I turn off the lamp, the light of the day, pooled in corners and hiding under the bed, slides out the door. There's just the glow from the ceiling, the fluorescent stars Thomas sticky-taped there for me, that match no constellation at all.

I stay awake, watching them blink out, one by one.

Until I'm alone with the darkness.

Zero

It's the last day of summer. Except it isn't, not really. I'm here and I'm not here. This is the first time I've been here, but also it isn't. Déjà vu. I'm watching myself, inside myself. It's a memory, it's a dream, it's a wormhole.

A wormhole. But it still hurts.

It's the day Grey died.

And I'm wishing. Not cross-your-fingers lightly, or how six-year-old me wished for my vegetables to magically disappear.

I'm pouring everything I have into wishing to a God I don't believe in.

How could I be sleeping with Jason in the sunshine three hours ago, and now I'm in the hospital?

Papa was nowhere to be found when I got here, but Ned was in the waiting room, green snakeskin on a grey plastic chair. We'd exchanged information: the note I found on the blackboard. The texts we swapped on that long bus ride. As though by knowing exactly what had happened, we could change the outcome.

"The paramedics say he was all right when they arrived."

"They think he might have had a stroke after getting to the E.R."

"He's in the ICU."

"He's in the stroke ward."

"Didn't you say?"

"I thought he was . . ."

Papa eventually showed up. Maybe he's always been here, invisible. Maybe when Mum died, Papa never left this hospital.

We follow him down the corridor.

Grey has shrunk. He was a giant, a grizzly bear. Now, he's under some evil wizard's spell. His face is a landslide.

He blinks at me, mewing, his hands frantically pawing at his flimsy hospital gown over and over again, unwittingly exposing himself, a baby.

And his hands!

There's a picture of Ned, newborn and wrinkled as a pickled walnut. He's just a frog in the palm of Grey's huge hand—a hand that's now translucent. A tube sticks out of it, covered in tape, surrounded by a bruise. There's a drop of blood on the sheet underneath.

Papa comes back and the doctors come in, and give us numbers.

Seventy-five percent chance of disability.

Fifty-fifty chance of making it through twenty-four hours.

Ten percent chance of further seizures.

Six months till we're out of the woods.

His blood pressure is a problem, they say. There are risk factors, underlying conditions. It could go either way, they say. He's sixty-eight, they say.

I stop listening, start thinking of Midsummer's Eve. Jason's kiss. But before that, Grey lit a fire to ward off the mist that rolled in from the sea.

We'd eaten roast chicken and potato salad with our fingers, and wiped the grease onto the grass.

"I want to die like a Viking!" Grey had roared, drunk on heat and red wine, leaping across the flames like an enormous Pan. "Burn me on a pyre; push me out to the waves!"

A brisk nurse, a different one from a couple of hours ago, rattles a plastic curtain around Grey's bed. Someone else, someone old, is wheeled into the next bay—

The bonfire smelled of smoke and spring.

The hospital smells of antiseptic. He can't stride into Valhalla from here.

Grey blinks up at me, tiny. The nurses roll him over so they can peel away his shit-stained sheets, and he's looking right at me and he doesn't see who I am.

I love you, *I think, holding a hand that can't squeeze mine back. His skin is slack under my fingers, loose and cold.* You are a Viking.

The nurses write numbers on a clipboard. Ned comes back from the canteen with weak, hot coffee that burns our hands through the thin plastic cups, and we don't drink any of it. Jason texts, a single question mark. Papa sits across from me on a plastic chair, his hand over his mouth. Staring at nothing. Waiting.

There were sparks in the air on Midsummer's Eve. Sweet wood smoke and a first kiss, a fire collapsing in a shower of light and flame.

The machines beep quietly over and over again. My grandfather lies on the bed, tiny and alone, and far away from me.

I close my eyes.

"Burn me on a pyre; push me out to the waves!" Grey leaps across the flames. "I want to die like a Viking!"

And I wish that for you, with everything I have.

Two hours later you are dead.

{5}
BLACK HOLES

$$S_{BH} = \frac{A}{4L^2_P} = \frac{c^3A}{4G\hbar}$$

The heart of a black hole, known as its singularity,
has zero size and infinite density. A black hole
is formed when a star collapses in on itself.
Gravity implodes, sucking in everything around it.
And it's called black hole entropy.

Sunday 17 August

[Minus three hundred and fifty]

I dream I'm in a spaceship, and Thomas is at the controls. He steers us through galaxies. We are all alone in the world, except for the stars. They rush past us as we speed through time and space, heading to the future. And when we get to the very edge of the universe, Thomas stops the spaceship and turns us around.

"You can see Earth from here," he says. "Everyone's there, waiting."

I look where he's pointing, but I can't see anything. Just darkness. And when I wake up, he's gone.

For a second, everything's fine. This used to happen every day last autumn, until Jason, and then not sleeping altogether. There'd be a brief, delirious moment after I woke when I'd have no memory of what had happened. A garden full of laundry, *Hey, Grey's home.* Then it comes roaring back.

Memories flood the room. Papa's confession. Kissing Thomas.

Stomping around the party, drunk and belligerent. Hiding from the wormhole. Trying to have sex with Thomas. Thomas saying *no*. I cringe under my duvet, but my brain won't let me hide: Sof yelling. Ned yelling. The tap exploding. Meg telling everyone about me and Jason. Our fight. Thomas running away.

And the last wormhole. This is what this whole year's been about. That wish, that stupid Viking wish. Who did I think I was, playing God?

Grey is dead and I wished it, I wished it, I wished it. And don't tell me wishes aren't real, because I've seen the stars go out and watched numbers fall like rain. It's as real as the square root of minus fifteen. But, oh—it was only for a split second

and

I take it back!

I want to yell. I want to claw through the earth with my bare hands, screaming for him to come home. I want to bury this memory deep and never visit its grave. I want a hundred thousand million things, but mostly, stupidly, hopelessly, I want him not to be dead.

I cry till I'm raw, fat hot tears of self-pity. I cry till I'm forcing it, till my throat hurts, punishing myself. Then I lie in bed, scratchy-eyed, watching the early-morning light deepen and take on the color of the day. As the sun filters through the ivy, guilt slowly washes over me. And it brings me to shore.

The worst is over, and I've survived.

I'll never reconcile myself over Grey's death. Over the wish I made. But I can get out of bed. I can yank open the window, breaking through the ivy, and throw open the door—the room is hot and stuffy and green, and I want air and light.

When I stumble outside, the garden is all aftermath: empty bottles and beer cans wink from the grass, and there's a table lamp in the plum tree. I lift it down and tuck it under my arm, heading for the kitchen.

Ned's already there, mopping. He's dressed down in black leggings and a giant, moth-eaten jumper. I recognize it as one of Grey's—Ned said he took the clothes to a charity shop in town, but clearly he kept some. His hair is subdued under a beanie.

I knock on the door frame, unsure whether I can come in. "How bad is it?"

He looks up, green-faced. Too hungover to take a photograph of my dishevelment. "You mean Papa? Or this?"

"This" is the puddle of water that covers the floor. It looks worse than I remember from last night: the color of Sof's mum's vegan soup, topped with cigarette butt croutons. The chairs are stacked upside down on the table, café-style. I peer through them, stupidly hoping to see a loaf of bread or a pile of pastries.

"You can come in," says Ned. He sounds amused. "You can't make it dirtier."

I put the lamp down and splosh inside, my sneakers instantly soaking. A disgruntled Umlaut sits on top of the woodpile, surveying Waterworld. The sitting room door is closed, which I hope means the destruction is limited to the kitchen. And that Thomas isn't going to come in and help. My stomach twists as I think about facing him.

I pick up an empty can that floats by, and stand there with it, waiting for Ned to tell me what to do. "I don't know where to start."

"Tea. Always start with tea," the expert advises.

I splash my way to the kettle, which is thankfully full—the tap is swathed in brown parcel tape like an amputated limb. By the time it boils and I'm rummaging for milk, you'd barely know anything had happened here. Only the tap and a garbage bag of bottles are evidence.

"Where is Papa?" I ask Ned, handing him a mug.

He slurps his tea, not answering.

"Are you not speaking to me?"

"Grots," Ned sighs. "Meet hangovers. Talking's like red-hot pokers."

"Are you annoyed at me?" I'm stubbornly stuck on this point, I don't think I can bear it if Ned's still angry at me.

"'Course not. Like I said last night, you ignore me all year, all summer—"

"Me?" I'm incredulous. "What about you?"

"What about me? I've been here, in case you haven't noticed. Fixing your bike, making dinner, rehearsing, whatever. I'm always around. But you're not—you stare into space, or creep around in your room avoiding everyone, you upset Sof on a weekly basis. Then Thomas bats his glasses at you, and you're all smiles—don't get me wrong, that's great, I'm glad you're happy—except you refuse to get involved with Grey's party, you won't even talk about it, then you show up and bellow at us all for no reason . . . Never mind. *'Course* I'm not annoyed at you."

"Oh." After last night's shouting, I'm awash with relief.

"That was sarcasm, you idiot." He laughs, plonking his mug down on the table. "Look, I know you hate it when I play the three-years-older card, but—"

"Two years and one month," I correct automatically.

"Same dif," he snorts. "I think you could be nicer to Sof. I think you should've come to me when Jason was sniffing around. But I also think it was probably nuts being here this year with just Papa for company. Maybe I should have come home at Easter. I get how hard it is, I do. It was shit, moving to London a week after he died. You're not the only one who was upset, y'know? Maybe in *two years and one month*, you'll see that a bit better."

"You're annoyed 'cause of Jason." I nod wisely.

"Rraaarrrgh." Ned yanks off his beanie, stuffing it in his pocket. His hair tumbles free and he looks like himself again. "I'm annoyed *at* Jason, and I'm pretty sure you should be too."

"It wasn't his fault," I say, because I've been blaming him for my unhappiness all year, and I need to let him off the hook. "I think he couldn't handle it, after Grey died. He didn't know how."

"He bloody well knew you were two years younger than him, though," says Ned, snorting. Not listening to what I'm saying. "The prick."

"Isn't he your best friend?"

"Can't he be both? The wanker."

Stubbornly, I try to explain again. "He loved me."

"Did he say that? Or did he clench his jaw and swallow so his Adam's apple jumped, and say—" Ned looks away mournfully, the perfect Jason impression, and I stifle a giggle as he says, " 'Do you love me?' "

I know what me and Jason had, that it was love. But we didn't have to be a secret. And he didn't have to make me beg for him to talk to me after he left. So I say: "The *dumm Fuhrt.*"

"C'mere." Ned twists me into more of a half nelson than a hug, rubbing his fist on my hair. "Too right. You don't keep things like love a secret. Christ. You know who I sound like?"

We stand there for a bit, me bent uncomfortably double and breathing through my mouth. Then he rubs my hair again, and releases me. I gulp fresh air while he straps on a fanny pack and, amazingly, makes it look cool. Only Ned.

"I'll have a word with Althorpe, tell him not to mess you around. But I'm gonna hang out at Sof's today."

"Why don't you invite her here? Her mum will give you vegan food."

I don't know much about hangovers, but instinct tells me I'm going to need pizza.

"Because Papa's going to yell at you." Ned grins, heading out the door. "I've already been through that, I don't fancy another one."

After he leaves, I take the garbage bag outside, then go back to the kitchen and wipe the counters with a dishrag and a squirt of something violently chemical that Grey would disapprove of. I force myself to eat a banana, make a pot of coffee. Then I put all the chairs back on the floor, sit in one, and wait for Papa.

I look at my hands, side by side on the table: this is what I did when I was little. Thomas and I would adventure, hell-bent on destruction, profit, or scientific inquiry (sometimes all three). When we got home, he would hide while I'd trot straight to the kitchen to await discovery, detection, punishment.

"Am I grounded?" I ask Papa as soon as he floats in, first checking his trademark red Converse won't get wet.

It wrong-foots him, I can tell. "Ah, *nein?* This was Ned's party, Ned's trouble. He tells me the tap was an accident?"

"Yes." I wait for the goose-hissing, but it doesn't come.

"And the kitchen is cleaned up? Maybe you can call plumber, and Ned pays." Papa pours himself a cup of coffee and sits down next to me. "I think I arrange the Book Barn shifts this time, until school starts again. Work together, no more fights. And maybe dinner as a family tonight, tomorrow, the next day . . ." He smiles. "I'll cook. Or your brother. No more baked potatoes or cereal, please. You cook like your mami."

"That's it?"

"You want a punishment for having fun?" He wrinkles his nose. "If Grey had done this party, it would have turned out the same. I do think, is you maybe owe Thomas a sorry. I don't know the details, what happened between you, but he was very upset when he left this morning—"

Papa's still talking as I push my chair back with a squeak. I stub my toe on the table leg as I turn and shove open the sitting room door, run through to Grey's, to *Thomas's* room.

The door isn't quite closed and it swings open under my hammering fists.

The bed is stripped, the Black Forest cake smears from last night, gone. There's a neat stack of cookbooks on the piano, borrowed from around the house and the Book Barn. A faint smell of whiskey still in the air. And *The Wurst*, hovering over the emptiness like a sad blue penis.

"He knocked on my door very early."

I turn around. Papa's standing behind me, watching.

"He was all packed up, and he told me . . ." He hesitates. "He said he couldn't stay here. That he was going to stay with a friend."

"Who?" I'm Thomas's only friend. Except for Sof and Meg and whoever he hung around with all the days I ignored him to dive into wormholes. He probably knows loads of people in Holksea. He did live here before, after all. "Where is he?"

"I checked that it was okay. And his mum knows. But, Gottie, *Liebling*." Papa reaches out for me, offering his arms, but I'm already pushing past him as he says, "He didn't want me to tell you."

Sunday 17 to Monday 18 August

[Minus three hundred and fifty to fifty-one]

I hit my room running, yanking the patchwork off my bed, balling it up and throwing it next to the door. The bike-crash blankets join it—it's summer, who needs wool blankets?—spilling out a million pairs of balled-up socks. Thomas's socks. Umlaut pounces on one and scuttles off underneath the bed with it.

What next? Thomas's cardigan is draped over the back of my chair, and I hurl it onto the laundry heap, yanking the chair over. I have to keep moving, keep doing something, otherwise I'll think: *Thomas hates me* and *Thomas is gone* and—

I'm so angry.

I can't believe he's pulled a disappearing act again!

A broken lipstick gets chucked in the trash, followed by a pair of earrings borrowed from Sof. I tip my little bowl of hairbands and bobby pins in as well, then throw the bowl after them. Every surface is littered with plates, a legacy of Thomas's baking and hours spent at my desk in search of lost time. When they're stacked by the door and everything's in the trash, the room seems a little less haywire—but my heart is still bouncing off the walls. How dare he do this.

I clamber onto the desk, flick the plastic stars one by one onto the floor. It's grimly satisfying. But when I gather the constellations in my hand, it's too much. I can't throw these away. I heap them on the stripped bed instead, where they're joined by a pile of coins from the window-sill. On top of the chest of drawers, the piece of seaweed from the beach. I take down everything from my corkboard, the email, the cake recipe, Polaroids of Ned's.

Then I'm done. I stand and look at the bed, breathing heavily. All of these *things*, a time capsule of our summer, and what does it amount to? A heap of junk, and broken promises. Thomas hasn't given me anything of meaning, not even his word. I barely know anything about him. I suppress the voice that says—*because you never asked*.

I had no choice, I was disappearing down wormholes.

Is that true? Grey's voice answers me. *Determinism, dude. Drive your own lawn mower.* What to do with all this Thomas stuff? Grey would call it a cleansing and have me burn it in a herb-spiked fire. Sof would donate it all to a charity shop. Ned would chuck it in the trash. But me, what would I do? Do I know myself well enough to make a decision?

I dig inside my wardrobe for my book bag, unused since the last week of term, and cram everything inside. The front pocket rustles. I fumble with the zip, and pull out a crumpled piece of paper—Ms. Adewunmi's quiz. How did I not notice she asked about the Weltschmerzian Exception?

I put the book bag at the back of my wardrobe. I put The Great

Spacetime Quiz! on my windowsill. Then I crawl into my unmade bed and sleep for the next sixteen hours.

I wake up in the middle of the next afternoon, to sun streaming green through the ivy. The first thing I see is the quiz. *Clocks are a way of measuring time . . . It's infinite . . . A spacetime boundary—the point of no return . . . what is the Weltschmerzian Exception?*

Good question.

Ten minutes later I'm out in the fens. The sky is huge, infinite and empty as I cycle along the deserted coast road. I'm the last person left in the universe. The whole wide world is in high-definition 3D, bigger and brighter than I've ever known it. Or perhaps that's me. Facing down that final wormhole, I feel like sunshine, burning the fog away.

When I reach school and chain my bike to the rack, there are students everywhere. Anxiety tweaks at me—has term started?

Ms. Adewunmi's classroom is unlocked and empty. It's strange, being at school when you're not meant to be. It makes me nervous— stools I'd normally sit on and whiteboards I'd normally take notes from are suddenly museum exhibits. Look but don't touch.

The whiteboard is covered in equations from last term, second-year stuff. It'll probably be cleaned off before lessons begin again in September, so I grab a pen and add the equation from Thomas's email, the one in my handwriting. I still don't know what it means.

"Whoa."

I jump. Ms. Adewunmi's in the doorway, and she's staring not at the whiteboard, but at me. "You changed your hair," she says.

"Uh, yeah." I prod my mullet self-consciously. "You too."

She puts the box she's carrying down on the desk, tossing her braids. "I like it. Very Chrissie Hynde."

"You're moving?"

"Getting ready for the new term." She starts unpacking: fresh board pens, reams of paper, plastic-wrapped sets of cardboard folders, a catering-size bag of lollipops, which she shakes at me. "Get a cola one before they all go."

I take the bag from her and fish out a lollipop at random, waiting while she finishes sorting her things out before plying her with questions.

"Sit down, smarty-pants," she says, gesturing to the desk. "Scooch. I'll be with you in a sec."

I perch on the edge of the desk and gaze at the whiteboard. *Am I clever?* I know I understand all the numbers I'm looking at. But it's no different from the way Sof can decipher a Renaissance painting or Ned can read music. How Thomas can translate a recipe into cake.

This summer is the world's doing, not mine—the wormholes could have happened to anyone. I just knew how to recognize them mathematically. Even so, the equations on the board—they're incredible. Maybe that's something I could do when I go to university. Learn all the ways to describe the world.

"All right, then, Ms. Oppenheimer." My teacher hops up next to me, talking round her lollipop like it's a cigarette. "You're a bit early. Term starts next month."

"I needed to talk to you," I say. "I brought my quiz back. And I wanted to ask about a theory—there's a page missing, in one of the books from your reading list . . ."

"Oh! That reminds me, I have something for you." She takes the quiz from me, but doesn't look at it, just puts it on the desk and rummages through her things. "Aha. I picked these up, was planning to bombard you on the first day, in exchange for your essay. But, well—here."

Ms. Adewunmi hands me a stack of brochures: Oxford, Cambridge, Imperial in London. But also faraway places I've not thought about, like Edinburgh and Durham, and ones I've not even heard of, like MIT and Ludwig-Maximilians. I run my hand over the glossy covers, trying to imagine myself in a year's time, who I'll be then.

She taps the stack with a long, lightning-bolt-adorned nail. "I got your theory notes. *The Gottie H. Oppenheimer Principle?*"

It takes me a second to remember: the emails I sent her from the Book Barn.

"It's good. A touch science-fiction, but still. Type that into something comprehensible, and world's your oyster."

"This might be a silly question, but—"

"Of course you'll get in wherever you want, Gottie. If money's a problem, there's funding available, especially for girls wanting to pursue STEM industry degrees, there's all sorts of programs, grants, and such. It's hard finding them, but they're there. You'll get my recommendation."

"Actually, I was going to ask if you could understand that equation I wrote on the board?"

"No. Oh, no, I can't." She turns to me, wide-eyed and terrified, and whispers, "You must be a *genius*."

I roll my eyes while she laughs harder than when she welcomed me to the Parallel Universe Club. Finally, she says, "Sorry. Oh, boy. It's a paradoxical time loop."

I quiz her with a baffled headshake.

"A joke," she clarifies. "An equation for something that doesn't exist. A sci-fi thing—c'mon, you don't watch TV?"

"Could you explain it to me anyway?"

"Eh, why not." She leaps up and wipes a space on the whiteboard clean, talking over her shoulder as she diagrams the equation.

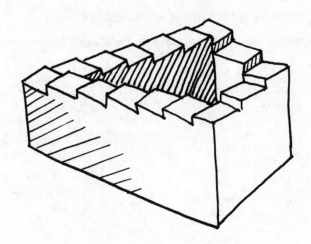

"It describes a loop, yeah? A tunnel to the past, created in the present. A two-way wormhole. But the joke is, it can only be opened because it's already been opened, in the past." She circles with her pen. "And the reverse is true. It exists because it exists. It's a paradox. Make sense?"

"Kind of." I point to the part that most confuses me. "What's this factor, though?"

"That's matter created when all this happened. A sort of overflow valve. Excess energy. The equation only works if you funnel off this solution into its own section—which means it'll never work. The whole thing is some bored physicist's idea of a joke."

"A joke," I repeat. I'm disappointed—I'd hoped it was the Weltschmerzian Exception. That's obviously a physics gag too, a hilarious mathematical urban legend. I'll never know what happened this summer. Ms. Adewunmi sits back down next to me, swinging her legs under the desk.

"All right, then," she says, "a joke. But it's some pretty cool math. That it, no more questions? Surely you want to be outside on a day like this."

I slide off the desk. When I reach the door, I turn back. "One more thing. On the reading list. How come you put *Forever*?"

She chuckles. "I thought you could do with some light reading. It's a classic."

Saturday 23 August

[Minus three hundred and fifty-six]

"Liebling." Papa appears from the ether, knocking softly on my door.

"I'm fine, Papa," I mumble into the pillow. "New shifts, remember? It's my day off."

"Ja, I know," he says, putting a cup of tea next to my head. It's been almost a week of moping, and he keeps trying to coax me out of it with "treats"—such as letting Ned play music at the Book Barn. This is the first time he's sought me out in my room, though. Maybe ever. Grey was always the one to find me when I was in a funk.

I peel one eye open and watch him as he looks around, noting the emptiness, the equations on the wall, lingering by the desk, running his hand over the brochures Ms. Adewunmi gave me. The diaries.

He turns back to the bed. "Sof's outside."

Bah.

Papa hovers while I gulp the tea—as though he thinks I'll book it out the window if he leaves me to it.

It's going to be a scorching day—the air already smells like toffee, and the sun is beginning to burn. I find Sof in the shade, sitting with her sketchbook among overblown raspberries, tangles of ivy, brambles, and nettles gone to flower.

"Hi." I half wave as Papa floats off, and plonk myself in the grass next to her, the dew soaking through my pajamas. Her sketchbook is full of doodles of the garden.

"You realize I can *literally* say it's a jungle out here?" Sof waves her pencil at the wilderness as Umlaut bounces, then disappears into the grass. All the flowers have long wilted and burst in the heat. They straggle across the bushes, limp balloons after a party. In the winter, Norfolk's beaches are shrouded in bleak white fog, and you can't imagine spring will ever break through. The garden has that same air of loneliness now.

"Do you think your mum would come over?" I ask. I don't have the right to ask her for a favor, but I know her mum would want to help. "Help us, I don't know, prune?"

I wouldn't blame Sof if she told me to piss off, if she was only here to say that. Or maybe she's here to see Ned, and Papa's misunderstood.

"Ask Mum yourself, later today," she says. "She's running the plant stall at the fair."

Ah, the fair. Holksea's annual jamboree of cake competitions and donkey rides marks the end of summer—for the village. For me, I had Grey's party for that. I always thought of the fair as the start of autumn. A new beginning.

"You could come with me . . ." Sof croaks so quietly, I almost miss it.

"You'd want me to? I thought you'd still be pissed off at me."

"I was," she says, then off my look, adds, "Okay, I still am, a bit. Look, last year? Not telling me you were ditching art, ditching *me*, it sucked. Worse than getting dumped. But I understand it, now. I mean, you lost your dad."

I blink at the oddity of her mistake. "My grandfather."

"Nah. I've been talking to Ned about this. He was your dad. Your papa's your dad, obviously. But Grey was his and your dad too. He was, like, all of our dads, or something."

"Yeah, he was."

I sigh and lean my head on her shoulder. She puts an arm round me and we sit there for a bit, both waiting for it not to be awkward. Maybe it always will be. I look at my feet, seeing how tanned they are. And dirty. The earth is definitely between my toes, and the cherry-red nail polish I put on at the beginning of summer is nothing but chips. I'm ready to fall asleep on Sof till autumn, when she pulls away.

"Please? I want to see pig racing! And eat cake—I'm going to go crazy and have gluten *and* dairy. And sugar! And the vegetable sculpting! Pleeease," she begs. "I can't go alone."

"What about Meg? And—is it"—I can't remember the name of her latest girlfriend—"er, Susie? Or won't Ned go with you?"

"Meg will be there. Susie's old news. And Ned's playing with Fingerband. But anyway, I wanna go with *you*." She prods me with her pencil, and I giggle, reluctantly.

"Fingerband? You didn't want to perform as Jurassic Parkas?"

"I like rehearsing," she muses. "And singing at the party was fun. But I think I prefer being behind the scenes. Being looked at is ugh."

She full-body shudders. I take in her gold-sequin T-shirt, Hawaiian-print trousers, pineapple hairdo. I don't know if we'll stay friends. But I do know that if Sof can simultaneously be spotlight-reluctant *and* wear this outfit, and all that contradiction can be contained in one person, well: we might be more than the sum of our past.

Without Thomas, the fair is devoid of drama. My righteous anger at him has burned away and I kind of miss the chaos he might have caused.

After the pig race, Sof and I wander through the village green—sheep shearing, bric-a-brac, the world's smallest petting zoo. Distantly, I can hear Fingerband squawking. By unspoken agreement, we avoid the cake competition tent.

"What about the Bunting Belles?" says Sof as we get to the food stands, peddling everything from organic veggie burgers to hot fried doughnuts. "Girls-only touring band visiting summer fairs around the country. All our songs have hand claps in them."

"Supported by doo-wop duo the Marquee Men. Bratwurst?" I point to a hot-dog stand. Sauerkraut will soothe my soul.

She shakes her head. "The worst. We'll travel in a gingham-themed bus."

"And live off farmers' market food."

Sof keeps wrinkling her nose at said food until I suggest ice cream, then gleefully scampers off to line up for soft-serve, while I sit down on the grass to watch the world. Children tugging on their parents' hands, a girl crying for her balloon that's floating off miles into the sky. People from school, a handful of faces from the party, swigging cider in milk bottles and eating jerk chicken and coleslaw from Styrofoam trays. A few wave at me as they walk by. I smile back shyly.

And then, sloping towards me through the sunshine: Thomas.

He's carrying two ice-cream cones, one a simple soft-serve, the other a toppling rainbow tower of scoops and sauces and nuts and wafers. Without speaking, he leans down and hands me the vanilla. I wordlessly accept. I'm more mixed up than his ice cream, which is practically an ice-cream sundae (barely) balanced on a cone. My heart is the cherry on top, and he bites it.

I gaze up at him as he contemplates me, blocking the sun.

"I bumped into Sof," he finally explains, swallowing. "She thrust these at me, pointed you out, then grabbed Meg, and they both booked it. Almost like they planned this. The ice cream was melting all over my hands, and I couldn't find a garbage can, so . . ."

"Oh. Thank you."

"It's ice cream. I don't forgive you."

"Oh."

Despite saying this, he sits down next to me. My skin runs hot and cold with confusion, sunshine and shade. He doesn't forgive me; I'm not sure I've done anything that needs forgiving. But he knows without asking that the vanilla scoop in a waffle cone is mine. I nibble at it, stealing glances at him and wondering what we'll say. How we'll get our friendship back. I think that might be all I want, for now.

"Meg and Sof planned this?" I ask eventually.

Thomas shifts, guiltily. "I stayed at Sof's the first couple of nights. Weird, right? I'm at Niall's now, on the sofa. Oh—and I entered the cake competition." He tugs his cardigan aside, showing me the rosette on his T-shirt. "First prize. Ban's over."

"*Mein gott*, Thomas—that's amazing." My voice sounds false, clangs too loudly. I'm annoyed and pleased and confused, all at once.

"Yeah, well. You know I worked in a bakery back in Toronto? Every Saturday since I was fourteen, and summers." He holds up his hand, counting off barely visible burn scars on his fingers. How have we spent a whole summer talking and this never came up? "Brownie. Mille-feuille. Tray bake. I'm not bad. I had some money saved up from that job. My dad kept telling me it was for college. I don't know what it was for— maybe to go traveling after high school. I'd like to see a shark. Or catering college. Move to Vienna and learn how to make strudel."

"What are you going to do with it?" I ask nervously.

"Well, it turned out I saved less money than I thought—cardigans don't come cheap. Not enough for a shark. Or Vienna. Once I sold my car, it about covered a one-way ticket to England. This mad thirty-eight-hour round trip via Zurich and Madrid, the soonest flight that I could afford after term ended. Left a note for my mom that I'd be living with you till she came over. She and my dad had pretty much decided I'd be staying with him in Canada. That's why she calls so much. It's Mr. Tuttle, ten-fold. I'm in trouble."

Ice cream. Brain freeze. Whoa.

I had no idea where his story was going, I was just happy to have him babbling at me again, but this is huge—Hadron Collider huge. Thomas cashed in his cannoli money to see me. And *why*?

Before I can ask, he glances at me and says, "I probably should have told you that before."

"Er, yes. Probably," I squeak, and try to refill my lungs, which seem to have collapsed. "Why didn't you?"

"Because it's nuttier than this ice cream?" He shrugs. "The moment never seemed right to confess. You might have noticed, I'm not the best at telling you stuff. And because . . . I knew I was using your email as an excuse. The idea of leaving Toronto and choosing to live with my mom—I'd been thinking about it for a while. If I did it, without giving them the choice, they'd have to stop arguing about it. And I didn't tell you about Manchester, and I didn't tell you I was half here to annoy my dad—"

Thomas is bat-grabbing again, sending drips of sticky ice cream flying through the air, and the gesture topples me like a domino. Every emotion falling into another—love and fondness and familiarity and want, an aching want for us to be okay. Whether that's friendship or something else.

"—or about any of it, because you seemed happy see me again, and I liked you."

He glances at me, checking for my reaction. Which is mostly just trying to keep up. I have at least a hundred questions, but I nibble on my cone and swallow them.

"I don't want you to think I was running away. I want you to think I was running towards. Making a grand gesture."

"A gesture like telling me you spent all your money on a plane ticket for me, when really it was to get away from your dad?" I cock an eyebrow.

"It was still a little bit about you. I wanted to know if you'd chin me again." He smiles, rubbing his jaw. Somehow, even when we're out of sync with each other, we still have a rhythm. "It's pretty funny that you actually did."

I put my half-finished cone down next to me and wipe my fingers on the grass. And I say to my knees, "It's pretty funny that you actually did run away again . . ."

"Yeah, well." He sighs. That's all I get—a sigh?

"Look." I shuffle around so I'm sitting cross-legged opposite him. Meet his eye. "I'm going to explain this once, about me and Jason, and then it's done. But you can't just disappear on me again. You promised you wouldn't. Deal?"

Without checking behind him, he flings the last of his ice cream over his shoulder, and reaches out his hand for me to shake. "Deal."

"All right. Okay. I'm sorry I lied."

Thomas nods, still holding my hand, waiting for me to go on.

"No, that's it. That's all I have to say—I'm sorry I lied, or let you misunderstand, or whatever. Period. Ned tells me I'm self-absorbed. I'm not sorry Jason and I had sex, or that I was in love with him before you, and I meant what I said in the garden—it's not your business, and I don't have to explain it, and you don't get to judge me on it or be jealous. And if you are, keep it to yourself. It's not even a thing."

After my little speech, I nod, firmly. I think Sof would be proud.

"Why did you? Lie, I mean," he asks. I take my hand back. "Sorry. It's just, if you'd told me . . . Okay, I'd still have been totally jealous. But it was like you were making fun of me."

"I was used to keeping it a secret," I say. "You know that thing you said—that I was the first kiss that counted? I thought it was a nice idea. You were my first best friend. But I'm not sure it matters anymore—first, second, the order you do things."

He doesn't say anything, just sits there quietly in a totally un-Thomas-like way. He's still. Did I freeze time again? Can he even hear me? Then he blinks.

"So what happens now?" I ask, my voice squeaky. "Are you going to come home? Papa, and Ned, and Umlaut, everybody wants you to. I know you're leaving in a week anyway, but it's true."

"Are you asking me to come back as friends, or as whatever we were?"

"I don't know." It's true, I honestly don't. "Can't you just come back, and leave it up to fate?"

"The trouble is," he says, "I still like you. And after the party, you just gave up! We wouldn't even be talking right now if I hadn't come over. And I like you so much, I would probably let you do this."

"This?"

"Not make a grand gesture in return. You email me, and I come from Canada for you. You ask me to come home, but you're not coming to me. When I lied about Manchester, I came and found you. Then you go and break my heart, and I'm still the one who goes looking for you."

There's a fairy tale Grey used to read to me called *Guilt and Gingerbread*. The princess's heart of gold is stolen and replaced by an apple. The apple rots inside the princess, there's a maggot. She sighs, she dies. That's me. Rotten. Where my soul should be, is a shriveled little dead thing.

"I'll make you a grand gesture," I declare.

"Hmmm."

"I will! I don't know what it'll be yet. Come back first."

He huffs, a half laugh. "And pack all my stuff AGAIN?"

I scoot round so I'm sitting next to him, and we both lean back against the fence. We're friends. We did promise each other that.

"I don't remember it being this tiny," Thomas says eventually, waving out at the fair.

"We're bigger now. Proportionally, it's tinier. If you're three times the mass you were then, and you used to be half a percent of the fair, there's now less of it in relation to you."

"Hey, I nearly understood that." He elbows me, then unfolds himself, brushing the dried grass off his jeans. "So . . . I'll see you before I go to Manchester, right? To say goodbye."

The sun has slipped down the sky, and now, when I gaze up at him, he's nothing but light.

"Okay," I say. And then he's gone, walking off into the afternoon. I sit there for a while, feeling like I missed a really big moment, and I can't even blame a wormhole.

———————————

When I get home, Papa is in the garden. He's lying on his back among the dandelion stars, staring up at the evening sky. There's a glass of red wine half-balanced in his hand, the bottle buried in the grass beside him, and it looks like he's been crying. It makes me want to run and run, hide inside the horizon, but instead, I sit down next to him. I'm saying yes. I'm running towards.

He smiles up at me, patting my hand.

"Grüß dich," he says. "How was the fair?"

"I saw Thomas," I blurt without preamble. "I'm sorry. I tried to get him to come back here, it was my fault he left, and the tap—all of it."

"Liebling," he says, smiling, "that can't possibly be true. Ned attacked it with a wrench."

"Yes, but—" I flail, tight-throated. I have an ocean of apologies to make and no one will accept them.

Papa sits up and takes a sip of wine, frowning at his empty glass and refilling it.

" 'It's all my fault, it's all my fault,' " he parrots. "This was how Thomas got his reputation as, what did you call that? A gremlin? The pair of you were always up to something. And afterwards you would always be racked with guilt. You'd be full of apologies and making amends—I'll be *gut* for a week, so *gut*!—and you were. Naturally, we all assumed everything naughty had been Thomas's idea."

"He keeps telling me everything was always *my* idea," I complain. "Did you know it was his idea to come over this summer, not his mum's?"

"Ha-ha," Papa says, goblin-gleeful. "Not at first—I thought it was you, like the cat."

"Papa," I say carefully. "*I* didn't bring Umlaut home."

"*Nein?* Anyway, after the party, I call Thomas's mum and she told me that he told her it was your idea." He hands me his glass. "I've missing you."

I take a sip—sour and vinegary—and say, "I've been here."

"Have you?" His voice isn't sharp, like the wine—but it stings. If everyone's telling me I'm only half here, maybe they're all right.

"I missed you too," I tell him. Papa draws his knees up, looking out to the tangled garden. "And I miss Grey." I gulp the wine again, to hide my embarrassment. We've never talked about this. We've snuck around, avoiding the subject.

"*Ich auch.*" Me too. "I don't know—did I get it wrong? Letting you and Ned find your own way? When your mami died, Grey did this for me. Stepped back. Let me discover." Papa trails off, plucking the wine from my hand. "*Liebling.* You've been reading his diaries. You know now he was ill, the radiation treatment?"

*R

*R

*R

Radiation? The wine and the second shock announcement of the day set me reeling in the twilight. I think of Grey's thunderstorm moods last summer. His early nights. All the times I'd cycled past the Book Barn and the door had been locked. Getting me a book for my birthday. Thomas's voice in the kitchen, saying, *morphine.*

And Grey, leaping over the fire. Shouting for a Viking's death.

"No. I didn't know." All these secrets, shattering.

"*Ja, Liebling,*" says Papa. He gulps his wine, till there's just a bit left, then he hands it back to me. "Go slowly. I already have Ned to deal with. Hodgkin lymphoma." He tests the words on his tongue, unfamiliar. "Cancer. For a while. The stroke was always a possibility. But anyway, even so. There wasn't much time, and he wanted you not to know. You and Ned had exams. You'd lost your mami. He liked when everything was happy, you know?"

And I thought we had all the time in the world. I've held on to a meaningless wish for a year. It stings a little, when I let it go. It had put down roots. Then I pour my wine onto the grass: a ritual. And at last, the guilt dissolves like smoke in the air.

Papa is watching me. "*Ich liebe dich mit ganzem Herzen,*" he says. *I love you with my whole heart.*

Ned chooses this touching moment to start pounding AC/DC through his open window.

"*Ist* your brother?" asks Papa, wincing.

"I'll get him." I unfold upright and stomp over to his window, taking out my feelings on the grass. Yellow tulips and wormholes and a wish. It's haunted me for a year; now it's gone.

"Ned!" I bang on the window. "We're getting DRUNK."

He pops his head out immediately. "What's the occasion?"

"Grey."

———

"Remember the slugs?" I ask.

"The sluuuuuuugs." Ned stretches the word from here to the moon as he flops backwards on the grass. We've been out here since I banged on his window, the twilight slipping into dark, sharing our favorite Grey anecdotes. Tree laundry. The frozen orange story. Slugs.

They were Grey's first test on the road to enlightenment. He read all these books, went temporarily vegetarian, started meditating. Fat Little Buddha statues sprang up all over the cottage, and bites sprang up all over Grey's legs because he wouldn't even swat a mosquito.

Summer and mosquitoes gave way to autumn and daddy longlegs. Around October, it started to rain. And rain begat slugs, and slugs begat more slugs, and slugs begat Grey slowly, softly, gradually, losing his temper. For a few weeks, he'd painstakingly pluck fat grey apostrophes off the pavement and tip them into the Althorpes' vegetable patch.

Then one night, we were woken at two in the morning by a bellow of "Bugger enlightenment!" and Grey banging a hoe on the pavement. A massacre.

"Did I ever tell you about him and the bells? He just stood out there"—Papa waves in the direction of the church—"yelling they should shut up."

There were bells after his funeral, ringing out through the afternoon. Everyone goes quiet. Ned wriggles upright.

"We should do something," he says, breaking the silence.

"It's late," says Papa. "Bedtime. No more parties, no more drinking."

"I meant"—Ned rolls his eyes—"about Grey. It's nearly a year. Shouldn't we ring bells or, okay, maybe not. Fireworks?"

"If you both wanted, we could scatter the ashes," says Papa. "They're in the shed."

"The *shed*?" Ned hoots. "You can't keep them in the shed! It's—it's—"

"Where else would you keep them, *Liebling*?" Papa asks, his face rumpled in confusion. "Anyway, Gottie put them there."

"I *what*?" I choke on my wine.

"I put them in one of the Buddhas, and you cleared them all away," he says, standing up, "so that's where they are."

"Papa, when you say they're in *one* of the Buddhas . . . Half of them are back out in the house. Do you know which one?"

"I know which one," he says. It's clear he's always known. Is he as vague and absent as I think, or do I just not notice him? "I'll find it. You all start to think about where we can do this. Maybe here." He disappears into the dark.

"Here . . ." I say. "You don't think he means in the garden?"

Ned snorts, and we're back to normal. "Bit morbid. I bet near the Book Barn, or in the fields. What do you think?"

I wait until Papa comes back from the shed, a cardboard box in his hand. He rests it gently on the grass between us. It's unreasonably tiny.

"Grots?" Ned prompts me. "Where should these go?"

"The sea," I say, because Grey wanted to die like a Viking.

There's nowhere else. The sea is the only place big enough, and the box is far too small. How can you hold the universe in the palm of your hand?

Sunday 24 August

[Minus three hundred and fifty-seven]

I wish I knew how the world worked, already. Because I wake up early with a pounding headache and Thomas's email clutched in my hand. And I can read it.

From: thomasalthorpe@yahoo.ca
To: gottie.h.oppenheimer@gmail.com
Date: 4/7/2015, 17.36
Subject: Trouble times two

The answer's yes, obviously.
But I think you already know that.
Hasn't it always been yes when it comes to us?
I want to see the stars with you.
And whatever you tell me, I'll believe.

Because remember—
Things can get dark, and fairly terrible
But the scar on my palm makes you fucking indelible.

I read it a dozen times, and it still doesn't make any sense. The stars—that's obvious, the plastic ones he put on my ceiling. But what is he saying yes to? What have I told him that he believes? And I want to throttle him—this is hardly the clear warning you give if you're flying across the Atlantic to visit! It is, however, thoroughly Thomas—full of heart and gesture and a little bit loony, with no thought to the consequences.

I think I know why I can read it, too, and it's got nothing to do with the Weltschmerzian Exception. I've finally forgiven myself for Grey's death. I'm allowed a little bit of love in my life.

And I know what I can do for a grand gesture. Still in my pajamas, I grab my book bag from the wardrobe and run through the misty dawn to the kitchen.

By the time I climb the apple tree, the day is full sunshine. While Umlaut chases squirrels around the branches, I check for frogs—I don't want to accidentally shut one in. Then, moment by moment, I empty my book bag, and fill up the tin box. The seaweed from the beach. Canadian coins, the treasure map and my constellation, the little plastic stars, a pair of Thomas's balled-up socks, my ice-cream-sticky napkin from the fair yesterday. The recipe he wrote out for me.

And the squashed and terrible results of my first solo baking attempt this morning—a chocolate cupcake.

I close the lid and padlock it for Thomas to open. This time capsule of our summer. It's the best I can do. Then I lean back against a branch and start writing him an email on my phone.

[270]

From: gottie.h.oppenheimer@gmail.com
To: thomasalthorpe@yahoo.ca
Date: 24/8/2015, 11.17
Subject: Bawk, bawk, bawk

Trouble times two, remember? Turns out, one is worse. I can't explain it, but I need you to come and open the time capsule with me. I know you've got no reason to. But I don't know how to be without you.

If you need more reason than that . . . Picture me now, holding out my little finger to you. And saying: Hey, Thomas. I dare you.

I look at what I've written. I think about Thomas's email, and that he told me it was a reply to mine. My fingers move on instinct, adjusting the date to 4 July. And I know it will work, because it already has. I hit send and shove the phone in my pocket, along with the key for the padlock. Now I just need to shower and go find Thomas.

I'm standing up and turning around on the branch, one foot reaching out into the air, searching for a knothole, when the time capsule begins to change. First, the old and tarnished padlock I took from the toolbox this morning becomes shiny and clean. Then the names on the top, *THOMAS & GOTTIE*, fade away.

"Uh," I say to no one, to Umlaut, as I pause, half in, half out of the tree. I thought all this nonsense had stopped after the party. After the last wormhole. Except for, *um Gottes Willen*, Gottie you moron, except for the fact you could suddenly read Thomas's email this morning! Talk about a screenwipe.

As I watch, captivated, the writing reappears, followed by the tarnish.

[271]

The lock re-rusts at warp speed. The time capsule pulsates back and forth, faster and faster: clean/dirty, letters/blank, rust/shiny. Past/future, past/future, past/future. The Weltschmerzian Exception didn't begin when Grey died. It's starting now.

And a drop of rain falls.

Upwards. There's not a cloud in the sky. As another drop of rain hits me, I scramble away from the time capsule, and "Oh, shit—"

I think I hear someone shouting my name as I fall out of the tree.

Five Years Ago

"Did you just SEE that?" Thomas shouts through the rain.

It's pretty dark, but I still saw the ginger cat run past us under the annex.

"Yeah, it's under here." I get down on my hands and knees, trying to peer under the building. The grass is gross—all wet and slimy—but my jeans are already soaked. It's just water though. I'm a twelve-year-old girl, not the Wicked Witch of the West.

"Here, kitty kitty."

"What? No," says Thomas behind me. "G, you have to see this."

"Mmm. In a minute."

"G," says Thomas impatiently. "Forget the cat for a minute. A girl just fell out of the tree."

"No, she didn't."

"Geee . . ."

I sigh. Thomas has been weird all day, ever since the head-butt kiss. I don't want to play his stupid game. I want to get the cat. But I stand up anyway, turning round, wiping my muddy hands on my jeans.

There's a girl lying on the grass under the apple tree.

Seriously.

It was just me and Thomas in the garden. Grey booted us out the Book Barn, then came home and booted us out the house too. Unbelievable! Thomas is leaving for Canada today, and it's my last chance to kiss him—to kiss ANYONE in my whole life—and we keep getting interrupted. Then the cat ran through. And now there's this girl. She sits up, rubbing the back of her head.

"She fell out of the sky-aye," Thomas sing-songs as he starts crab-walking towards me.

"Actually," says the girl, standing up tall tall tall. "I fell out of the tree."

She shields her face with a hand from the rain and peers at us. At me. "Hi, Gottie."

I stare back, spooked. How does she know my name? She looks like my mami, who I've only seen in photos. They all look the same as this girl: dark and skinny, with a big nose, and choppy hair like mine.

"Aren't you cold?" I ask. I'm wearing rain boots, jeans, a T-shirt, Thomas's jumper, and a Windbreaker. The girl is wearing pajamas and a book bag and no shoes. She must be friends with Grey. And she's not wearing a bra. I can tell. Her toenails are cherry red and chipped.

"Did you hit your head?" asks Thomas. I sidle next to him and take his hand. He squeezes mine back.

"No, I hit the hedge." She giggles.

She's loopy: there isn't a hedge back here. The ginger cat comes running to her, and it purrs and rubs against her ankle.

"I *knew* I should have called you Schrödinger!" she says to it, then turns to look up into the apple tree. "Holy long division—it's a paradoxical time loop."

What is she talking about? Thomas looks at me, and, slowly so she doesn't see it, I point my finger at my ear and move it round in a circle. Mouth: "Cuckoo."

But how can he smile when he's going away today? Doesn't he mind?

"But why here? Why does it open today and not somewhen else? Is it the time capsule?" the girl murmurs to the tree. Then she looks over at us. "Hey, Trouble Times Two. Can you do me a favor?"

"No," I say, at the same time as Thomas says, "Yes."

I glare at him.

"After I'm gone, climb this tree and see what you find," says the girl, taking something out of her pocket and throwing it through the rain to Thomas. It's small and silver.

"I've got a knife!" I blurt. It's true.

"I know." She winks. "And you really shouldn't. Gottie. Listen. I know I should say something so *ficken* wise to you right now. Like, talk to Papa. Eat your vegetables. Phone Ned when he's in London. Pay attention to the world. Say yes when someone asks you to bake a cake. Make grand gestures. Be bold."

She laughs. "But . . . eh, we're going to forget, and do everything wrong, anyway. But be careful with that knife, okay? We could get hurt."

I think *We?* But the girl's already darting off through the garden and Thomas is tugging on my hand, saying, "There's something in the tree, I've got the key. C'mon."

And he's leaving me for forever in an hour and we have a blood pact to swear, so I climb up after him, the knife in my pocket.

Since it's already happened, I can't stop my idiotic younger self from getting stabbed in a tree, so I go and hide from the rain in Grey's car. It's parked askew, half in the hedge. One wheel is missing, propped up on bricks. We got an ambulance to the hospital today, so I'm safe here. I won't bump into anyone else.

What did I cause by meeting myself just now? When Thomas asked me about time travel, I'd been absolutely certain in my explanation of why this could never happen. Cosmic censorship. Clearly, I was wrong—you *can* see beyond an event horizon. But, then, this: I still don't remember what happened with the blood pact, but I do recall the part beforehand, when Thomas and I were in the garden, in the rain. It's coming back to me.

And there definitely wasn't a cat. There definitely wasn't another me. What's different about this time?

Rain slashes at the car windows as I try to figure out what's missing from my theory, what could cause the memory gap. Then I hear a yell and turn to see little Thomas, running across the garden, clutching his bleeding hand, screaming fit to bust for Grey, for Papa, for tree girl—*that must mean me*, I think—for anyone, to come quickly.

Papa pokes his head out the kitchen door. When he sees Thomas, he turns green, turns away. A few seconds later, Grey strides out of the house.

And I'm *verklemmt*.

It's been one thing, seeing him in my memories, reading his diaries. Remembering him, over and over. But this, this is him here now, flesh and blood and here and alive . . .

I ache with how much I miss him.

He starts crossing the garden, half running to the apple tree as Thomas wails and runs behind him.

Grey. Grey, alive, and *here*, and I'm here too, and if I could just follow him through the garden—he's disappearing beyond the shrubbery, almost gone, if I could just talk to him . . . My hand is on the door handle, ready to leap out, to run across to him, one last time—

If I could just.

But I can't. It's the wrong time. It's the wrong place. It's the wrong me.

And anyway, Grey is moving out from behind the rhododendron now, carefully and urgently. He's carrying other Gottie in his arms. I'm already with him. Another me, in another time, always I'll be with him.

I laugh, a little, through my tears. Seeing my younger face, its stubborn, gremlin-y achievement, muddled with pain and confusion. And pride! I think that I look safe. I think that Sof was right—Grey was all of our dads. He was my daddy. There I am, in his arms.

All the love we've lost hits me like an ocean wave.

There are sirens now; Papa must have called the ambulance. And there's shouting, and there's pain.

God. Why can't I remember this?

Is it because there are two of me? And why weren't there two of me when I went back a week to the kitchen? I made all that stuff up, about the universe hiding you in a tiny cannoli—but perhaps it's true, and that's where my memory has been all along.

Or, perhaps, it's this: when only seven days had passed, I was the same person, unchanged. I couldn't meet my week-ago self, because of causality. This is different. Me at twelve, and me at seventeen—there's a chasm of grief between us. I lost myself when Grey died, and there isn't a single particle left of who I was. I can meet my younger self, because we're not the same person. I'll never be that girl again.

Thomas scurries to keep up with Grey's seven-league strides. I squint, trying to see what he's holding. As he runs across the garden, his unhurt hand forms a fist. The Canadian coins? There's chocolate cake round his mouth. And I hope, in his pocket, there's a recipe. He doesn't look left or right, or at me in the car: he runs after Grey, after me, into the kitchen. And then we're gone.

It's time to go home.

The rain is easing as I climb out of the car and cross the garden. Under the tree, I retrieve the discarded knife from the grass. Water has washed the blood away. I stuff it in my pocket, then climb up into the branches.

Umlaut is waiting for me, next to the open time capsule. The padlock is lying next to it, and all that junk I put in there before—the seaweed, the coins—is gone. Was I really going to woo Thomas back with a pair of old socks?

I settle myself on my usual branch, take a notebook out of my book bag, and I start to write.

The Gottie H. Oppenheimer Principle v 7.0.
A general theory of heartbreak, love,
and the meaning of infinity, or:
the Weltschmerzian Exception

Dear Thomas,
You promised me that whatever I tell you, you'll believe.
Remember? So here it goes.
Time travel is real.
Five years ago, you and I accidentally created a paradoxical time
loop. It's fate.

What's a paradoxical time loop? Okay, so you bake a cannoli . . .
Kidding! It's a wormhole that exists because it exists. You know
the equation I wrote on your email? My physics teacher called it a
joke. It describes a wormhole opening in the present, because at the
same time, it's opening in the past. Impossible, right?

I disagree.

It's real. And I think its power comes from the negative energy, or
dark matter, that naturally exists in the universe.

I think it comes from grief.

I'd already lost my mum. There was already grief in my world.
The circumstances for a Weltschmerzian Exception (more on this
later) were ideal. And you were more than my best friend. We were
unquestionable. When you went away, all I had left was a scar, a
hole in my memory,* and the thought that you didn't want to kiss
me. I broke your heart? You broke mine first. So we're Even Stevens.
That's why the loop comes back to this day in particular (I'm writing
this from our tree, the day you cut my hand, by the way).

When my grandfather died, I imploded. This second heartbreak
completed the loop. Could I have traveled down a wormhole to five
years ago if Grey hadn't died? Would his death have shattered me, if
I hadn't already lost you? To put it another way: would losing you
have hurt so much, if I hadn't lost Grey in the future?

And then there's this summer. You're not supposed to be here.
You're here because of an email I sent. But I only sent it, because
you're already here. When you came back to Holksea, time went
wackadoodle. I think you triggered something. What did we find,
that day in the tree? I still can't remember, but I'm going to guess:
Canadian coins, which you took to Toronto with you. Did you buy a
comic with them, and bring it back on the plane this summer? You

wrote me a recipe for chocolate cake this July and discovered it five years ago—is that why you want to be a baker?

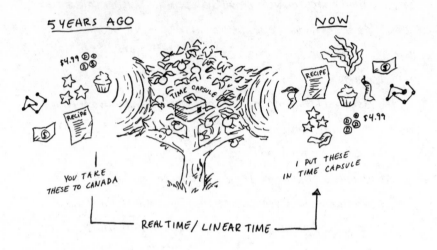

The universe has been tying itself in knots trying to correct all these paradoxes.

It's called the Weltschmerzian Exception.

The rules of spacetime don't apply. When you broke my heart, the world split into a thousand timelines. In your version of the universe, you got an email from me. Want to know why I was so weird this summer? Every time you mentioned it, we jumped to a new timeline. You know how particles get to their destination without traveling there? That was me. Sometimes time froze, like a knot in a thread. Or it bent and distorted completely, letting me step from my bedroom one rainy night into a warm kitchen the week before. Where I kissed you. (There's a secret I never told you!)

There are years of twists and turns, but the world kept bringing me back to last summer most of all, because that's where I needed to be. And for that, I wanted to say: thank you.

Indelibly yours,

G. H. Oppenheimer x

PS *That memory is in a tiny cannoli somewhere. Lost in spacetime. I don't need it anymore.*

I write the future date, 24 August, at the top, then I put the letter in the time capsule, close the lid, and padlock it.

The effect is instantaneous. First the apple tree bursts into blossom. Within seconds, the petals are falling like confetti. The sun rises and sets, rises and sets, a heartbeat in the sky. The clouds race by.

"It's okay," I whisper to Umlaut, scooping him into my lap. "We're going home."

I'm no longer afraid. I can see all the loops and snags and knots I've made in time. I can see all the universes at once.

The timelines layer over each other. I watch a dozen different Gotties running through the garden, appearing and disappearing, faster and faster. Mathematically speaking, all this will happen over and over again, a hundred different heartbreaks in a hundred different ways. One of the Gotties will wake up underneath this tree at the beginning of summer, drenched in déjà vu, sad, and alone. My heart goes out to her. But for me, that's in the past.

I'm ready for *now*.

The years pass more quickly now, snow then sunshine then snow. The garden is a blur. As the sky gathers into one last autumn and the leaves come fluttering down, a torn scrap of paper floats by. I stand and catch it: a page from a future textbook. The yet-to-be-written equation for the Weltschmerzian Exception. And I see my name next to it, and the title "Dr."

In a moment of complete clarity, I know: I won't remember everything. That I *shouldn't* remember everything. Especially not this. So I hold the page out to the wind and let it fly away in the snow. It vanishes into thin air. This is a secret that the universe can keep. The sun comes out, first spring, then summer. Then I close my eyes, and I jump out of the tree . . .

Now

I land in the grass, my pajamas still soaking wet.

Dazed, I sit up, peeling off my book bag, and look around the garden. The lawn is freshly mowed and has the scent of cut grass. There's no more rotting fruit on the ground. Yellow roses, hundreds of them, tumble over the kitchen window.

I tilt my head back and see my room, upside down. The ivy is clipped back, and I catch a glimpse of curtains inside the windows. Beyond them, against all odds, I think I can see a glow of stars.

Curtains in my room. Yellow roses, not peach. Thomas's cosmos, back on my ceiling. A thousand tiny details, a thousand incremental changes. I've remade the universe. Better. It's the end of my weltschmerz.

A sudden burst of Black Sabbath blasts across the garden from Ned's room. Some things stay the same. And when I tilt my head forward again, Thomas is peering down at me from the apple tree, leaf-dappled. Was it him calling my name, when I fell?

"Welcome back," he says. A smile tugs at his face.

"Um. Hello." I stare up at him. "What are you doing?"

"Reading your letter." He waves the pages at me, through the branches. If he's surprised by what I wrote, or the fact that I'm dripping wet in pajamas on a blazing sunny day, or that my feet are smeared with mud, he's not letting on. Unless . . . Memories of the summer drift down around me like dandelion fluff.

Remember? That day with the time capsule. You had short hair that day.

The time capsule. Maybe we opened it too soon.

Bake at 300 degrees for an hour. Even you can do this. Trust me.

"I meant here," I say, letting my thoughts scatter. Not caring what he knows, or if it even happened this way at all. "In my garden. Up a tree."

"Oh. Hang on." There's a rustle of leaves and a sparkle in the air, as something small and silver lands in the grass next to me.

I pick it up. The key to the padlock, the one I tossed through the rain to Thomas five years ago.

"You kept it?" I ask, even though I know he must have. How else would he get my letter—take a chain saw to the time capsule? Actually, since it's Thomas . . .

"After the fair yesterday, Niall's mum booted me off the sofa," he explains. "I found it in my suitcase while I was packing. And I got to thinking about the day we opened the time capsule, and how there was nothing in it. You'd promised me a grand gesture. I thought it was finally the right time . . ."

He looks down at me. I look up at him. We share a scar. And we don't need to explain anything to each other at all.

"Oh, you got one thing wrong," Thomas says. "It wasn't July, it was April. Your email? I'm Canadian. We reverse the dates."

April . . . You've got to be kidding, bored physicists! *That's* the multiplying factor of the paradoxical loop, the thing we created to make all this balance out? Umlaut?!

"I'm sorry," Thomas voice drifts from the tree and I refocus on him. "Look. When I got your email, that was the original grand gesture." He waves the notebook pages again. "I couldn't be sure . . . but it was worth all the bakery money in the world to find out. I thought you and I were fate. Unquestionable. Then that gimp in his leather jacket! I was jealous."

"And now?"

"I sat up in the tree just then, freaking out that you'd disappeared, waiting for you to come back. Remembering about you and Grey that day, how much he loved you—he gave me the ass-kicking of my life over that scar on your hand. Anyone would be fucked up, after he died. I didn't take it seriously enough. Everything you were going through."

My eyes search his face, his freckles too far away to be visible. He's leaving in a week. But here we are. I'm covered in teeny-tiny blades of grass, he's hiding in a tree—we might be nuts enough for this to work out.

"Hey, Thomas," I say. Making a fist, sticking it straight out into the air—pointing my little finger. "I dare you."

When he lands next to me in the grass, I roll over and look at him. I don't reach for his hand quite yet. I just take it all in. My pajamas are still damp from long-ago rain, but it's a nice smell. Not quite petrichor. Something new.

"Do you think if we'd written to each other after you left, we could have skipped all this?"

"Nah," Thomas says. He reaches out and plucks a blossom petal from my hair, frowns at it, then lets it fall. "Then it might not have happened. Cannolis, and all that. Now, ask me again why I'm in your garden."

He presses his forehead to mine, a clunk of glasses on my nose.

"Why—"

"I couldn't move to Manchester and not promise you I'll come back. Visit. Write. Email. Make my iced-bun fortune and meet you halfway across the country before you go off to science school and forget about me."

I can tell he wants to bat-grab, but it's difficult when you're lying down.

"Let's make a new time capsule," I say, my mouth moments from his. "Give you a reason to come back. Maybe we could put Ned's stereo in it."

Thomas laughs. "G, I know how to be without you. But life is *so* much more interesting with."

"And I suppose that," I tell him, taking his hand, "has always been the point."

This time, when we kiss, the world doesn't end. The universe doesn't stop. Stars don't fall from the sky. It's an ordinary kiss.

The kind where you can hear both your hearts beat. The kind that's about discovering each other again, mouths and hands and laughter— like when Thomas finds the knife in my pocket, or the clumsiness as I try to take his glasses off. The kind that leaves you both breathless, and covered in grass, saying goodbye, and making promises.

The kind that stops time, in its own way.

Monday 1 September

[One]

A week later, we give Grey his Viking funeral. I tell Papa I'll meet them at the beach—there's something I have to do first.

It's dark inside the bookshop, but I don't turn on the lights—I won't be here for long. In the attic, in a tucked-away alcove that no one comes near, I take Grey's diaries out of my book bag. Turn the pages, see his handwriting, alive in ink: I RAGE AT THE UNIVERSE. BUT GOTTIE REMINDS ME, IT'S ALL GOING TO WORK OUT. I AM A VIKING.

There's no time loop here, yet it's winter all around me. Snow covers the books. I remember—

sitting at the kitchen table with my back to the wood stove, studying for English, wondering how I can explain $E = MC^2$ but I can't understand a gerund.

*I'm texting Sof—*Is it a type of dog?*—when Grey comes in, filling the room. The table wobbles as he strides to the kettle, humming ebulliently.*

A mug is plonked in front of me, then he half settles at the other end of the table, chuckling at the newspaper. I sip my tea, and jump when a giant hand slams my textbook shut.

"Come on, dude," he says. "Let's go for a drive."

I squeak about revision, but let him steer me out into the icy garden anyway. Clinging onto the car door as he speeds us bumpily away from Holksea, happy to be out of the house.

"You know I used to do this with you, when you were a baby? We'd drive around, up and down the coast. You'd stop crying, and you'd watch me. Probably thinking, 'Hey, old man, where are we going?' Ned hated being driven. But you and me, kid, we'd motor to the sea. Sometimes I'd chat to you, like you were listening. Sometimes not, maybe we'd have on music, or just silence, like now. Whatever, you know, dude."

He glances over at me.

"What you're saying is . . ." I pretend to think. "You don't know where we're going?"

Grey laughs, a huge sonic boom.

"Metaphorically speaking?"

"Driving speaking."

"Where do you want to go?" Grey asks me. "This is for you—one day's escape from reality. I'm just the chauffeur. The world's your oyster."

The phrase gives me déjà vu. I check the dashboard. "About fifteen miles of gas is our oyster."

"Then let's get oysters," he chuckles, flipping on the signal.

It's too cold for that, so we get chips in paper cones, dripping with vinegar, and eat them sitting inside the car, watching the waves through the fog. The wind turns the sea to foam.

When we get home, he goes straight to bed, even though it's only six o'clock.

"All that talking," he tells me, dropping a kiss on my head, "it's worn me out."

The next day, I go back to sitting at the kitchen table, wrestling adjectives. Grey ruffles my hair with his giant hand every time he walks by, and takes to cooking stews to keep me company. We tune the radio to static, and we sing along to nothing. We're happy.

Tick-tick . . .

Tick.

Tock.

The clock brings me back to the bookshop. And I let it. I consecrate a smile to the memory of my grandfather, driving me up and down the coast. Then I stop living in the past.

I stack the diaries on the shelf. The Book Barn is the right place for Grey's secrets. Maybe someone will try to buy them. Or maybe they'll disappear. As I hide them behind some paperbacks, I think I hear a *meow*. I think I see a flash of orange, scuttling away across the universe.

And all that time falls through my fingers.

The wrong date on an email and a cat who shouldn't exist. A time capsule we found in a tree five years ago, and the boy who gave me a summer. A best friend from the fifties and a brother from the seventies. A father who fades in and out and a mother I will never, ever know.

And Grey. Grey, who it still hurts my heart to think about. Grey, who I will always mourn. Grey, who I will always be able to find again.

This is what it means to love someone. This is what it means to grieve someone. It's a little bit like a black hole.

It's a little bit like infinity.

Ned is waiting for me when I come down the stairs. He's leaning against the desk, flipping through a book, his foot tapping to an invisible beat. He looks up and takes a picture as I approach, his face behind the lens all eyeliner and nose. My twisted big brother.

"Yo, Grots. Everybody's waiting outside," he says. "You coming?"

"Right behind you," I tell him.

He bounds ahead of me to the door, cape billowing. On the porch, I stand for a minute, my eyes adjusting to the light. When I can finally see, everyone is piling back into Grey's car, through the one stupid door that works. Ned, clambering over into the front passenger seat. Sof sliding in behind him, a sequin sparkle, then Thomas. He twists around to wave through the back window. We've got one more day.

Papa waits patiently outside the car for me, his Converse as bright blue as the sky.

I'm still standing on the edge of the step, rocking on my toes, holding my breath as I see the future spinning out ahead of me—getting in the car driving to the beach scattering the ashes saying goodbye going home lighting a bonfire writing an essay—when Thomas sticks his head out the window.

"G!" he yells. "Hurry up—you're missing everything!"

He's right. I don't want to wait another second. My heart fills with yellow as I step outside, because it all starts—

Now.

∞

Find a piece of paper. On one side, write down: "For the secret of perpetual motion, please turn over." Then, on the other side, write down: "For the secret of perpetual motion, please turn over."

Read what you've just written. Follow the instructions. And just keep going.

Acknowledgments

In memory of my grandmother, Eileen Reuter. Above all, this book is a love letter to my family—who will read it and say, "Well, it didn't happen anything like *that*." My parents, Mike Hapgood and Penny Reuter; my sister and brother, Ellie Reuter and Will Hapgood; and all of Rabbit's friends-and-relations (most especially Martha Samphire).

And a hundred heartfelt thank-yous to:

My thoroughly wonderful agent and friend, Gemma Cooper, at The Bent Agency, who changed my life. It is as simple and as extraordinary as that. Her guidance, insight, and joy turned my writing, and me, inside out. The brilliant writers of Team Cooper. And the exceptional co-agents and scouts across the universe (I'm shooting for a moon edition . . .) who worked tirelessly to champion this book and only took the piss out of my "internet translation" German a little bit. I am so, so *glücklich*.

At Roaring Brook Press, my editor, Connie Hsu, who graciously let me bitch about Britishisms and cling to commas while she quietly and cleverly reshaped this book into something bolder and brighter than I dared imagine—thank you. Elizabeth H. Clark for capturing Gottie's world so perfectly on the US cover, Kristie Radwilowicz for the charming illustrations, and the entire publishing team for saying "*Ja!*" to an oddball little English novel full of Wellies and vicars and Mr. Whippy.

In the UK, my other editor (like martinis, two is the perfect amount) Rachel Petty wooed me with Judy Blume and wine, and encouraged me to immortalise my skinny-dipping days in print. Rachel Vale for my golden cover, and everyone at Macmillan Children's Books for their boundless enthusiasm.

The coven! Don't go into the writing cave without one. Jessica Alcott, who sends the longest emails (seriously, the delete key is, like, a thing?) and makes fun of me just, y'know, *constantly*. Mhairi McFarlane, who kindly read the first three chapters, didn't hate them, and quoted Batman when I most needed it. Alwyn Hamilton, side by side in the edits trenches. John Warrender, grudgingly, I guess. Whatever.

For blatant name thievery, Bim Adewunmi, Megumi Yamazaki, and Maya Rae Oppenheimer. For the books, Stacey Croft. A. J. Grainger for being a class act, Keris Stainton for the writing lessons, Genevieve Herr for sending me Gemma's way, and Sara O'Connor for the novella crash course. For in-the-nick-of-spacetime physics advice, Georgina Hanratty and Dr. Luke Hanratty—all errors very much my own. Everyone at YALC, Team #UKYA, and the book bloggers. And for sitting on top of the manuscript at every opportunity, shout-out to my cat, Stanley.

Finally, I could not have written a word without my friends. I'm forever astonished and grateful that they continue to welcome me back to the pub after I abandon them for months in favor of imaginary worlds. Catherine Hewitt. Jemma Lloyd-Helliker. The 5PA: Rachael Gibson, Isabelle O'Carroll, Laura Silver, and Emily Wright. Video Club: Dot Fallon, Anne Murphy, Maya (again!) and, more than anyone, Elizabeth Bisley—world's greatest human and navigator.